The Fair Queen

Lyndsey Hall

First paperback edition August 2020

Cover design by Natalie Narbonne
originalbookcoverdesigns.com
Interior Formatting by Evenstar Books
evenstarbooks.com
Editing by Lara Ferrari
writinglaraferrari.com

ISBN 978-1-8380911-0-1 (paperback)
ISBN 978-1-8380911-1-8 (eBook)

lyndseyhallwrites.com

For Joseph

PART ONE

Monday's child is fair of face.

— MONDAY'S CHILD (TRADITIONAL)

1

Today was the Summer Solstice, and that meant one thing. The Hartwood summer fayre.

Aria weaved through the crowd, her hands full of hot coffee in paper cups. The entire village of Hartwood had ventured out by the looks of it. She smiled as she squeezed past neighbours and a group of kids she recognised from the year below at school.

As she made her way back to where she'd left Jasper in line at the doughnut van, her cotton tote bag slipped down her shoulder and jolted her arm, slopping coffee onto her favourite leather boots. She bent down and placed the cups on the ground, taking a napkin out of the bag to wipe it off before it left a mark. As she reached in, her fingertips brushed the box in the bottom, the birthday present she'd bought Jasper and was waiting for the right moment to give to him. She'd do it later, when they were alone.

Satisfied that the coffee wouldn't leave a stain she straightened up, and paused as a creeping sensation washed over her. Her flesh rose with goose bumps, the feeling of eyes on her, but when she glanced around at the other fayre-goers no one stood out. It wasn't the first time it had happened this week, either.

After another look around, she shook off the feeling and headed for the doughnut van. She was being paranoid, Hartwood was about the safest place on Earth. A quiet, rural town in the middle of England, with a maypole in the centre of the town square. It was all very idyllic.

But then, a lot of new people had arrived with the fayre. Performers and musicians and the like. Strong-looking lads she took for roadies and techies.

"Aria? Aria!" She could see Jasper standing on tiptoe, trying to catch a glimpse of her copper hair over the crowd surging between the tents. He hadn't even noticed her leaving, had been too busy staring at the blue-eyed, blonde-haired boy working in the doughnut van, probably working up the courage to flirt with him when his turn to order came around. She pushed the thought away and plastered a grin onto her face.

"Here!" She lifted a cardboard coffee cup in the air. "You have to drink coffee with doughnuts, it's the law." She handed him a cup and took the bag, reaching inside to take a bite of the hot, sugary contents. "I did tell you I was going, but you were too busy drooling over doughnut guy." Jasper blushed and her stomach clenched, he was so adorable when he was embarrassed.

"Whatever, shove a doughnut in it and come on."

As they strolled around the tents, sipping their coffee and killing time until the next performance on the big stage, Aria noticed the brass band for the first time. They were playing the usual sort of music you'd expect at a summer fayre, but it sounded wrong somehow, off key.

Like a music box as it wound down, warping the notes, the tiny dancer twirling slower and slower before grinding to a halt. It sent a shiver down her spine.

Despite her name, Aria didn't have a musical bone in her body. Her parents had chosen the name out of their own love of music—her mother was a cellist, performing with an orchestra for years before becoming a music teacher. That was where they had met, at a concert. Aria's dad was writing a review for the local paper and her mother had agreed to speak to him after the show.

She sometimes worried they were disappointed in her lack of musical talent. She wasn't much of a writer either, so it was unlikely she'd follow in her father's footsteps. She felt adrift, like there was nothing tethering her, and no map or guide for her to follow. Her future wasn't written in the stars, hadn't been mapped out from the day she'd been born, no matter how much she wished it was at times.

As they strolled between the stalls and food vans, the scent of roast pork and apples filling the air, Aria and Jasper passed a performer on impossibly tall stilts who held out a fanned deck of cards. Jasper took one and flashed it to Aria. The Jack of Clubs. Except it wasn't a normal Club, she realised, it looked like a leaf.

Jasper slid the card back into the pack and, with a flourish, the magician whipped off his top hat and held it out. Aria leaned forwards, peering into the hat. Jasper's card was inside. They applauded and the man bowed deeply before turning to a group of women sitting on deckchairs, drinking wine and laughing.

Aria spotted a hook-a-duck and dragged Jasper towards it. "Come on, let's have a go."

"But, you're crap at these—" She punched him in the arm. "OK, sorry!" He laughed, rubbing the spot she'd hit. She rolled her eyes.

"Don't pretend that hurt."

They paid the stall operator and he handed them each a long pole with a hook on the end. "Step up, step up! Three attempts to win a prize. Black spot on the bottom of the duck means a win."

Aria approached the duck filled pool and hooked one of the nearest. She turned it over, but the underneath was blank. The next duck was the same. On her third attempt she finally won and chose a stuffed bear from the array of prizes.

"The dogs will love this. And then destroy it in three seconds flat."

Jasper stepped up to the pool and as he reached out over the congregation of rubber ducks with the pole, a shadow fell over the stall. Aria glanced up to see a boy in a black t-shirt with chin-length black hair walking by. As though feeling her gaze, he turned his head and their eyes met. A jolt went through Aria, like an electrical current from her finger tips to the roots of her hair. The way the sunlight hit his face, for just a second his grey eyes had looked like molten silver. It was…distracting.

She stumbled and reached out to steady herself, knocking the pole in Jasper's hands.

"You cheat!" He pulled the pole back and turned over the duck she'd knocked him into. "Yes! Winner. Serves you right for trying to cheat."

Aria looked around but the black-haired boy had gone. Vanished into thin air. Weird.

She turned back to Jasper and rolled her eyes. "Of course, you won on your first try. *Of course*, you did." She shook her head in mock disbelief. "Lucky git."

Jasper grinned, and chose a second stuffed bear as a prize. "Here," he offered it to her. "Now Max and Leo won't have to share." Aria smiled and took the toy, tucking it in her tote bag along with the other one, and Jasper's present.

They continued their stroll around the fayre, nibbling their still warm doughnuts. A unicyclist in harlequin face paint meandered towards them, pulling a bunch of fake flowers out of his sleeve as he passed and handing them to Aria, who laughed and feigned a swoon.

The sun was warm on Aria's pale, freckled skin and the smell of sugar doughnuts and candyfloss was intoxicating. She wished this day would never end, that they could wander between the tents and stalls, laughing and talking forever.

It felt like the last day of summer, rather than the first. The last day of their youth.

When September came around Jasper would be leaving Hartwood and heading off to university, and Aria would be left behind. It wasn't fair that three months' age difference meant a whole school year apart. Her final year of primary school had been bad enough, but they'd still been able to hang out after school. Now, Jasper would be an hour away in Axton, making new friends and probably forgetting all about her. All she wanted was one last summer together, just the two of them, before everything changed.

Jasper chose the High Striker next, lifting the enormous hammer with apparent ease. Aria watched as his biceps flexed, the muscles rippling under his tanned skin. He must have been working out, he was lean from playing football for years, but she'd never noticed how muscular he'd become until now.

Jasper swung the hammer with a grunt and set the bell ringing, lights flashing and crowds cheering. Typical. He was good at everything he tried his hand at, especially sports, unlike Aria whose hand-eye coordination left a lot to be desired.

Aria stepped up to the plate, rolling her shoulders and flexing her arms like she'd seen athletes do on TV.

"Come on, Riri! You've got this."

She hefted the hammer in her hands, it was heavier than she'd expected. She lifted it onto her shoulder and swung as hard as she could, putting all her strength into it.

Nothing happened. No bells, no lights, no adoring crowds chanting her name.

"Don't worry about it, it's obviously rigged." Jasper slid an arm around her shoulders and squeezed as the stall operator glared. Aria gave Jasper a smile and wrapped her arm around his waist as they wound their way back through the throng towards the Big Top.

His bronzed skin made hers look almost translucent. She envied his ability to tan with minimal sun exposure, what with being a quarter Spanish on his mother's side. Her redhead genes seemed to rule out anything other than freckling.

People were pouring out of the big red and white tent as they neared. The previous show must have run over, it'd be at least ten minutes before the next one.

Aria noticed a multi-coloured tent nearby with chiffon curtains hiding what was inside. "Come on, we've got time for one more game before it starts." She dragged him towards the curtained entrance until he spotted the sign hanging above it.

"A fortune teller?" He quirked an eyebrow at her. "I don't think so."

"Come on! Please? It'll be fun." She grabbed his arm and tried to pull him towards the fortune teller's tent. His feet didn't budge.

"Aria, you're not getting me to see a fortune teller. It's not happening."

She huffed an exasperated sigh. "You're such a scientist."

"I think you mean realist." She gave him a dry look, but he just pressed his lips together in a hard line. He'd always been a fan of facts and proof, it made watching films together a bit tedious, but she could usually forgive him his lack of imagination.

"Fine. You can wait out here." Before he could say another word, she ducked under the curtain and into the fortune teller's tent.

She was instantly enveloped by an overwhelming warmth. Outside, it was a beautiful summer's day, but walking into this tent felt like sinking into a bath, fully clothed.

"Welcome, my dear." The voice was high and girlish. "I am Divina, medium and mystic, here to answer your questions to the universe."

A woman sat at a small table, lit candles cast flickering shadows across her heavily made-up face and a warm breeze fluttered the curtains, carrying the scent of vanilla and sweat. "Come and take a seat."

Aria hesitated. Maybe this was a mistake. She should go or they'd miss the show.

Divina's smile widened and grew warm. She reached out, beckoning Aria. "There's no need to fret, dear. It's just a bit of fun." She picked up the dull crystal ball and rubbed it on her sleeve, before setting it back on its silver stand.

Aria hovered by the door, scuffing the poorly-laid carpet with the toe of her boot. The fortune teller cocked her head. "What is it, dear? What do you wish to know?"

Aria bit the inside of her cheek. Maybe Divina would be able to put her mind at rest. And the quicker she sat down, the quicker she'd be out of this tent and back in the fresh air.

She took a step forward and slid into the chair opposite Divina before she could change her mind. The fortune teller's robes and headscarf were made from cheap polyester in garish colours, and the crystal ball looked more like a paper weight, but she had a kind face. From this distance it was clear she was much older than she had first seemed. Her eyeliner had smudged into the deep wrinkles that cradled her watery eyes, giving them the look of precious jewels nestling within folds of leather. The sheen of sweat on her forehead and upper lip made Aria want to reach out and dab it with the tablecloth. Smoke from the candles stung Aria's eyes, she could feel herself beginning to perspire from the heat and hoped she wouldn't come out looking like the fortune teller, makeup-smeared and sweaty.

Divina's expression was patient but curious. Finally, Aria took a deep breath, exhaled slowly, and asked. "Will I ever get out of Hartwood?"

The fortune teller's thin eyebrows shot up, and Aria assumed she'd been expecting the usual 'who will I marry?' or 'how many children will I have?'. Rearranging her expression into something akin to admiration, the woman said, "Take my hands. Let's ask the ball." She laid her hands palm up on the table, either side of the spherical lump of glass she called a crystal ball. Aria reluctantly placed her hands atop the woman's, recoiling internally at the feel of Divina's clammy skin. Divina closed her eyes and began to chant under her breath, something that sounded like gibberish to Aria.

Her eyes shot open. They'd become glassy and unfocused, as though she saw something other than the girl sitting in front of her in the candlelit tent. She gripped Aria's fingers like a vice, and when Aria looked down she realised the crystal ball no longer resembled a dull lump of glass. A white mist had begun to swirl inside it. She knew it was all rigged up to make the experience more authentic, but Aria's heart raced. She had to admit, Divina put on a good show.

The fortune teller stopped chanting abruptly and a sudden breeze extinguished the candles. More smoke filled the room, making Aria choke. Divina began to speak in a strange voice, several octaves lower than her normal timbre. *"When kingdoms unite and flame and aether collide, the Fair Queen shall return. She shall bring forth the fall of a false king and usher in a time of—"*

Cool air rushed into the tent as someone ripped open the curtain and burst inside. Aria whipped her head around, wrenching her fingers out of Divina's grip, to find a boy with an impish grin and auburn hair standing in the doorway. He spotted Aria and Divina sitting there in a cloud of smoke and bowed, the smile spreading across his handsome face like an infection.

"My mistake. Apologies, ladies, do continue."

Divina, her eyes now clear and grey, stood and shooed the boy out of the tent. He gave Aria one last grin before ducking back under the curtain.

"Where were we?" Divina sat back down and reached for Aria's hands, but the spell had been broken. Aria stood and staggered towards the torn curtains and the promise of fresh air, her skin still crawling from Divina's touch and the way she'd sounded moments before, like she'd been in a trance.

"Sorry. I mean, thanks. I have to go." Her toe caught on the carpet where she'd kicked it up earlier and she stumbled, grabbing the curtain for support and almost tearing it down. Divina called after her, but Aria ignored her, fighting her way through the chiffon curtains and out of the tent.

2

ARIA STOOD OUTSIDE GULPING DOWN COOL AIR and squinting in the too-bright sunlight. She'd just wanted a bit of fun, maybe a generic platitude to reassure her that she'd one day escape her hometown and make something of herself. She hadn't expected to be so freaked out. She couldn't even put her finger on what had bothered her so much.

She didn't believe in psychics and mysticism and Divina's words hadn't made any sense, but the creeping sensation that Divina's performance had caused still prickled under her skin.

She hadn't told Jasper how she'd been feeling lately—trapped and powerless. Like she was bound for a life of mediocrity and mundanity. She didn't want him to feel sorry for her, or worse, guilty for leaving her behind.

The realisation dawned that she hadn't paid for the fortune, that must be why Divina had called after her.

She turned to go back inside and pay, but her shoulder connected with something hard. She sprawled on the floor, hands burning as they scraped on the dry grass. Groaning, she rubbed her knee through her jeans. Luckily they weren't torn or she'd have been pissed. Her favourite boots and her favourite jeans ruined in the same day?

"Awfully sorry—oh, it's you!" The auburn-haired boy held out his hand to help her up. He wasn't a local by the sound of his clipped accent. Aria didn't recognise him from school or around the village either. He must have been visiting someone, or maybe he had arrived with the fayre. He certainly had the air of a performer.

She ignored the hand and got to her feet, brushing herself down. His smile faltered for a second, and then returned, doubly bright. "That's twice I've disrupted you now. You must let me make it up to you. How about a beverage?" His expression was open and he was good-looking, she had to admit, with those piercing blue eyes and roguish smile. "The name's Bazyl, by the way."

Aria opened her mouth to tell him thanks but no thanks, glancing around for Jasper, who was nowhere to be seen, when a shadow fell over the boy's face. She felt a hand on her lower back and relaxed. There he was, finally.

"Are you alright?" He asked, concern distorting his voice.

"I'm fine, I just—"

Aria looked up into her friend's face, and started. The boy with his hand on her back wasn't Jasper. It was the black-haired, grey-eyed boy she'd seen by the hook-a-duck stall.

"Can I help you?" The boy asked Bazyl. His voice sounded polite on the surface, with a coolness underneath, like steel wrapped in silk. His chin length hair curled around his ears, grey eyes narrowed at the other boy, who looked surprised and slightly irritated at the intrusion.

"No, thank you. I was actually just speaking with…?" Bazyl looked expectantly at Aria, but she didn't hear him. She was gazing into the cool grey eyes of the other boy. She couldn't remember what she'd been about to say.

"You…" Aria breathed.

Bazyl frowned. "You know each other?" He sounded surprised. His eyes darted between them, a look of growing consternation twisting his elegant features.

The black-haired boy snaked his arm around her waist and pulled her tightly in to his side. "Of course. She's here with me." Aria's mind raced with questions and she looked to Bazyl, unsure what to say or do. She was paralysed, stunned into silence by the newcomer's boldness.

Confusion filled Bazyl's eyes and Aria felt a pang of guilt that she couldn't explain. He made his apologies and backed away, still glancing between the black-haired boy and Aria, disbelief and irritation flitting across his face like clouds across a stunning blue sky. He disappeared into the crowd, leaving her alone with the black-haired boy.

Aria finally pulled away, feeling a chill run down her side where his warm touch had been seconds before. Now that he was a safe distance away, she couldn't believe how frozen she'd been. What the hell had come over her?

"You're welcome." The boy wasn't looking at her, he was squinting as he scanned the crowd, making sure Bazyl had really gone.

Aria balked. "I'm *welcome*? For what, exactly?"

"You looked like you needed rescuing. I rescued you. You're welcome." He said it matter-of-factly, still avoiding her eyes. Maybe he thought Bazyl would come back and bring a gang of friends to kick his teeth in. Worryingly, he didn't look afraid. He looked ready for a fight.

While he was distracted, Aria took the opportunity to study him.

He was tall, over six feet, and muscular. He wore a black t-shirt and dark jeans with canvas trainers. He looked like any other boy her age. Except for those pewter eyes.

He finally turned his attention back to Aria and caught her staring at him. He suppressed a smile and she looked away, heat rising to her cheeks. "Let me know if he bothers you again. You don't want to associate with his sort."

This threw Aria off balance. Bazyl had seemed harmless enough to her. Charming, even. "What do you mean?"

"Just trust me," he said over his shoulder, and then he strode away without a backwards glance.

Who the hell did this guy think he was? Trust him? He hadn't even told her his name. And how exactly was she supposed to contact him if Bazyl did turn up again? Scream for help? Not likely.

She marched after him, determined to give him a piece of her mind. Or, at least that's what she told herself. Deep down she was curious about him, the odd feeling that had washed over her when he was near, and those steely eyes. She followed him as he slipped between two stalls and disappeared into a tent. The sign read Hall of Mirrors.

Lifting the tent flap and stepping inside, Aria was confronted with a dozen images of herself, every one distorted. Music came through hidden speakers inside the tent, loud and jarring, the notes clashing together in a cacophony that made Aria's flesh rise with goose bumps, despite the warmth. She took a step and twelve other Arias stepped forwards too. She glimpsed movement in one of the mirrors and turned to see the black-haired boy, or his reflection.

"Hey." She moved towards the mirror and his image disappeared. "Wait, I want to speak to you!" The music drowned out her voice and footsteps, disorienting her. She would have to rely on sight, try to separate the real boy from the reflections. Spinning around, something caught her eye in one of the mirrors and she darted towards it. There he was, except it wasn't quite him. The mirror warped his features. He looked sharper, somehow. His cheekbones were higher, his bone structure finer, and his ears seemed to taper. His grey eyes flicked to her, glinting in the dim light.

"Who are you? Have you been following me?" She approached the mirror, and as she did the boy vanished. She stood in front of it alone, her own reflection staring back at her. The effect was the same as it had been on the boy, her features were honed, elongated. Her brown eyes appeared to be lit from within. Pointed ears poked out from her shoulder-length copper hair.

Aria took another step closer. Slowly, she reached up to brush her fingertips over the tops of her ears, eyes fixed on her face in the mirror. She hesitated, fingers millimetres away from her ears.

Her phone vibrated in her pocket, sending a jolt of electricity through her nerves. She dropped her hands and fumbled for her phone, heart beating a rhythm against her ribs. It was a text from Jasper, asking where she'd disappeared to. The show was about to start.

She shoved the phone in her pocket and ran out of the tent without a backwards glance, feeling a dozen pairs of grey eyes on her back as she went.

3

"I'M HOME!" Aria opened the front door of her parents' bungalow and was instantly assaulted by the dogs jumping up to lick her face. She crouched down to take the two stuffed toys out of her bag and the dogs dropped into a sitting position, patiently waiting. Her fingers brushed against something hard at the bottom of her bag and she groaned. She'd forgotten to give Jasper his birthday present.

"In here." Her father's voice came from his study. Max and Leo, now mollified by the stuffed toys, trotted into the kitchen, leaving Aria alone in the hall. She punched out a quick text message to Jasper:

Forgot to give you your present. Come round x

She popped her head round the door of her dad's study. "Hey Teacup, how was the fayre? Did you win a goldfish?"

When Aria had been a little girl, her tiny stature and fiery personality had earned her the nickname Storm in a Teacup. Her tantrums had been the stuff of legend, according to her father. Over the years, the name had been shortened to Teacup. It had surprised everyone when Aria had continued to grow throughout her teens, quickly surpassing her petite mother for height, and almost matching her father, who, at just five foot ten, was not a particularly tall man. Even Jasper towered over him at six foot one.

"It was fun, we won a couple of teddies for the boys. No goldfish, sadly." She stepped into the room and closed the door gently behind her. "What are you working on?"

The sun had begun to set and the lamps in the study were already lit, giving off a warm, inviting ambience. The room smelled of furniture polish and the extra strong mints her father chomped on constantly while he was writing. His greying-brown hair was a mess from running his hands through it, and his cable-knit sweater had a hole in the shoulder. He was endearingly shabby, although her mother found it somewhat less endearing.

"It's a new piece actually, about the history of Hartwood. For a collection of essays." His face lit up. Aria loved listening to her father speak about his work, he was passionate and curious, and Aria thought he could write about absolutely anything and find a way to make it universally interesting. "I'm mentioning your mate, the White Hart." He winked at her, blue eyes twinkling in the lamplight.

"I'll see if I can get you an exclusive," she joked back. She'd told everyone she'd seen the mythical white stag when she was a little girl, wandering the woods behind the bungalow one dark winter's night. No one had believed her, and now she wasn't sure it hadn't been one of the neighbours walking their dog, the light from a torch giving the animal a pale glow. "What's for tea?"

"Check the fridge, your mum made lasagne, or there might be some leftover pizza."

Aria closed the door behind her, leaving her father to his writing, and headed to the opposite corner of the house. Her bedroom opened out onto the back garden, which was now barely visible in the fading light. Her mother had draped solar powered fairy lights along the fence and they shone prettily in the dimness, casting tiny halos of light that made the surrounding darkness seem impenetrable.

Aria dropped her bag onto the bed and turned on her laptop. The last song she had been listening to before she left the house resumed playing through her speakers. She sang along absently with Ed Sheeran, going to the mirror and brushing her long hair. She ran a fingertip over the top of her ear, tucking her hair behind it, and wondered again how the mirror at the fayre had worked. She'd caught the sun today, she realised, leaning in closer to inspect the freckles that had appeared across her nose and cheekbones.

Jasper's distinctive knock sounded at the French window, and she went to open it. "Hey, you." He stepped into the room and went straight to lie on her bed, long legs dangling over the edge. "I love this song." He sang along, his voice like silk. It was infuriating how talented he was.

"Hey, you—did you change your clothes?" She took in his clean white shirt and dark jeans. He'd redone his hair too. And put on aftershave. "Birthday meal?"

He was blushing. "I'm going back to the fayre."

"Doughnut guy?" She kept her tone light despite the tightness in her chest.

"His name's Mark." He grinned and Aria's heart gave a painful squeeze. She busied herself, picking up her bag and tipping out a box wrapped in blue paper. She handed it to Jasper who tore off the paper and opened the box. He pulled out a watch with a brown leather strap.

"It's engraved." Aria dropped down next to him on the bed, so close their arms and legs were touching.

Jasper turned the watch over to read the inscription on the back. "Ninety-four days, sixteen hours and forty-one minutes." He looked at her, brow furrowed. "Is that…how much older than you I am? Calling me old on my birthday, that hurts." He laughed and Aria rolled her eyes as she took the watch from his hands and started to fasten it around his wrist.

"*That* is exactly how long you lived without me in your life." She focused on fastening the buckle and fighting back the tears that threatened to spill over if she so much as blinked. She hated getting emotional in front of him. "It's the only time you will *ever* have to live without me." She let go of his hand and looked up at him, eyes shining.

Jasper pulled his best friend into a tight hug. "Aria, I love it. And I love you."

She fought to keep her breathing steady. Once upon a time, she had dreamed of hearing Jasper say those words. As more than a friend.

They'd lived next door to each other their entire lives and the two had been inseparable from the beginning. They'd walked to school with each other every day, sat at the same table at lunch, and even insisted on eating the same sandwiches, much to their mothers' chagrin. They'd managed to remain best friends when Jasper moved on to secondary school at eleven, and Aria had been forced to wait a year before she joined him. And as they'd grown up and hormones had raged, the natural assumption had been that they would become more than friends. Or so it had seemed to Aria.

But she was over her childish crush now. She didn't even think about what it would be like to kiss him anymore. Or run her hands through his wavy brow hair…

Jasper hopped off the bed. "I'd better get going." He reached the French windows in two strides.

"Yeah, you don't want to keep *Mark* waiting." She teased, but he didn't take the bait.

"Wish me luck." He opened the door and stepped out.

"Jazz."

"Yeah?"

"He doesn't stand a chance." Jasper grinned and disappeared into the night, now inky black and cooling quickly. Aria got up and pulled the curtains across, leaving the door ajar to let some air in. She crossed to her laptop and scrolled through her music, looking for something that suited her mood. She was still a bit on edge after the fayre, although she hadn't told Jasper about the weird fortune, or the grey-eyed boy and the hall of mirrors. She hadn't been able to find the right words, the thought of saying it out loud made her feel strange. Almost silly.

Lana del Ray's haunting voice flowed from the speakers. Moody, and just a little bit sad. Perfect.

Telling herself the crazy old lady in the headscarf probably said the same thing to everyone didn't help. It wasn't even her words that had made Aria's stomach drop and her blood turn to ice water. It was the way the fortune teller had looked at her. The unfocused eyes, the steel grip, the swirling white mist inside the crystal ball.

When Bazyl had burst into the tent and interrupted them it had been a relief. He'd had the brightest blue eyes, like a clear sky, and his hair had been like night to Aria's day—deep auburn where hers was palest copper.

Then there was the black-haired boy. She hadn't caught his name…

Jasper's distinctive knock, one slow rap followed by two in quick succession, sounded at the window again. He must have forgotten something. "It's open, Jazz." She reached down beside her bed to plug her phone into the charger, the sudden breeze from the open door lifting her hair from the back of her neck. The sweet scent of honeysuckle drifted in from the garden.

"Was the date that bad?" She said without turning around. The curtains billowed in the breeze and Lana del Ray sang about summertime sadness.

When Jasper didn't reply, she lifted her head, but before she could turn around something hard connected with the back of her head and she fell forwards.

If she hit the floor, she didn't feel it.

4

ARIA WASN'T SURE HOW MUCH TIME HAD PASSED when she woke up, opening her eyes and seeing only blackness. The back of her head felt like it might split open at any moment, if it hadn't already. She reached up to touch it, hoping there wouldn't be any blood, and realised with a jolt that her hands were tied. Her ankles, too.

She took a shaky breath and tried to slow her racing pulse. She couldn't let herself panic, she needed to work out where she was, and try to get out of her restraints. A cool breeze rushed over her—she was outside, then. Nightjars sang nearby, and as her eyes adjusted to the moonlight she could just make out the trees towering over her. She was in the woods. Shit, she could be anywhere within a five-mile radius, how the hell was she going to find her way home?

She pushed up onto her knees. Dizziness and nausea hit her like a fist.

"I wouldn't do that if I were you." A low male voice, quiet and unnervingly close by. Aria froze, terror almost weakening her bladder.

A fire roared to life, dispersing the darkness a little. She was in the middle of a small clearing, and she wasn't alone. "You probably have a concussion. Apologies about that, I may have been a little heavy handed."

The boy was sitting on the other side of a small fire, fiddling with something that glinted in the firelight. Aria was lost for words, her limbs leaden with fear. He looked strangely familiar, but she wasn't sure where she'd seen him before. "I am sorry we had to do that, but there was no other way. You would never have come willingly, and there was no time to convince you."

White hot rage burned through the terror and Aria finally found her voice. "Who the hell are you?" She regretted shouting immediately when her head exploded with pain. In a quieter, but no less angry voice, she said, "What do you want with me?"

He paused, turning over the thing in his hands. "You're not who you think you are, Aria."

Taken aback, she just stared at him for several seconds. "What the hell does that mean? And, how do you know my name?" She didn't actually care, she just wanted to keep him talking. That was what you were supposed to do, weren't you? Keep your kidnapper talking, try to find out something about them, some leverage you could use to convince them to let you go. She'd read that in a book, or heard it on a podcast. So she'd keep him talking and distract him as long as she could.

Because she could feel the ropes around her wrists loosening as she fought against them.

"Your father sent us."

That caught her attention. She stopped struggling against her restraints momentarily. "My dad?"

"Your *real* father," he corrected. "The Salamander King."

Her fear was a living thing, clawing at her insides. He was insane. She pulled as hard as she could on the ropes binding her wrists, desperation numbing her senses. She had to get away from this boy, as fast as she could.

"My real father?" She stammered, grasping for a way to distract him while she worked her way out of her ties. "The—what was it?"

"The Salamander King. King Ossian."

"Salamander. Right. So, my real dad is a lizard?" She could have laughed, but the ice-cold fear gripping her wouldn't allow it. She was painfully aware of her own vulnerability, especially with her limbs incapacitated.

A spark caught her eye, and the sound of metal scraping drew her attention to the thing in the boy's hands. He was sharpening some sort of weapon.

Aria's insides turned to liquid and she sobbed out loud. He was going to kill her. He was going to slit her throat, or stab her, or any number of horrifying things you could do with a sharp object.

"A *lizard*?" Somehow, he managed to make her sound like the crazy one. "No. No, that's just what we call the Fair who are gifted with fire."

Well, that made *much* more sense.

Pulling harder against the rope, she finally ripped a hand free. She held tightly onto the rope to stop it from dropping to the floor and making a sound. If she could just get her ankles free…

The boy paused his sharpening and set down the blade. "I didn't expect you to believe us, that's why we had to take you by force." The fact he kept saying 'we' scared Aria more by the minute. Where was his accomplice? Exactly how many of them were there? It would have taken more than one person to carry Aria this far from her house without waking her, or being seen.

A thrill went through Aria at the thought of someone having seen them, alerting the police or her parents. Jasper leading a search party to find her.

"Your father is very sick, Aria. And, as his eldest child, you are the rightful heir to the throne."

A strangled sound escaped Aria, and she instantly regretted it. Fire erupted inside her skull. She took a deep breath and let it out slowly. She needed to buy some time, he would tire of this strange game soon and then she would be in real danger.

"I'm a princess?" From where she sat, with the fire between them, she could make out the boy's head and shoulders—short, dark hair, dark t-shirt, blue eyes—but not much below that. She hoped with everything she had that he could only see the same amount of her. Slowly, she slid her left foot out of her boot. "Does that mean I'm rich?"

The boy narrowed his eyes, something like distaste in his expression. "Rich?" He shook his head. "Wealth is not the concern right now, you need to come with us and take your rightful place as the Salamander crown princess."

Aria slid off her right boot as quietly as she could, and started to roll down her sock with her toes. She didn't care if running through the forest barefoot was a bad idea. Better to have bloodied feet than…No, she would not consider the alternative. She had to get away from this psychopath. *Had to.*

"I don't have time to convince you, Aria. You're in danger." His voice was low and rumbling, almost a growl. His words vibrated in her bones. He didn't have to tell her she was in danger, she was acutely aware. "The boy who spoke to you at the fayre, Bazyl Demitree, he is one of the Celeste King's men. He was there to take you, on the Celeste King's orders."

The fayre. It felt like days ago, not hours. She had the sudden surreal feeling that she was still sitting in that fortune teller's tent, asking if she would ever escape her small town, and that this was some kind of strange wish fulfilment. She imagined she would wake up any second and be back there in that tent, the fortune teller cackling as she staggered to her feet and out into the fresh air.

"Aria, if you don't come with us, they will come for you. And they will not be as subtle as we were." She almost snorted at that. The pain that throbbed in the back of her skull took exception to that description. "And they will kill anyone who gets in their way."

Aria's heart stopped. Her socks lay on the ground, the ropes around her ankles almost loose enough to slip off. But she sat frozen to the spot, her parents' faces in her mind. Jasper's.

You don't want to associate with his sort. Just trust me.

No. She didn't believe it. Why was she listening to him? He was the danger, not some clumsy boy who had offered to buy her a coffee as an apology. This one, who had knocked her unconscious and taken her from her own bedroom and tied her up in the woods.

She needed to run. *Now.*

A twig snapped in the trees behind the boy and he turned his head just a fraction, distracted momentarily. It would have to be enough.

Aria stepped out of her restraints and ran.

Branches snagged at her hair and whipped her arms and legs, but Aria kept running as fast as she could. Her breath came in short gasps and the pain in her skull was excruciating. She didn't stop, though. She kept putting one foot in front of the other, stumbling through the woods in what she hoped was the direction of Hartwood.

She couldn't let her kidnapper catch up with her. She had to get away, find her way home or get some help.

She thought back to earlier that evening, when she'd been in her bedroom listening to music and Jasper had come round. He'd opened her gift, told her he had a date, and left. And then he'd knocked again…

Everything after that was a blank. Had he come back? Was it even Jasper who had knocked? It'd sounded like him.

She couldn't remember, and it terrified her. Her memory was a blackhole up until she found herself in that clearing. She thought back to earlier in the day, trying to anchor herself in those memories, but she kept coming back to the empty space where the last few hours should have been. It hurt to think about, like a tongue probing the gap where a tooth has been removed.

Something hard and unyielding struck her shins and she flew for no more than a second, but it felt like forever. Until the ground rose up to meet her, hard, and she sprawled across the dirt and pine needles, groaning.

A light appeared between the trees, moving from side to side. "Are you alright?" A hand appeared in the beam of the torch, reaching out to her. She recoiled instinctively, shielding her eyes from the light. "Sorry," the male voice said, and the torch clicked off, plunging them back into darkness. "It's a little late for a stroll through the woods, isn't it?"

She knew that voice. That arrogant, mocking tone.

As her eyes readjusted to the dimness, she recognised the black-haired, grey-eyed boy from the fayre. "It's you. Please, you have to help me. Some guy abducted me, he tied me up. I managed to get away, but

I—" Aria stilled, the words dying on her lips. What was *he* doing in the woods in the middle of the night?

"*What?*" He sounded genuinely appalled. "Come on, let me help you get home." He reached a hand out again and this time, after a few seconds of deliberating, she took it. "Are you hurt?"

"Just a bit of a headache," she admitted. Blood rushed to her head as she stood up and it made her sway, threatening to steal her consciousness. The grey-eyed boy draped her arm over his shoulder and took some of her weight, helping her to walk in a straight line.

"Seems like a little more than a headache to me. You might have a concussion." She did feel a bit nauseous. And tired. It was nice to lean against him and feel the warmth of his body as he guided her through the trees towards the village. He felt strong and solid, muscles tensing in his stomach as she clung on to his t-shirt.

"Hey," Aria said after a few minutes of walking, and the boy paused to look at her, an odd expression on his face. "What's your name?"

He hesitated for a moment and she thought he might not reply, but after a few seconds of uncomfortable silence, he spoke. "Xander."

"I'm Aria. Wait, I already told you that at the fayre. Thank you for helping me, Xander." Her mind had started to cloud with dizziness and fatigue. She could see moonlight filtering through the tree line now, they had to be close to Hartwood village.

But instead of stepping through the trees into the open, they stepped into a large clearing. A smoking pile of sticks where a fire had recently been was in the centre, and a pile of discarded ropes.

The nausea tripled and Aria staggered away from Xander, who was holding his hands up and looking at her like a deer that might bolt.

"You're with him?" She said, sick realisation dawning. "What is this? I don't understand. I don't—"

"Aria, I'm sorry, but you need to come with us." He didn't sound sorry. The moon shone down into the clearing, deepening the shadows and chiselling his jaw and cheekbones. Aria couldn't see his eyes, but it didn't matter. She wouldn't have trusted him anyway.

A chill rippled through Aria as the other boy, the one who had been sitting by the fire earlier, stepped out of the darkness of the trees behind Xander. She saw the similarities now, the strong jaw and straight nose. They looked like brothers.

"I told you it wouldn't work," the other boy ground out.

"Not now, Kiefer," Xander growled.

Aria took a step back and her foot slipped on a loose stone. She put a hand out to grab onto something—anything, to prevent her from falling, and felt a hand catch her arm, holding her upright.

"Steady there." Aria whipped around, wrenching her arm from the third boy's grip. She had to crane her neck to look at his face, he must have been well over six feet tall, this newcomer. And built like a bear. Facial hair hid a large portion of his face, and when his lip started to curl in some sort of grimace, white teeth flashed in the moonlight.

Aria backed away, bumping into Xander as she did. When she whirled around, trying to keep all three of them in her sights at once, she realised two more boys had materialised from the shadows, completing the circle around her. A whimper escaped her before she bit down, the coppery tang of blood filling her mouth as she looked from one to the other.

5

"**S**HE ISN'T GOING TO MAKE THIS EASY FOR US, IS SHE?" Kiefer tucked his knife into his waistband and ran his hands over his slicked-back, dark hair.

Aria sat on the ground in the clearing, hands and feet bound again, tighter this time, a strip of material between her teeth as a gag. She glowered up at the five young men who stood in a loose circle around her. She had kicked and fought, and even bitten one of them as they restrained her, screaming and shouting for help, until Kiefer had cut a strip off his shirt and shoved it in her mouth.

Now that the adrenalin had worn off, she sat shivering, knees drawn up to her chest, an overwhelming exhaustion tugging at her consciousness.

"You had your chance, Xander. She didn't believe us," the tall, bearded one said, his voice deep and gravelly.

"I know, I know," Xander replied. He glared down at Aria, jaw clenching and unclenching. "How far to the crossing?"

Aria could feel panic rising in her chest. Where were they taking her? She remembered another piece of advice she'd heard on some true crime podcast or other—never let a kidnapper take you to a secondary location. It never ended well in the stories she listened to. But how was she supposed to escape from five men?

"A few minutes' jog."

"We should leave soon, before Demitree and his men reach us," said a boy with dark-brown skin and something that looked like a bow strapped across his back.

Demitree?

Was it true, then, that Bazyl was after her, too? Aria got the sudden, sick feeling that this was all some kind of twisted game. Two teams of hunters, and her the prey caught between them. Her stomach churned at the thought.

"We need to cross through the Veil before they catch up to us. They probably had someone watching the house, they may already know we have her," Kiefer said.

Xander rubbed a hand over his face. "Rainer, can you carry her?"

"Sure," Rainer, the bearded one replied. "Coulter, watch our rear. We need to leave now."

"On it," the dark-skinned boy said with a nod, removing his bow and drawing a long, feathered arrow from his quill.

Aria stared at Rainer, eyes wide. She shook her head vehemently— no way was he carrying her anywhere.

Only one of the boys hadn't spoken up yet, the youngest by the looks of it. He stood with his head down, casting furtive glances at Aria, something like shame in his light eyes every time she caught them. He shared the dark hair and strong jaw of Xander and Kiefer, but lacked the hardness of the older boys.

"Quade, fall in."

"Xander, I don't think—" His voice was quiet and soft.

"Now!" Barked Xander, and the younger boy took up a position to Rainer's left, gnawing at his bottom lip. Kiefer moved to Rainer's right, hand on the knife in his belt, and Xander headed the diamond formation.

"Apologies for this, Princess." Rainer took a step towards Aria

"No, no, no, no, no—" She tried to protest, but it came out garbled around the gag. He lifted her like a sack of coal and threw her over his shoulder. The world flipped and so did Aria's stomach, threatening to empty its contents onto the forest floor.

The sky had darkened to an impenetrable black, she couldn't make out much beyond the shoulder-length hair of the man who held her. It smelled surprisingly of sandalwood, and she wondered distantly if he oiled it.

Her head throbbed painfully and she squeezed her eyes shut, hoping the blackness would ease her nausea. It did, a little.

The sound of bodies moving through the forest, of twigs snapping and feet thudding reached them from a distance.

"Demitree's men," Coulter said, his voice coming from in front of Aria, now that she was draped over Rainer's shoulder. "We need to go if we want to avoid a bloodbath."

They took off at a fast jog.

After several minutes of Aria bumping against Rainer's back with every step, bile hit the back of her throat and she vomited down his back.

"Hang in there, Princess." He didn't break his stride.

After what felt like hours of hanging upside down and being constantly jostled, Rainer slowed to a stop and turned to face the others. From her position over his shoulder, Aria could just about make out a pair of pine trees that had grown towards each other instead of the sky, twining to form an archway underneath. Through the arch she could see yet more dark forest.

"Coulter, Kiefer, you two go first, then Quade and Rainer," Xander ordered. "I'll follow. Hurry."

Kiefer stepped forward, removing his dagger from his belt. Aria felt nauseous again at the sight of the blade. With the concussion and the abject terror, she felt lightheaded and weak. She had all but accepted the fact she would die at the hands of these strange men. She didn't even think she could muster a scream, let alone fight back.

The only thing holding her together was the thought of her parents and Jasper, safe in their beds. If what Kiefer had said was true, then Bazyl and his men were even worse than these boys, and they would have murdered her parents in order to get to her. In other circumstances, she would have willingly died to protect her mum, dad and best friend, but she wasn't ready to give up quite yet…

Coulter unsheathed his own knife and the two boys shared a grin, some understanding passing between them, before they approached the archway. They stepped between the trees, weapons held up defensively.

And disappeared.

"What the—" Aria thrashed in Rainer's arms, trying to get a better look at the place where the two boys had vanished from sight.

"Our turn now, Princess," Rainer muttered, his grip on her tightening as his other hand pulled out a deadly-looking hatchet. "Hold on tight." He gave Xander a nod, turned towards the archway, and strode forwards without hesitation, Quade scrambling to keep up.

Xander watched them go, expression unreadable.

A moment later, Aria felt a strange sensation, like static electricity tingling her skin, and Xander disappeared from view.

6

RAINER SET ARIA DOWN ON THE GROUND, her bare feet connecting with cool, damp grass. She stumbled when he let go of her, ankles still bound, and his hands gripped her upper arms gently, steadying her.

"Easy, easy." He held his hands up when she writhed away from him. "Here, let me untie you." He reached into the satchel strapped across his broad chest and pulled out first, a wicked-looking blade, and second, her socks and boots. He removed her bindings, moving slowly and letting her watch as he sliced the ropes. "Here, put these back on. It's not far to the horses, but it will be better for your head if you walk."

With her hands free, Aria tore the makeshift gag from her mouth and tossed it on the ground. She pulled her socks and boots on, grateful for the warmth and comfort. Plus, it'd be much easier to run with her boots on.

Coulter appeared then, jogging towards them. "All clear."

Kiefer emerged from the trees on their other side. "Clear!"

Aria barely heard them, she was looking around at the trees that lined the pale gravel path that began just beyond the arch and seemed to lead deep into the forest. They looked just like the trees that had surrounded them on the other side of the archway, but somehow different. More vital. A breeze whispered through the leaves, making them dance, and she could almost hear words under the gentle shushing sound.

The air felt charged, like right before a thunderstorm, and a faint layer of mist swirled around the base of the trees. She shivered, and not from the cold.

"Where's Xander?" Quade's voice was tight. They all turned to look at the archway.

"He was right behind us, he'll be here—"

A ripple disturbed the image inside the arch and Xander appeared in front of them as if from thin air, a blade in each hand. Aria's brain fought to process what she was seeing. It had to be a trick of the light. He couldn't have materialised from nothing…

"Thank the Earth." Quade muttered.

"Q, it's only been thirty seconds." Kiefer rolled his eyes, but Xander tossed a wink at his younger brother as he tucked his knives into his belt.

Aria couldn't take it anymore. "I'm not stupid, you know." She wished she didn't sound so pathetic. She locked her knees to keep them from shaking. "I know you're going to kill me. Why don't you just get it over with?"

She wasn't sure why she said it, but she didn't want them to see how afraid she was, she wanted them to think she was brave. Not that it mattered what they thought, but she certainly wasn't going to cower and beg, or go willingly.

The boys were silent, Coulter rubbed the back of his neck and Quade hung his head, unable to meet her eyes.

Finally, Xander stepped towards her. "We don't have time for this." He reached for her and she backed away.

"Just let me go," she sobbed, her throat thick with unshed tears. Realising that nobody was restraining her, in a moment of madness she sprinted towards the archway and threw herself through it.

She hit the ground with a thud.

Groaning, she rolled onto her back and saw the archway above her. And the five boys standing on the other side, staring at her. Kiefer and Coulter seemed to be stifling laughs, and Quade's mouth was a perfect O, but Xander's expression terrified her. On the surface, he appeared calm, but when she looked into his eyes her mouth went dry. The anger there burned cold and clear.

Rainer strode towards her and held out a hand to help her up. "It doesn't work like that," he said in a low voice, out of earshot of the others.

She ignored the proffered hand and got to her feet, brushing the dirt from her clothes.

"What are you talking about?"

"Aether magic is…complicated," he said, confusing her even further. "At any rate, the crossing is closed to you, so you may as well come with us." He gestured towards the group of boys standing a few feet away. They all seemed to be looking anywhere but at Aria. All except Xander, who was as steely-eyed as ever, studying her with an intensity she could almost feel on her skin like a physical touch.

"Come, the horses are just a few minutes away." Rainer's tone was gentle.

Xander's was the opposite, when he added, "Do we need to tie you up and carry you, again?"

Aria looked around and, seeing little choice, shook her head, which sent a spike of pain through her skull. She swallowed, her throat tight, and started to walk.

Five sleek horses grazed in a small, moonlit paddock next to a wooden stable with a row of empty stalls.

Xander approached a black stallion, slipping his hand into a leather saddlebag and pulling out an apple. The horse proceeded to chomp on the fruit while Xander stroked the animal's neck.

He glanced at Aria, saw her watching and looked away quickly.

"You'll ride with me." She almost didn't hear him, distracted by the sudden change in his features.

It wasn't just that he seemed softer, somehow, as he showed affection to his horse, or the flattering silvery moonlight that bathed the clearing. His eyes shone like metal, almost shimmering, like raw silver. His jaw and cheekbones were sharper, chiselled almost, the shadows carving hollows where there had been none before. And—surely her eyes were playing tricks on her now—were his ears *pointed*?

"I hit my head," she muttered, unable to look away from his face. He was still the boy she had met at the fayre earlier that day, just more defined.

As the others reached the clearing and stepped into the pool of light, she noticed the same thing about every one of them. Sharper features, like they had left standard definition behind in Hartwood and were now in high definition. Iridescent irises that sparked when they caught the light. Ears that came to a point and poked out of their hair.

"I have a concussion." Aria stumbled backwards, shaking her head and regretting it.

Coulter snorted. "I may not be a healer, but I'm pretty sure that shaking your head will not help if you do." Rainer flashed him a reproachful look.

"Is it the ears?" Quade asked. "You'll have them too, what with you being one of us." He stepped towards her and reached out a hand as though to brush her hair back behind her ear and prove his theory. His brow furrowed and he dropped his hand. "Well, it will probably be a while before your body remembers that you're not human." He shrugged, apologetically.

Aria's hands shot up to touch the tops of her ears. "*Not human?*" She gasped. When her fingertips found the smooth, rounded skin of her ears she sagged with relief.

Rainer stepped between Quade and Aria, giving the other boy a sharp look. "Of course you are human."

Now that he was standing in the middle of the clearing, flooded with light, Aria studied Rainer. He looked to be a couple of years older than the other boys, perhaps in his early twenties, while the others looked like teenagers. Xander, Kiefer and Coulter could pass for nineteen or twenty, while Quade looked closest to Aria's own age, maybe even a year or two younger.

"We are all human," Rainer said pointedly. "He just means that you are not from *there*, you are from *here*." He gestured around them, as though that clarified things. "You are one of us, Princess. One of the Fair." Aria hadn't thought she could get any more confused. She opened her mouth, and was immediately cut off by Xander,

"We don't have time for explanations. We have to leave before

Demitree and his men manage to cross through the Veil." He checked the saddle and bridle on his horse and untethered him. "Aria, it's just a few days' ride to your father's stronghold in the Salamander Kingdom." He studied her face with his cool gaze, "He'll explain everything. If you still wish to leave after you've heard what he has to say, I'll return you to Hartwood myself. You have my word."

His word? Like that meant anything.

He held out his hand to help her climb into the saddle. She stared at it, wary. With a sigh, she put her hand in his and stepped into the stirrup.

Once she was atop the horse, Xander swung himself up easily and settled into position behind her. She could feel him pressed against her back, his legs lying along the outsides of her thighs, and it made her skin crawl. His warm breath moved the fine hairs at the nape of her neck and a shudder went through her.

When he wrapped an arm around her waist, pressing her to him, she pulled away and he didn't fight it. But when the horse began to trot, picking up speed and jostling her in the saddle, she found herself pushing back against him to stop herself from falling. Anger and revulsion coursed through her, but better that than to be thrown and killed.

If she couldn't have her own horse, there was no way she was going to get away. She would have to go with them, for now.

She closed her eyes and gripped the horse's mane, her knuckles whitening with the effort. The pain in her skull was building to a crescendo and she thought she might throw up again, but the cool breeze as they rode through the dim forest was soothing against her face.

She wasn't sure where they were headed, but she knew they would have to stop at some point, to sleep or find something to eat.

And when they did, she'd find someone who'd help her escape.

7

THE SKY HAD BEGUN TO LIGHTEN, streaks of pink and orange shot through the inky blue as day broke. It must have been hours since Aria had woken in the woods, wrists and ankles bound. It felt longer. She hadn't slept as the horse trotted over the uneven ground and splashed through shallow streams, as branches tore at her hair and clothes. Her eyes stung, her mind barely able to focus on a single thought.

The trees thinned, allowing more light to break through their ranks. The horses slowed to a walk as they reached another clearing, this one larger than the others with a blackened circle in the centre, marking the place where a fire had been. Xander dismounted without preamble and the sudden rush of cold was a shock to Aria. His body heat had become a comforting presence, to her surprise.

She slid out of the saddle and watched as the others dismounted and Quade led the horses a short distance away. Rainer and Coulter were unpacking bed rolls and blankets, a copper kettle and some sort of spit for roasting meat over a fire.

Xander dropped his saddlebag on top of a pile of blankets and unbuckled his weapon belt. "We'll rest for a couple of hours and then carry on. Kiefer, Coulter—you're on food duty." They grinned at each other and bumped fists. It was strangely comforting in its normality. They grabbed their bows and quivers and jogged into the trees in opposite directions.

"Q, build a fire." Quade, who had returned from tethering the horses nearby, groaned and trudged off to find kindling. "Rainer, I need you to stay with Aria."

Aria studied them both. She still hadn't figured out why Xander seemed to be the leader, when Rainer was clearly the older, and larger, man. He seemed like the more obvious choice to her.

Rainer dipped his head. "Of course." He adjusted a bed roll, arranging one of the blankets as a pillow, and gestured towards her. "You need rest, Princess. Come and lie down. I'll keep watch while you sleep."

Aria didn't argue. She was completely at their mercy, and too tired to fight it. She slid between the blankets, a wave of utter exhaustion overwhelming her. "Just for a minute," she mumbled, closing her eyes and letting the sounds of the forest slip away as sweet nothingness enveloped her.

When she woke, the sun was high in the sky and the smell of meat cooking made her mouth water. She realised she hadn't eaten since the fayre, almost a day ago. Had it really only been a day?

She could hear the boys talking quietly amongst themselves, and the sound of a fire crackling and spitting as fat from the meat dripped into the flames.

Rainer's deep voice was low, she had to strain to hear him. "Perhaps sharpening your blade was…ill-advised."

"It was pretty intense," Quade said apologetically.

"Yes, thank you, Q. I don't believe I asked for your opinion." Kiefer bit back.

"I should never have asked you to speak with her," Xander said. "I should have known you'd fuck it up."

"Well, then you should have done it yourself, shouldn't you?"

"You know I couldn't," Xander growled. "She would have recognised me instantly."

It was warm now, and Aria was sweating under the weight of the horse blankets. She rubbed her eyes and ran her fingers through her greasy hair, trying to flatten it before the boys noticed she was awake.

"By the Elements," Kiefer began, but before he could finish Coulter's lilting voice broke over the camp.

"Good morning, Sleeping Beauty!" He'd spotted her moving. She hoped they didn't think she'd been eavesdropping.

Which she had.

She pushed the blankets off and sat up, ignoring the dull ache in the back of her skull. The boys were sitting on wooden logs around a roaring fire, several skinned animal carcasses skewered on a spit, which Coulter turned with a gloved hand. "We waited for you to wake before eating breakfast. If you call rabbit and pheasant breakfast in your realm." He grinned and patted the empty log between Xander and himself with his other hand. Xander watched her wordlessly, expression closed.

She realised they had all changed clothes while she slept. Instead of t-shirts, jeans and trainers they now wore linen tunics, boots and some kind of leather armour with dull metal studs. And, she noticed, mouth suddenly dry, various sheathed weapons lay on the ground next to them.

"I beat Kiefer. Again." Coulter threw the other boy a wicked grin. His pale linen shirt and trousers complemented his dark-brown skin and eyes. His black hair was shorn close to his head, and he wore a string of opalescent beads around one wrist. "He only caught three rabbits, and I caught two rabbits and two pheasants."

Kiefer was busy whittling a branch with a small, sharp knife. He was dressed in dark-green linen, as were Xander and Quade. His black hair was short at the back and sides and longer on top, tied in a knot on top of his head, and one ear was studded with silver rings from the lobe right up to the pointed tip.

"I demand a rematch." He punched the air theatrically. "And next time," he added, shaving a sliver of wood off the stick, "I'm bringing back a deer."

"Then, I'll catch two." Coulter smirked and Kiefer made a vulgar gesture.

"It's not a fair contest anyway, Sylph."

Coulter shook his head with a smirk. "Jealous, Gnome?" He lifted the spit and began to slide the roasted meat into a metal tin.

Seeing her watching with a less than keen expression, Rainer asked, "You do eat meat, Princess?"

"Yes." She took the tin when Coulter held it out to her and picked out a leg of what she thought was pheasant. She nibbled it cautiously at first, but when she saw the boys tucking in with wild abandon, she joined them. The tin made a full circuit and she took two more pieces of meat. tearing into it, not caring how she looked or sounded as hunger consumed her.

Coulter unscrewed a flask, took a swig and held it out to Aria. She took it and drank deeply, expecting water. When the liquid inside burned her throat she coughed and spluttered, dribbling it down her chin. Tears sprang to her eyes and she wiped her mouth on her sleeve.

"Not much of a drinker, Princess?" Coulter's liquid-brown eyes danced as he took the flask back from her and passed it to Rainer, who drank heartily.

"It's barely morning!"

"Call it brunch, I know how you humans like your bottomless brunches," Coulter said with a wink.

Quade lifted the kettle out of the fire and filled a metal mug, holding it out to her. "Here. Try this, Aria." She accepted the mug, hesitant this time, blowing on the hot liquid inside before taking a small sip. She spat it back onto the ground.

"What was that?" She spat once more to clear her mouth out, rubbing her tongue clean on her sleeve. When she looked up, Quade's cheeks were pink and he was looking at his feet.

Kiefer groaned. "Who let Quade make the coffee, again?" He took the mug from Aria's hand and sniffed the contents. "You always make it too strong, Q. You don't even drink coffee!"

"Yes, I do!" Quade turned redder. "I like it this way." He snatched the mug out of Kiefer's hand and took a big gulp. His face crumpled and the others burst out laughing, making him turn puce. "Shut up. Make it yourselves next time." He got up and stormed into the woods. Kiefer called after him, laughing, but he didn't turn around.

"Let him go," Xander said, wiping his hands on his trousers. "He'll be back once he's calmed down."

"Or when it goes dark and he gets scared." Kiefer chimed in, and

Coulter barked a laugh.

Rainer gave them both a dark look, but Aria could tell he was holding back a smile.

They fell into silence. Xander using a long stick to poke the fire. He stared into the flames like he could see the future in them.

Aria still wasn't sure what was going on here, but she knew it wasn't your average abduction.

Sitting around a fire, sharing their food and drink, and listening to their familiar banter, it was as though they'd all forgotten how they'd knocked her unconscious and taken her from her home against her will not twelve hours ago.

"Have you had enough to eat, Princess?" Rainer asked, holding out the tin with the remaining rabbit and pheasant meat.

"OK, let's get one thing straight," she said, and they all paused to look at her, Coulter with a pheasant leg halfway to his mouth and an eyebrow quirked. "My name is Aria. Not Princess." She held up a hand when Kiefer looked like he was going to interject. "I don't care if you think I'm the daughter of a lizard king. I'm just Aria, OK? So, please stop calling me Princess."

The boys all looked to Xander. He considered for a second before nodding once.

"Thank you."

A few minutes passed in silence as they finished chewing their roasted meat and passing Coulter's flask around. Aria had grown accustomed to the harsh taste and burning effect of the liquor. She had drunk alcohol before, shared a bottle of wine with her parents over dinner, sneaked the odd rum and coke at family parties. She wasn't a seasoned drinker, though, and after just a few sips she could feel warmth coursing through her veins, making her bold.

"Do you think you could maybe tell me who the hell you are now?"

Rainer coughed, and it sounded suspiciously like he was covering a laugh. Aria turned to look at him. He raised a hand to his forehead in a two-fingered salute. "Captain Conroy Rainer, Gnome King's Guard."

Aria raised an eyebrow. *Gnome King's Guard?* Were they part of some re-enactment group? Or just really into LARPing?

Either way, they took the game way too seriously.

She looked to Kiefer next. He took an elaborate bow without standing up. "Prince Kiefer Alexander, second son of King Lonan of the Gnome Kingdom." There was something in his tone.

"A prince, eh? I don't suppose we're related?" She was being sardonic, but before Kiefer could respond, Xander's cool voice cut in.

"No. You're not a Gnome." He was staring into the dying flames of the fire, elbows resting on his knees, hands clasped. "Your father is King Ossian."

"Right. The lizard." She rolled her eyes. "Coulter?"

"Coulter Egan, at your service." Coulter saluted lazily, a lopsided grin on his full lips.

"What, no rank or title for you?"

He shrugged. "Well, you know, I don't like to flash it around like these guys. But, since you ask," he flicked imaginary dirt off his shoulder, "I'm a lieutenant."

"Is that right." Aria shook her head. When were they going to give up the charade and tell her the truth?

Reluctantly, she turned to Xander, who was still staring at the fire with a focus that had to be intentional. His chin-length, black hair hung like curtains, framing his face, as he leant forwards with his hands clasped between his knees.

"Last, but not least?"

He looked at her then, studying her face for several seconds before opening his mouth. "Prince Xander. Crown Prince. Heir to the Gnome throne." He said the last part with an unexpected bitterness.

He took a swig from the flask and gazed into the flames again. His expression was clear, he wasn't interested in sharing any more than that. Aria watched him for a moment, the firelight turned his eyes to molten silver and cast shadows across his face that sharpened his features into something terrifying and deadly.

A moment later, realisation struck her. "Wait. You're brothers, you two?"

Xander nodded without tearing his eyes away from the fire. "And Quade."

"So, you're telling me your parents named you Xander Alexander?" Aria bit her lip to keep in the laugh that threatened to burst out of her. This was all too absurd for words.

Xander looked at her, his steely eyes cutting to her core. "No—"

"Was your mother still high on pain relief when she named you?" She was enjoying the look of pure fury on his face, but the others had all gone quiet and were suddenly very interested in their surroundings.

Aria didn't care if she pissed him off, what difference would it make if they were going to kill her anyway? Screw his feelings, he had *kidnapped* her, for fuck's sake.

"My parents did not name me Xander—"

"Were you teased as a child?" Her tone turned venomous now as she stuck the knife in and twisted it.

Xander stood abruptly, his fists clenched at his sides, tension clear in the muscles of his neck and jaw. "My name is not Xander Alexander." It was more of a growl than words. Aria stared at him. His eyes were quicksilver. "Xander is a nickname."

"Oh." The other boys didn't move. It seemed to Aria as though they were hardly breathing. The effect Xander's voice had on them was astounding.

"What is your name then?" She probed. She wasn't afraid of him, she would not save his feelings. Not after what he had done to her. She was enjoying riling this boy who held everything back, revealed nothing. He had taken everything from her and she would take what she could from him.

He ran his hands through his hair, smoothing it back behind his ears, and licked his lips. "Just call me Xander."

Aria shrugged. "OK, Mister Mysterious."

He turned away from her. "We need to move. We've already been here too long. I'll go and find Quade."

Once Xander disappeared into the forest, it was as though the spell had broken and everyone unfroze. They started to roll up their blankets and repack the saddlebags. Aria watched Rainer rinse the cooking tins with water from a flask, wiping them with a rag.

"The Xander is the eldest son of the Gnome king." Rainer spoke in a low voice while he worked. "It's the nickname given to the eldest son of the Alexander line. King Lonan was a Xander until he was crowned, and Xander will be until his own coronation."

Aria pondered this. Whatever game they were playing, they'd put a lot of thought into their back stories. "What if something happened to him? If he died, would Kiefer become the Xander?"

"No. In that case, out of respect for the firstborn, the name is passed on to the next generation. Kiefer's firstborn would become the Xander."

Aria looked to Kiefer, who had finished packing his things and was listening in. One corner of his mouth quirked upwards in a half smile, but it didn't reach his eyes. Aria sensed a tension between him and Xander. Was Kiefer angry that he hadn't gotten to be the crown prince?

The liquor and the heat from the fire had given Aria a warm glow and heavy eyelids. She longed for her bed, the comfort of her own home, her parents. Jasper. She no longer felt the ice-cold terror that had filled her when she'd woken in the forest, but she was still afraid. Afraid that they were lying about why they had really taken her. Lying about her real father.

And afraid that they were telling the truth.

But they couldn't be. It wasn't possible.

Tears prickled at the backs of her eyes. She tried to blink them away, but the combination of exhaustion, fear and alcohol was working against her. Would she ever see her parents again? Was anyone looking for her? She didn't even know where she was, how would anyone ever find her?

The sky had begun to darken overhead, a navy-blue stain spreading quickly and overtaking the cloud-dotted cerulean. The boys had noticed it too, Coulter gave Rainer a worried look.

Xander reappeared then, with Quade in tow. He turned his eyes skywards, and moved a hand to the hilt of his sword, brow furrowed.

"How long was I asleep?" Aria asked, bewildered by their reaction to the coming dusk.

Rainer went to stand beside Xander, both of them looking up at the now midnight black sky. "About two hours."

"But, that would make it—"

"Mid-morning," Coulter finished for her. All five boys were now standing and Aria had to crane her neck to look at their faces. In the light cast by the campfire their expressions were exaggerated, their faces grim masks. Aria's stomach clenched, dread weighing heavy in her gut.

"What is it? What's happening?"

The boys drew their weapons and formed a circle around Aria, facing outwards.

"What the hell—"

She stopped short as a deep growl rent the air in the clearing. She froze, hair standing on end, unable to detect the direction the sound had come from.

A twig snapped behind her and she whirled around to see an enormous black dog stalking towards them. In the firelight, the creature's huge teeth and claws were bone-white and deadly sharp.

"Barghest." Kiefer's voice was barely above a whisper. A snarl on Aria's other side signalled the arrival of a second beast. She backed up several steps, bumping into Quade's back, trying to keep both creatures in her line of sight. Her heart pounded against her ribs like it was trying to escape through her chest. She was wide awake now.

8

XANDER KEPT ARIA AT HIS BACK, the other four boys closing around her in a tight circle. All eyes were on the two large beasts that continued to prowl towards them.

Aria looked into the red eyes of the nearest barghest, they burned in the dimness, reflecting the flames of the campfire. She felt like the creature was looking back at her. *Into* her. A strangled sound escaped her throat before she could clamp a hand over her mouth.

"Protect the princess!" Xander brandished a sword at the beast in front of him, tension thrumming through his body, so electric Aria could almost feel the charge in her own bones.

Rainer hefted a hatchet in one hand, every muscle in his body straining towards the creature. Kiefer trained an arrow on the second beast, while Coulter had opted for a lethal-looking, curved blade, and Quade gripped a small, sharp knife in each hand.

Aria had no weapon. No way of defending herself.

Terror ran razor-sharp claws down her insides.

A growl behind her made Aria start. She spun around to discover the source of the sound. A third barghest watched her from the edge of the clearing. This one was even bigger than the others, its head level with Aria's shoulders. Ropes of saliva hung from its jaws, elongated canines flashing in the firelight. Its eyes burned into her, she could see only hunger and rage in them and her mouth went bone-dry in response.

The creatures didn't seem to take any interest in the heavily armed boys surrounding her, their eyes were on her and her alone. They must have singled her out as the weakest member of the group, marking her as prey.

The tension in the clearing was palpable, the only sound the laboured breathing of the three enormous beasts. Aria couldn't make out much in the darkness that had descended, but the barghests' flame red eyes and glistening white teeth shone in the firelight.

One of the barghests leaned back on its haunches, getting ready to pounce with those skin-shredding claws and bone-crushing teeth.

Kiefer caught sight of the beast and spun around at lightning speed, loosing an arrow at the exact moment the barghest leapt, teeth bared, jaws wide.

Kiefer's arrow was true. It struck the creature in mid-air, square in the chest, piercing its heart.

With a growl and a thud, the silence was broken. The two remaining barghests charged towards the group, snarls ripping through the air. Xander lunged with his sword, catching one of the creatures in the side and throwing himself into a roll, coming up in a crouch, hair swept across his forehead, blood slicking his blade,

Rainer's hatchet swung and connected with the beast, sending blood spraying across the ground and Rainer's tunic. Coulter launched himself after the wounded animal, thrusting his curved blade into its chest.

Kiefer nocked another arrow and aimed it at the third and largest barghest. He loosed the arrow, it clipped the barghest's ear and buried itself in a tree.

Aria could do nothing but watch as the boys battled the enormous creatures. Blood splattered the ground and oozed from wounds inflicted by blades and arrows.

She couldn't help but picture her beloved dogs back home in Hartwood. Their sweet faces and cheeky personalities.

One of Quade's knives whistled past her head, just barely missing the barghest's head.

Aria finally snapped. "No!"

Xander whirled to face her then, eyes wide with concern. He scanned her face and body, searching for injuries—any indication as to why she had screamed. Satisfied that the blood spotting her clothes and skin wasn't her own, he turned back to face the beast, ready to end its life with one swing of his sword.

But the creature swiped with claws as long and as sharp as knives. Xander leapt back, but not fast enough. The barghest's claw slashed through his trouser leg, slicing the flesh beneath. Xander collapsed to the ground, but not before slipping his sword between the creature's ribs.

The beast died with a whimper.

Silence settled over the clearing. Aria pushed between Quade and Rainer, stopping short when she saw the enormous beast lying on the ground just inches from her, its life draining away as blood pooled around it on the ground. In death, the animal had lost most of its fearsomeness. It looked like an overgrown dog.

Aria glanced around at the abundance of blood-stained steel glinting in the light of the dying fire, the bodies of the other two slaughtered barghests just feet away. Her breath came in short, painful gasps.

The inky blackness that had stained the sky receded quickly, revealing a beautiful, cloudless day. In the sudden light, Aria felt exposed. She felt light-headed with relief, she'd been convinced the beasts would tear them all to shreds. It had all happened so fast, her body hadn't had a chance to catch up, and now all she could do was stand and stare at the huge black shapes on the ground.

"Xander, your leg." Quade dropped down in front of his brother, carefully he peeled the bloody strips of linen aside to see the damage. One of the barghest's long claws had left a deep wound in Xander's shin, it was at least six inches long and Aria could see the pink tissue inside his leg. "It isn't bone-deep, at least."

Xander took Quade's remaining knife and cut away the shredded material up to his knee.

"What the hell were those things?" When she blinked, Aria could still see the flame-red eyes of the beast, could still hear its wet, panting breath, the snarl that tore from its throat as it lunged at her.

Quade stood, brushing the dirt from his knees. Distantly, she thought it was pointless when his clothes were spattered with blood. "They're called barghests. They're sort of monstrous hounds with razor-sharp teeth and claws."

"I'm sure she saw that for herself." Xander spoke through a clenched jaw, prodding at his wound, trying to pinch it closed.

"They're an omen of death," Coulter muttered, crouching over one of the creatures, checking to see it was truly dead. Apparently unsatisfied, he took his curved blade and slit the creatures throat.

Aria winced.

"What was with the sky? Why did it suddenly go dark?" She stood trembling, arms around herself, unable to look away from the bodies of the three dead creatures.

"They usually only come out at night," Rainer said, wiping his bloody hatchet with a rag. "Looks like the Celeste King has been experimenting again. This time, he's found a way to allow them to attack during the day."

Coulter laughed darkly, "Lucky us."

Kiefer retrieved his arrows from the tree trunk and the heart of the dead barghest. He gripped the shaft, planted his boot in the beast's chest and pulled. A sickening tearing sound came as the arrow ripped free of its body. Bile rose up Aria's throat. She turned away, forcing it down.

Xander cut another strip of material from his trouser leg and started trying to bandage the wound.

"You need stitches." They all looked at Aria, surprised. Her eyes connected with Xander's for a second, and for the first time she could see the fatigue beneath the façade. It was as though the pain of his injury had lowered his defences.

And then, before her eyes, the walls slid up again. "I'll be fine." He reached for a flask of water and poured it over the wound. He grimaced as the cool liquid came into contact with his torn skin. "We don't have time. We need to leave."

"I'm serious. It's not going to stop bleeding until we stitch it up. Do you have a first aid kit?" She looked around at the blank faces of the boys.

Rainer, her best hope, shrugged. "I'm not a medic. We rarely go on missions like this without one." He rifled through his pack and pulled out a small black box. "I have a sewing kit, will that help?"

Aria squinted. "You carry a sewing kit, but not a first aid kit?"

"We lose buttons more often than we lose limbs." His mouth curved upwards at the corners.

Aria stared, shaking her head, and took the sewing kit from his outstretched hand. "I guess this will have to do then. And give me the flask of liquor. He's going to need it."

Quade and Rainer went to load up and saddle the horses, while Coulter and Kiefer scouted the area to make sure there were no more barghests lurking. Or other dark creatures that might attack them at any moment.

Aria and Xander were alone.

She poured some of the liquor over the wound, making Xander suck in air sharply through his teeth. She handed him the flask.

"Hold still." She gripped his leg tightly, pinching the torn flesh together, and pushed the needle into his skin. Xander gritted his teeth and squeezed his eyes shut.

A small part of her enjoyed the pain she was causing him, although her trembling hands made her job more difficult than it should have been.

"Could you not find a smaller needle?" He lifted the flask to his lips and took a long draught.

"There wasn't exactly much of a selection in Rainer's sewing kit." She focused on the task at hand, pulling the thread taught. She was using black thread so that she could see where she had already stitched. It gave Xander's leg a Frankenstein's monster look. It also showed up

Aria's sloppy work.

"Where did you learn to suture?" He ground out. Obviously looking for a distraction from the discomfort, but he sounded genuinely intrigued.

Aria paused, her blood-stained hand hovering over the wound, the needle millimetres from his skin. She looked up at Xander's face, his eyes were still closed, frown lines forming between his thick black brows. His lashes were long, brushing the tops of his cheeks like the wings of a dark moth.

Aria looked away quickly, not wanting to be caught staring. She pulled the thread, drawing the skin together a little too tightly, and Xander winced. "I was a first aider at the library where I worked. I had to take a course. Learn how to do the Heimlich manoeuvre, treat minor burns, put people in the recovery position."

She poured cool water over his leg to wash away the blood staining his pale skin, she'd almost finished the stitches. She could tell he would be glad when it was over. He hadn't complained once, but she knew it must be uncomfortable, if not outright painful. The needle was too thick for the job, and the thread was definitely not designed for sutures.

"They taught you to suture to work in a library?"

"No," she admitted. "But I enjoyed the course, so I took another one." She looked at Xander's face again. His eyes were still closed, but the crease between his eyebrows had softened, as though listening to her voice was soothing, distracting him from the needle she kept sticking into his leg. Her lips twitched almost against her will. "I learned to make a sling out of a t-shirt, how to bandage a wound, splint a broken arm."

She had finished the stitches, but he looked so peaceful listening to her, so unlike the cold, hard boy she had seen so far. She didn't want to ruin the moment. She rested her hand on his knee and pulled the thread taught. His brow furrowed slightly as she watched.

She couldn't let this opportunity pass her by without at least trying.

"Xander," she began. His eyes flew open and she was momentarily taken aback by how beautiful they were, this close up they glistered like electrum. "Where are you taking me? Please, just tell me the truth."

The tears that had threatened earlier pricked the backs of her eyes once more and she fought them back. Xander studied her in silence, his expression softer than she'd ever seen it. "You could let me go," she whispered. "I won't tell anyone. I'll say I went for a run before breakfast and got lost, or…I don't know, but I could just go home right now and make something up. Please."

A war of emotions flickered behind his eyes. He sighed. "Aria, I am sorry for how we—for taking you from your home and…but the truth remains, you are the daughter of a king. Here, in the Fair Realm. We were ordered to find you and bring you to your father. He's sick. Dying. You're his true heir." He rubbed his face, raked his hands through his hair. For a brief moment, Aria witnessed the exhaustion that he hid behind the cool façade, buried under layers of strength and determination.

What could make someone as young as Xander look so bone tired, so emotionally drained? Like the weight of the world was on his shoulders.

"You don't have to believe me, but I will ask that you trust me." He held up a hand when she opened her mouth to speak. "I know you have no reason to, but please, just trust me anyway. You'll understand soon enough."

Aria could only stare, mouth agape, as the tears that had threatened now spilled down her cheeks. He wasn't going to let this go. Wasn't going to let *her* go.

It was ridiculous. She wasn't a princess, she was just a pawn in a game she didn't understand. These boys were toying with her and she needed to find out why.

But, the barghests that had attacked them, she couldn't have invented those. Their size, their red eyes burning like embers, their razor-sharp teeth and claws that had torn Xander's leg. The sky had darkened in their presence, when the Sun should have been at its highest. She knew she hadn't imagined that.

And then there was the ethereal strangeness of the boys' features. Was it just clever makeup that she hadn't observed in the dark of the woods?

She was concussed though. And she been drinking from Coulter's flask. It could contain anything, now she thought about it.

The sound of boots crunching over twigs brought them both back to the present. Aria quickly tied off the thread and snipped it short with the tiny scissors from Rainer's sewing kit.

"All done." She stood and brushed the dirt off her trousers, keeping her eyes down. She could feel blood rushing to her cheeks, and she didn't want the others to see that she'd been crying.

She needn't have worried, her appearance was the least of their concern when Kiefer appeared in the clearing, bow and arrow in hand.

"Salamanders, headed this way."

9

"**D**EMITREE? SHIT." Xander jumped up, and cringed. He stretched his injured leg, testing its mobility. He put it down slowly, waving off Kiefer's silent offer of assistance, only to wince when he put any weight on the leg. "How did they find us?"

"They must have spotted our fire when the barghests attacked and the darkness descended."

Xander swore again. "Aria," he said, "You'll have to ride."

She felt a faint flutter in her stomach. He was trusting her to take charge of the horse. "OK."

Perhaps she could knock him out of the saddle and ride away, retrace their steps until she found Hartwood. Being in control of the horse definitely gave her options.

Xander nodded at Kiefer, who slung his brother's arm over his shoulder and they began to move as quickly as possible in the direction of the horses.

The make-shift paddock was only a short distance from the clearing. Aria heard the stamping and snickering of their mounts before she saw them. As they got closer, she could hear Rainer issuing orders to Coulter and Quade as they prepared to leave.

Something had started to fall into place in Aria's mind, jigsaw puzzles clicking together. She slowed to a stop, making the boys stumble.

"Wait a second." Xander and Kiefer looked at her with different shades of the same bewildered expression. "You said the Salamanders are coming?"

Kiefer nodded, not understanding her, and anxious to reach the others. "Yes."

She turned to Xander. "And then you said, 'Demitree'."

Xander paled, apparently catching her drift.

"Bazyl…is a Salamander?"

The look of desperation that crossed Xander's face terrified her. It only lasted a second before disappearing behind his usual cool façade.

"Aria, we haven't got time for this. I'll explain while we ride." He slid his arm around her waist and tried to hobble towards the horses with her in tow. She slipped out of his grasp with ease and stood, feet planted, arms crossed.

"Tell me now, or I'm going nowhere." She knew it was a gamble, that even with Xander incapacitated Kiefer or one of the others could throw her over their shoulder, but she had to try.

"Your choice, tell me and we can go, or refuse and we wait for them to get here and explain to me themselves." A look passed between the two brothers and Aria swallowed, clenching her fists at her sides to keep her hands from trembling. "Who ordered you to take me?"

Xander tensed his jaw. "Your father."

"But you said my father is the Salamander King, so why would he send you—what did you call yourselves, Gnomes? Why wouldn't he send his own men?"

The sound of bodies moving quickly through the forest reached her ears then, and she saw the boys hear it to. She raised her eyebrows at Xander, waiting.

He flared his nostrils. "Fine, but remember you asked. Bazyl Demitree isn't just a Salamander soldier, he's the king's son. Your half-brother." She could tell he had expected her to be shocked by the revelation, but she was struggling to believe a word out of his mouth, so it felt like yet another in a long line of lies.

"That doesn't explain anything, why didn't he send Bazyl for me—" she stopped herself, understanding settling like a stone in the pit of her stomach. "He did send Bazyl, didn't he. And you didn't want him to get to me first, so you kidnapped me." She took a step back, stumbling on a loose rock. "Why?"

Xander shook his head. "No, Aria, that's not it."

They were interrupted as Rainer, Coulter and Quade appeared atop their mounts, the two other horses' reins held in Rainer's hand.

"Xand, we need to go," Kiefer said with quiet urgency.

Aria wrapped her arms around herself tighter, suddenly cold. "Just tell me the truth. Please, you owe me that."

He looked straight at her, eyes boring into her, as he said, "Bazyl is your half-brother, but he wants the throne for himself. Your father sent us because he couldn't trust his own men, he didn't know which of them were loyal to his son. Bazyl wants you dead. He'll stop at nothing. We're protecting you, Aria, I swear it."

Kiefer helped Xander climb up onto his horse before throwing a leg up and over his own horse and settling into the saddle. Xander reached a hand down to Aria. "Please, just come with us."

A crash and a clatter of metal signalled the arrival of four young men in some kind of light chainmail over leather, weapons held high as they fanned out, facing the Gnomes. Caught between them, Aria's heart beat a rhythm against her ribs.

Xander and the others unsheathed their own weapons as the horses snorted and danced from side to side, unhappy with the tension. Aria felt as though the air had turned solid in her lungs.

"Let her go, Alexander." She recognised Bazyl from the fayre, his auburn hair and crystal-clear blue eyes, the smattering of freckles across his nose. He held a sword not dissimilar to the one Xander wielded, a long blade, polished to a mirror shine, with a short grip. Simple, and eye-wateringly sharp.

In this strange game, he was her brother. But he wanted her out of the way so he could be king, if what Xander had said was true.

"Go home, Demitree," Xander growled, and his horse tossed its mane in agreement. "The Solstice is over. You're trespassing on Gnome lands."

"She belongs with us, just let her go and we'll leave you in peace." Bazyl reached out with his free hand, trying to encourage Aria to come to him. "We met at the fayre, remember?" He couldn't quite hide the desperation in his eyes.

She looked between their outstretched hands, torn. Bazyl could be her only chance to escape the Gnomes. But they hadn't hurt her—not since knocking her out in her room—and if Xander was telling the truth then Bazyl could mean her harm.

She didn't know who to trust.

Bazyl took a step towards her, and Xander pushed his horse forward, swinging his sword at the Salamanders, who leapt back and resumed their defensive stances. "I know what you're doing, Alexander. You're making a huge mistake."

"Is that right?" Xander's words were a snarl. "Aria, get on the horse. Now."

She looked up at his face, the anger that burned there, and something else. Fear, in the tightness of his mouth and the crease between his brows.

"We saw the barghests," Bazyl said quickly, making another rash move towards Aria. "It's not going to stop, you know that as well as me!"

She made up her mind.

She launched herself towards Xander, gripping his hand and putting one foot in the stirrup. With a yell, the Gnomes' horses took off at speed, and Aria heard the tell-tale whistle as Kiefer loosed an arrow in the direction of the Salamanders, preventing them from following. She heard a crack as it embedded into a nearby tree, but by then they were moving too fast for the Salamanders to catch up.

Xander held tightly onto Aria's hand, holding the reins with his other, and helped her up into the saddle without slowing a single step.

Breathless and unsure whether she'd made the right choice, Aria sank her hands into the horse's mane and squeezed her eyes shut.

Better the devil you know.

She prayed she hadn't cursed herself with that thought.

They didn't slow down for a long time, and when they finally did, forced to adopt a slower pace due to uneven terrain, they still didn't stop.

It was hours later when they finally reached a small stream and paused to let the horses drink. Aria stretched her aching legs, she'd gripped the horse with her thighs harder than necessary for the first several miles, terrified of slipping off as they galloped away from the Salamanders.

Coulter crouched at the edge of the water, filling any available container with fresh water, including the flask that had held the liquor—Xander had drained the last drop while she stitched his leg.

Rainer and Quade unsaddled the horses and rubbed them down with rags, wiping off the sweat and dirt of the journey. Kiefer settled himself down against a tree and took his small, sharp knife out again, picking up a twig and beginning to shave off layers. Aria could only assume he enjoyed the mindlessness of the task, as he didn't seem to actually make anything with his carving. Unless you counted a small pile of wood shavings.

She walked along the edge of the stream a little way, Xander close behind. Making sure she didn't bolt, she guessed. She might have thought about it if her legs hadn't turned to jelly, she didn't think she'd get more than three metres before collapsing.

And, despite her reservations, she had to admit she'd begun to grow curious. If she left now, she may wonder her whole life what she might have discovered if she'd stayed.

What if.

It was her favourite question. Sometimes her anxious mind ran through worst case scenarios while she lay in bed at night—what if she got knocked off her bike on the way to school? What if she failed all her exams and had to work at the library for the rest of her life? There were worse places to work, she knew that. She loved the free books and unlimited reading time, but the thought of working in a tiny village library in the middle of nowhere her whole life made her chest tighten.

When those thoughts took hold and her heart started to race and her palms grew sweaty, she'd force herself to stop and think about other *what ifs*. What if she could fly? She'd imagine the feeling of the wind in her air, the weightlessness and pure thrill of soaring over rooftops and above the clouds, until her heart was racing with excitement instead of dread.

She tried the same thing now. What if it were true? What if they really had stepped into another realm with actual monsters, and her parents really weren't her parents, and she truly was a

She sat on the bank, crossed her legs and wiped her sweaty palms on her filthy jeans, taking a long, slow breath.

It surprised her when Xander sat down beside her, reached into his satchel and held out an apple. She narrowed her eyes at him, then took it without a word and bit into it.

They sat in silence for a little while, listening to the soothing babble of the river and the rhythmic scraping of Kiefer's whittling.

"You came with us," Xander said eventually, eyes never leaving the water. "I didn't think you were going to for a second there."

Aria watched him out of the corner of her eye, he almost seemed to be holding his breath. There was a stillness about him that made her uneasy.

"Neither did I, for a second there." He glanced at her then and she twitched her lips in an almost-smile.

Xander picked up a stone and casually tossed it towards the stream. It skipped once and landed on the opposite bank. "Why did you then?"

She shrugged her shoulders, then leaned back on her elbows, stretching her body out and feeling all of the tension in her sore muscles. She needed a good night's sleep in a real bed, all of this riding and sleeping on forest floors was playing havoc with her lower back.

If she was honest with herself, she'd been afraid. Afraid of what might happen if she made the wrong choice. Afraid that she'd never find out the truth if she did, if Xander was right and Bazyl actually wanted her dead. She'd chosen on instinct, something pulled her towards Xander and the Gnomes, there was more to what was happening here, more they hadn't told her. She needed to know what it was.

"I don't know." She pushed back up to a sitting position and turned to face him. "Look, I'm not saying I believe you about—well, anything. But there's a lot going on here that I can't explain, so I need you to be honest with me. Or don't be, but tell me. Why am I here?"

Xander studied her, then leaned forwards, elbows on his knees. His voice was low enough that she had to crane her neck to hear. "Our realm—the Five Kingdoms—has been at war for over a century. My people are suffering, Aria. Hungry. Sick. Poor."

He looked down at the ground, shame sharpening his already angular features. He hesitated, and then looked her straight in the eye, sending a shiver down her spine. "There's a sickness, a fever. It's spreading through the realm and has already killed thousands. There's no cure, but Celeste healers might be able to stop it. Except, they're forbidden by the Celeste King from crossing the borders or treating any Fair who isn't a Celeste."

Aria considered this. "So, the Salamander King," she refused to call him her father, "has this fever?" Xander nodded. "Why send for me?"

"Your family needs you home. Your kingdom needs its heir, Aria."

10

ARIA CHEWED HER BOTTOM LIP, MULLING IT OVER.

Even if she was the daughter of a king in this strange place—and she was far from convinced—she hadn't grown up a princess. She couldn't rule a kingdom. She'd only make the situation worse for the people. Someone, this Celeste King who seemed to have a vendetta against her, would invade her kingdom and overthrow her.

Never mind the fact that her own half-brother was apparently dead-set on taking the throne for himself, and half the Salamander army were on his side.

She shook her head. This was mad.

Xander was watching her. "You probably think we're insane, or playing an elaborate trick on you." His insight took her aback, but she worked hard to keep a straight face. "I know it's not an easy thing to ask, but I need you to trust me."

His words took her back to the fayre, when he'd first warned her away from Bazyl.

Just trust me.

She still wasn't sure she was ready to.

The others had gone very quiet while Xander and Aria talked, and when she turned to look they all resumed their tasks, trying to hide the fact they'd been listening. Kiefer even started to whistle while he whittled. She narrowed her eyes and he raised an eyebrow, but he couldn't hide the slight quirk of his lips.

"Alright," she said, turning back to Xander. "So, there are four kingdoms?"

"Five. Gnome, Salamander, Celeste, Sylph and Ondine."

She stared blankly at him.

He sighed, pushing his long black hair out of his face and tucking it behind his ears.

"Gnomes--that's us—manipulate earth," he said slowly. When he saw her frown, he added, "Nature. Plants and crops, we encourage them to grow."

"Some of us can do a little more than that," Kiefer said from where he sat, not pausing his whittling or taking his eyes off the twig he carved.

Xander's piercing silver eyes narrowed at his brother. He went to continue, but Aria cut in.

"What does he mean? What can some of you do?"

Xander shook his head. "He doesn't mean anything, just some Fair have stronger abilities than others." Kiefer snorted, but Xander ignored him. "Most only have a weak affinity for their element, they understand it and can manipulate it to some extent."

She tilted her head. "You said 'they'. What about you?"

He muttered something under his breath, but she didn't catch it.

Rainer picked up where he left off. "Some of us—a very rare few—can control our element. Nothing major, not anymore," he added quickly. "Magic has been growing weaker for decades, and the Fair with strong abilities are fewer than ever."

"Why?"

"No one really knows." He shrugged apologetically.

She looked to Xander, but he didn't make eye contact, still quietly seething at Kiefer. "And the other four kingdoms?"

"Salamanders can manipulate fire, Sylphs control the air, and the Ondine have command over water," Quade rattled off.

"Fire? You think I can control *fire*?"

They all stared at her in silence.

Coulter finally asked, "Can you?" He sounded sceptical.

"No, of course I can't!"

Kiefer tucked his knife away in a sheath on his belt. "Your ability's probably weak, like the rest of us. It might grow stronger now you're back in the Fair Realm though. Like the ears, it kind of fades in the Human Realm."

She'd forgotten about the ears. She tucked a strand of hair behind one ear, using her little finger to check it was still smooth and rounded. It was.

"Didn't you call Coulter a Sylph before?" She looked to Kiefer ,who darted a nervous look at his friend.

Coulter raised an eyebrow. "It's alright. I am a Sylph, Aria. My mother came from the Sylph Kingdom. My father was a Gnome though, a member of the King's Guard, so I was given honorary Gnome status by King Lonan."

Coulter could control the air. No wonder he was such a talented archer.

"What about the Celeste King? What's his element?"

Rainer cleared his throat, but Xander spoke up first. "The Celeste control aether."

Aria raised her eyebrows. It sounded like something she'd already forgotten learning about in Chemistry class. "They what?"

"Celeste abilities are probably more akin to what you'd call 'magic' in the Human Realm," Rainer offered. "But all it really is, is the manipulation of the fabric that makes up the world and everything in it. Aether, as we call it."

"Oh right." She pretended to understand. "And the kingdoms are all at war with each other?"

"For almost one hundred and fifty years," Kiefer said. "Thanks to our great grandpa. Or is it great, great grandpa?" He frowned, tapping the stick he'd been whittling against his lips.

"What did he do?" Aria turned fully around, interested.

"It wasn't his fault," Quade offered, stroking his horse's chestnut neck. "It was the Celeste Queen, Finula. She wouldn't bless Tobiah and Ianthe's marriage."

Coulter shook his head. "The way I heard it King Phelan was the one who opposed the marriage. He was prejudiced against the Celeste. Didn't want his son marrying into their line and giving him aether-tainted grandchildren. Even though Tiberius was the Xander, not Tobiah."

"That was the problem," Rainer said, biting into an apple and talking around it. "Queen Finula wouldn't allow her only daughter to marry the spare to the throne, she wanted Tiberius to marry Ianthe. Only thing was, Ianthe and Tobiah had already fallen in love, and Tiberius was betrothed to another. A Sylph princess, if I remember rightly." His eyes darted to Coulter and a small smile passed between them.

Aria absorbed everything she'd heard. "So the Celeste Queen started a war because she didn't like her daughter's boyfriend?"

The boys all appeared to consider this.

"Yeah, that about sums it up," Kiefer said.

"King Phelan attacked first," Xander said from behind her and she shuffled round so she could see him. "He was insulted that Finula wouldn't accept Tobiah as a son-in-law. Tobiah was the youngest and his father's favourite." Xander's eyes found Quade, who looked down at the ground, the tips of his ears turning pink. "Phelan launched an attack on the Celeste Kingdom, but in the midst of the battle, Tobiah and Ianthe snuck away and were married in secret." Xander's silver eyes burned into her, shining like mercury as he spoke.

"When they revealed their marriage to Finula, she banished Ianthe rather than have anything to do with the Gnomes. King Phelan reneged on the arrangement with Sylph and insisted that Tiberius marry a good Gnomish girl," he added bitterly. "Which, of course, enraged the Sylph Queen and she sent her armies to join the war against Phelan."

Aria's eyes widened. "What happened then?"

"The Ondine stepped in to defend the Gnomes, and the Salamanders were forced to choose a side. But they refused, so there was a stalemate. For decades."

She swallowed, waiting for him to go on. When he didn't she raised her eyebrows. "And now?"

Xander turned back to the river, wordless. Aria frowned and looked to the others for an answer.

Rainer sighed. "Now, the tradition of the Fair royal families marrying into each other and maintaining strong bonds between the Five Kingdoms is history. The Fair keep to themselves now, on pain of death in some kingdoms."

The look that crossed Xander's face at Rainer's words chilled her to the bone.

11

THEY RODE ON FOR A FEW MORE HOURS, before spending that night camped out under the stars on the edge of the wood. They opted not to light a fire, not wanting to draw attention, but the boys emptied their packs and shared whatever food they had left.

Apples, strips of salted, dried meat, some stale bread and a couple of flapjacks Quade had smuggled back from the fayre, laid out on a blanket. Aria hesitated, watching the boys grab what they wanted, biting off chunks of bread and apple, washing it down with water from the flasks and bottles Coulter had filled at the stream.

Quade saw her holding back and picked up one of the flapjacks, holding it out to her.

"We'll be at Hitherham by tomorrow night. We'll be able to get a good meal there, and refill our packs. It was originally an outpost—it's the closest village to the Veil so they're used to people passing through."

"The Veil?"

He nodded. "The portal we came through. The Veil is what separates the two realms and protects the Fair Realm from accidentally being discovered by humans. I mean, non-Fair," he corrected himself quickly.

"Right," Aria said, licking the butter and sugar off her fingers. "So, we're not in Hartwood anymore?"

"Um." Quade frowned, looking to the others for help.

"Yes and no," Rainer said. "It's complicated aether magic, but the way I understand it we're in a sort of pocket dimension."

"Kind of like an undetectable extension charm?" Aria asked.

"A what?"

"Nothing. Never mind."

After they'd eaten the last of their meal they slid under their blankets, staring up at the stars. Xander took the first watch, and Aria lay awake for a long while, stomach rumbling and thousands of questions circling in her head.

The next day, they rode on and off from dawn until dusk.

Night had begun to fall and Aria was exhausted. She had barely slept in the last two days, waking at every sound, fearing another barghest attack, and being disturbed every time the boys changed watch. Her eyes threatened to close and her body slumped against Xander, who sat stiffly behind her in the saddle.

She blinked her tired eyes, spots of light appearing on her retinas. A constellation of fireflies twinkled ahead of them, appearing between the sparse trees like will-o'-the-wisps. As they neared, she realised the lights were actually coming from windows.

Hitherham.

It was too dark to make out much, but she saw candles flickering on window ledges, lighting the square, leaded panes. They stopped briefly at a guard post where Xander conversed in a low voice with two young men in dark uniforms. After a few moments, the men saluted sharply and the horses walked on towards the village.

They dismounted and walked the horses into a cobbled courtyard surrounded by squat stone buildings and wooden structures that almost seemed to be hollowed out trees with doors carved into them. The scent of honeysuckle permeated the night air, and the sounds of conversation and clinking mugs drifted out to greet them.

A cracked stone fountain in the centre of the square provided a makeshift trough, which the horses drank from greedily.

Rainer handed the reins of his horse to Coulter. "I'll find us some lodgings."

He reappeared a moment later and led them to a stable around the back of a tall, stone building, where two young boys took the reins and led the horses away.

They returned to the square to find a thin, sharp-featured woman in a black dress at the door to the inn. Her greying hair was pulled back in an austere-looking bun.

At least the yellow light escaping from the open door was inviting, Aria craved a soft bed and a good night's sleep.

"Come on in," the innkeeper said in a warm, husky voice that seemed incongruous with her severe appearance. "My name's Audrey, welcome. I'll get Bonnie to bring you all hot water for a bath, and when you're ready you can come down to the den and we shall see what we can whip up for your supper. How many rooms will you be needing?"

"Three," Xander replied.

Aria liked the sound of a hot bath after riding all day and night. They followed the innkeeper up a wooden spiral staircase to their rooms, which were next to each other on the second floor.

Xander hovered as Aria opened the door to her room, and when she tried to shut it behind her he put a hand out to stop it closing.

"I'll let you take the bath, and the bed, but I can't let you out of my sight." His mouth was a hard line, but Aria could see the muscle flickering in his jaw.

"I don't get my own room?"

"I'm sorry, I can't risk you trying to run," he said in a low voice. "I'll wait out here until you're done bathing."

"Oh thanks," she sneered, and slammed the door behind her.

Slumping against it, she exhaled for what felt like the first time in days. How was she going to get away if she had to share a room with Xander? He probably slept with one eye open, so there'd be no chance of sneaking out in the night…

She'd have to wait for another opportunity.

She was desperate to climb under the blankets, but first she needed to get cleaned up and eat a proper meal.

To keep up her strength for tomorrow, when she would make her move.

The room was sparse, but comfortable. The walls and floor were wood, and a small window looked out onto the dark square. A wooden bedstead stood in the corner with a thin mattress that appeared to be stuffed with straw, and a pile of thick woollen blankets on top. A dresser stood next to it, with a mirror and a small vase of pink foxgloves. In the opposite corner stood a copper bathtub, small enough that Aria would have to sit with her knees drawn up to her chin to fit into it.

She couldn't picture Rainer squeezing his six foot five, cage fighter build into a bathtub that size.

There was a knock at the door, and a pretty, young girl with curly hair and tanned skin pushed it open, two buckets of steaming water in her arms. Aria rushed to hold the door for her. "Your bath, miss. Would you like any assistance?" She poured one of the buckets into the tub and lavender scented steam filled the room.

"No, thank you. I'll manage." The offer threw her slight, she hadn't needed help bathing since she was eight.

The girl, Bonnie the innkeeper had called her, nodded and opened a draw, removing a well-worn, but clean, white towel.

Bonnie left to fetch baths for the others and Aria stripped off, leaving her filthy clothes in a pile on the floor, and slid into the warm, scented water. She closed her eyes as the steam enveloped her, soothing her muscles and loosening the knots that had formed over the last two days. The lavender scent was so relaxing, she could have fallen asleep right there in the tub.

A scrubbing brush and bar of soap had been left on the edge of the tub, and she set to work cleaning her filthy nails and blood splattered arms. She slipped under the surface, rubbing her greasy hair between her hands.

Once clean, she reluctantly stepped out of the tub and dried off with the towel. She wrapped it tightly around her as another knock sounded at the door.

Bonnie had returned, holding a pile of neatly folded linen. "Audrey asked me to bring you some clean clothes, Miss. They were mine, they should fit." She quickly took in Aria's towel-wrapped form before casting her eyes down. She spotted the heap of dirty clothes. "Would you like me to wash your clothes for you, Miss?"

Aria nodded and Bonnie stepped into the room, placing the pile of clean clothes on the bed and picking up Aria's dirty ones from the floor. She was kind enough to not wrinkle her nose as she did.

"Thank you," Aria said, clutching the towel around her and giving Bonnie a small smile. A pang of longing struck her, the image of her mother picking up her clothes from her bedroom floor and yelling at her for not using the washing basket ran through her mind. She shook it away, she'd be home soon.

"You're very welcome, Miss. We don't get many female guests, it's nice to have a lady about the place." Aria balked at that. Never in her life had she been called a lady. "The gentlemen you arrived with, they're downstairs in the den. They said to send for you as soon as you're ready." She bobbed a quick curtsy, arms full of Aria's mud and blood-stained clothes, and left the room.

Aria would have told her to burn them, but she didn't want to lose her favourite jeans, and she didn't expect the clothes Bonnie had lent her to be to her usual style. She picked them up now, unfolding the beige linen tunic and brown woollen trousers. They were plain and worn thin in places, but seemed warm and comfortable, and only a little bit too snug across the chest and hips.

She stood in front of the mirror and combed her damp hair with an antique wide-toothed comb she found in a draw. She tucked a loose strand of copper behind her ear.

Still round and smooth.

She wasn't sure if she was relieved or disappointed.

She left the room and descended the rickety staircase, following the sounds of merriment to the den. She found a small tap room to one side of the door they'd entered through, with a wooden bar lining one wall with a row of stools tucked underneath and a range of bottles on top containing various shades of brown liquid.

Xander, Rainer and Quade were seated in the far corner, frothing mugs in front of them. A few locals were drinking quietly or chatting amongst themselves. Two men played a card game at one of the tables, a few bronze coins on the table beside them. Kiefer and Coulter were standing at the bar talking to a couple of very pretty girls. Kiefer's hand was on the brunette's lower back.

Aria stood in the door watching them all—Kiefer and Coulter flirting and laughing, Xander and the others talking animatedly and sipping mugs of ale. They looked happy, relaxed.

What if she ran right now? She could slip out of the door and disappear into the night while they were distracted. She'd be long gone before they even realised she'd left her room.

But it was pitch black outside now, without a single street lamp, only the moon and stars lighting the square outside, glinting off the water in the crumbling fountain. She'd get lost in the woods, or fall and injure herself.

She might stumble across more barghests. Or something worse.

And if she did run now, she'd never know the truth. Would never be able to answer the million questions that flitted around her mind like fireflies, dancing at the edge of her consciousness and snagging on her thoughts.

She could no longer blame her head injury for the strange, ethereal looks of the Gnomes, or the otherworldliness of this place. But if she wasn't hallucinating, that meant this was real, and she wasn't quite ready to accept that…

Quade spotted her and beckoned her over. She'd hesitated in the doorway too long.

Well that made her decision easier. For now.

Quade scooted over to make room for her and she sat on the edge of the threadbare upholstered booth. He pushed a mug of frothy liquid in front of her and she quirked an eyebrow in silent question.

"It's mead. You'll like it, I promise." Aria questioned how he could possibly know what she would like after only two days of knowing her, but she lifted the mug to her lips and took a sip. Surprised, she found that she did like it. The mead was sweet, with a hint of honey, and some fruit that she couldn't put her finger on.

"It's made with jostaberries. It's a Gnome speciality." Quade grinned with pride as she took a second big gulp, enjoying the frothy texture and fizzy, warming sensation in her stomach.

Audrey appeared with a platter of meats and cheeses, two small loaves of bread and a dish of butter. "Here we are, ladies and gents. It's not much, but it is all we have tonight. There's a delivery arriving the day after tomorrow. Just in time for the festival."

Xander reached across and clasped Audrey's hand in both of his, several gold coins glinting between his fingers. "Thank you for your kindness and generosity, Audrey. And your discretion." He dropped his voice on the last part. She accepted the coins and nodded gratefully before turning to leave. "We'll be leaving first thing in the morning."

The landlady turned back to the table, surprised. "Oh, but you must stay for the festival! We're holding a celebration in the square. Everyone is welcome. I'll be serving my famous jostaberry wine, it's been maturing for weeks." Aria wasn't sure what jostaberry wine was, but if it was anything like the mead, she wanted to taste it. "A group of good-looking lads and ladies like yourselves, you'll be very popular when the dancing starts." She winked at Rainer, who almost spat out his mead in response.

Aria saw her chance and took it. "That sounds wonderful, Audrey. I'm sure we can spare a few more days before we have to be on our way. Can't we?" She grinned at Xander, hoping to appear like a normal teenage girl who just wanted to go to a party. And not a hostage who'd spotted an opportunity to escape.

"Come on, Xand, let's stay for the festival!" Quade pleaded. "We always celebrate at home. It might be fun to go to an actual festival for once."

Xander's expression was controlled, too polite to show his annoyance. "Thank you, Audrey," he said. "We have to be on our way."

Rainer cleared his throat. "Xander, the delivery doesn't arrive for a couple of days. We need supplies. It might be prudent to stay at least until then."

Aria watched with interest as Xander stared at his friend, expression stony, only the slightest flicker of resignation in his eyes.

"We will stay until the morning after the festival," he ground out through gritted teeth. "Thank you, Audrey."

Quade grinned. Audrey nodded again and went to refill her other patrons' mugs.

Rainer was watching Kiefer and Coulter, who were still talking to the two girls at the bar. He had a wry smile on his face, which froze when he spied Aria watching him.

"Wishing it was you over there, Rainer?" She teased, wiping foam off her top lip with her fingertips. "If it's any consolation, I think Audrey's got her eye on you."

Rainer snorted, shaking his head. "No, I certainly do not miss that particular meat market." He took a long draught of his mead, froth clinging to his moustache. "It's a dark and dangerous place, and nobody escapes with their dignity." His eyes danced with mirth, and the mead.

They tucked into the meal Audrey had kindly prepared for them, a selection of cows' and goats' cheeses, thin slices of ham and beef, and a choice of breads, freshly baked and delicious smelling. It was a simple meal, but Aria enjoyed every single bite after the stale bread and hard cheese she'd endured earlier that day.

Eventually, Coulter appeared at the table, sliding into the seat next to Rainer and tearing off a hunk of bread from a seeded loaf. He dunked it in the butter and popped it in his mouth, washing it down with a swig of mead. Aria glanced over at the bar, where Kiefer was now kissing the brunette. The other girl must have left when she realised her friend was the boys' preference. Or, maybe she just didn't fancy Coulter.

Aria couldn't believe that herself. He was very handsome, his full lips balanced out by a strong jaw, and his brown eyes shone and shimmered like smoky quartz when he grinned. She could certainly imagine being attracted to him herself, if he didn't happen to be one of her captors.

"What did I miss?" He asked around a mouthful of ham.

"We're staying to celebrate the Festival of the Fair Queen." Quade beamed. He was building a tower out of the remaining bread, ham and cheese, stacking it as high as he could before trying to cram the whole thing in his mouth.

"Really?" Coulter asked, an odd look on his face. "I knew it was soon, but…You'll get to see what a real party looks like, Aria." He winked at her, but it didn't have the same sparkle as before.

They retired to bed as soon as the food was gone. Kiefer reluctantly said goodnight to his new friend, promising to find her tomorrow at the celebration.

Aria's mind was foggy with sleep, she wanted to close the door and collapse onto the bed. But she wasn't alone.

Xander coughed. "You take the bed, I'll just find Bonnie and get some more blankets." He left the room and Aria exhaled.

Bonnie had kindly left a cotton nightshirt on her pillow, which she quickly pulled on, tossing the linen tunic and trousers into the corner.

The mattress wasn't the comfiest, but the blankets made it bearable, and anything was better than a hard floor or a moving horse. After the last couple of days, she desperately needed a good night's sleep. She'd need all of her energy to put her escape plan in motion tomorrow.

When Xander returned with the blankets, she kept her eyes closed and pretended to already be asleep. She could feel his gaze on her as he created a makeshift bed on the floor, but she didn't open her eyes and he never uttered a word.

Her heart raced and she struggled to keep her breathing steady, knowing he was so close by, unarmed and undressed. The tension in the room weighed heavy on her already tired bones.

It wasn't long before darkness reached up and dragged her down.

12

ARIA WOKE EARLY THE NEXT MORNING, but when she looked over to where Xander had lay the night before there was nothing but a pile of neatly folded blankets. He must have woken even earlier than she had.

Some type of bird sang loudly outside the small window, and the sun shone in, warming the cosy, wood-panelled room. Reluctant to get out of bed, she lay under the blankets and stared out at the bright blue, cloudless sky.

It was a beautiful day for a ride through the forest.

She'd slept better than expected, even with her own personal night watchman. Xander didn't snore, thankfully, and the exhaustion of the past few days had carried her through until morning without disruption.

She had paid close attention to the way the boys spoke and behaved when they arrived at the inn, there had been no indication that she was their captive. The inn staff—Audrey, Bonnie and the two stable boys—

had no idea that she wasn't a willing travel companion. She hadn't had chance to escape in the night thanks to Xander, and she had needed sleep anyway, or she wouldn't have made it more than five miles before needing to stop and rest.

But, after a good night's sleep and a proper meal or two, she would be ready.

She planned to spend the day exploring the village, looking for the best route to take when she got a chance. She'd smile, chat with the boys, make them think she'd given up her plan to escape.

She'd try to get more information out of them about what lurked in the woods, just in case she stumbled across anything on her journey. Hopefully, Xander's horse would be quicker than any beast.

With any luck, the boys would fall for her act like the gullible fool they clearly thought *her* to be. And later, she'd make some excuse about needing to use the bathroom and she would slip away.

A knock at the door made her jump out of bed, crashing into the dresser as she tried to pull on her borrowed trousers.

"It's only me, Miss." Bonnie's soft voice came through the door. "I brought you some breakfast."

Aria pulled the nightshirt down over her trousers and opened the door. Bonnie was carrying a tray with a steaming teapot, a bowl of porridge drizzled with honey, and a small dish of fresh berries. Aria's now clean clothes were tucked under her arm.

"Thank you, Bonnie."

She placed the tray on top of the chest and opened one of the drawers, laying the t-shirt and jeans inside. "You're very welcome, Miss. Your friends are downstairs in the tap room, they said to join them when you're ready." She bobbed a curtsy and turned to leave.

"Bonnie," Aria started. "Can you…do you have to get back to

work, or can you stay and talk? Just for a minute." Bonnie glanced at the door, chewing her lower lip.

Aria's heart sank. She hadn't realised how much she missed having a friend to talk to, and whilst she couldn't tell Bonnie what she was going through, she could at least make friendly conversation, regain some sense of normalcy. Or, she could get some answers. "It's just, I've been traveling with the boys for so long, it would be nice to talk to another girl for once."

"I guess I can stay for a minute," Bonnie said, seeing Aria's glum expression. She smiled and sat down delicately on the edge of the bed. Aria straightened the blankets and placed the breakfast tray in front of her, sitting cross-legged.

Dipping her spoon into the porridge, she asked, "So, this festival. What's it for?" She shovelled a heaped spoonful of the warm, sweetened oats into her mouth. It was deliciously fragrant, the honey was like none she had ever tasted. She murmured in appreciation, picking the dish of berries up and tipping the contents into the porridge. She stirred them in, watching the creamy oats stain pink, red and purple.

"It's the Festival of the Fair Queen, when we celebrate Queen Oriana, the first Fair Queen, and the creation of the Fair Realm."

"The *first* Fair Queen?" Aria poured a cup of tea and offered it to Bonnie, who politely declined. Aria inhaled the steam that rose from the cup, closing her eyes momentarily. She took a sip. "When was the Fair Realm created?"

"Around five hundred years ago, according to the histories. Queen Oriana used her magic to create this place. Somewhere people like herself would be safe, protected from those who would do them harm."

"What do you mean?"

Bonnie's expression turned sad. "Well, before the Fair Realm existed, many Fair were executed for having abilities. And those that weren't killed were forced to live outside of society, so they tended to cluster together and keep to themselves. Oriana decided to create a place where all of the Fair would be free to live as their true selves without fear of persecution."

"She sounds like quite a woman, this Queen Oriana," Aria mused, mouth full of porridge. "And powerful. To create an entire realm? How do you even do that?"

Bonnie shook her head. "No one really knows. Aether magic is mysterious and complex. Especially to those of us who are not Celeste."

"Are you a Gnome?"

"Yes. But, not a powerful one. Strong magic is rare." She picked at a hole in her apron, mouth pinched, cheeks flushing.

"I heard. My companions aren't powerful either, apparently," Aria said.

Bonnie frowned. "Except Prince Xander. He's said to be very talented. The most powerful Gnome for generations. And he's quite handsome." She blushed a shade darker and looked down at her hands, folded in her lap.

Aria's eyebrows shot up. "You know him?" The hope of Bonnie helping her escape that had begun to kindle within her died instantly. If she had a crush on the prince, she'd be more likely to throw Aria under the bus if she discovered her plan to get away.

The maid nodded shyly. "He is known all across the Five Kingdoms. I have seen him before," she said excitedly, "when he travelled to the village to meet with our elders, as an envoy of his father."

Aria poured another cup of sweet black tea while Bonnie talked. It was different to the builder's tea she drank at home, somewhere between a black tea and a herbal tea, giving off a light floral scent.

Bonnie went on. "He never stayed at the inn before, though. They always set up camp outside of the village. There are usually a lot more than six of them." She frowned.

Aria considered Bonnie's words. Xander, and maybe the others, had been to this place before. Perhaps more than once. They would know it well, having chosen suitable campsites and patrolled the surrounding area, no doubt. It might make her escape plan a little more difficult. But, not impossible.

"If you don't mind me asking, Miss," Bonnie said, bringing Aria back to the present. "You're not from here, are you?" She said it like a question, but the answer was obvious from Aria's rounded ears and lack of knowledge. Aria nodded. "Why have you come?"

It was a shockingly blunt question coming from Bonnie, who had been unfailingly polite up to now. Aria was a little taken aback, but not offended. She wasn't sure whether Bonnie meant Hitherham, or the Fair Realm. She drew a breath and let it out slowly, trying to formulate an answer that wouldn't spark concern in this sweet girl. How would she take the knowledge that Aria had been brought here against her will, and intended to flee her kidnappers?

Before she could open her mouth to speak, Bonnie said something that turned her blood to ice inside her veins. "Are you she, Miss? The one the prophecy speaks of?" Her voice was barely a whisper. "Have you come here to save us?"

Aria's mouth fell open. The weird fortune she had gotten at the fayre came back to her in a sudden rush.

When kingdoms unite and flame and aether collide, the Fair Queen shall return.

It had slipped her mind, what with everything she'd been through the past couple of days, but now Divina's words were all she could hear. They grew louder and louder in her head until Aria thought her eardrums might burst.

Audrey's voice rose from the bottom of the stairs, startling the two girls. She was calling for Bonnie, impatience sharpening her tone.

Bonnie grabbed up the breakfast tray. "I have to go."

"Bonnie, wait." Aria jumped up, but the girl had already disappeared from the room, door slamming shut behind her.

Aria dropped back down onto the bed, mind racing and heart pounding. She stayed there, unable to formulate a single coherent thought other than the fortune, for a long time.

In the harsh light of day, the village looked more dishevelled than charming. Crumbling masonry and peeling woodwork had been overrun by climbing plants. Nature appeared to be trying to take back the landscape, erasing the blemish humans had inflicted on it.

It looked like a fairy tale. Not the Disney kind, more like The Brothers Grimm.

In the square, the villagers had begun to decorate in preparation for the festival the next day. They hung paper bunting and floral garlands from building to building, arranged mismatched tables in lines and covered them in white sheets. A small stage was being constructed out of wooden pallets, and a large pile of wood that Aria assumed would be a bonfire had started to form on the nearby green.

She perched on the edge of the fountain in the centre of the square, which had been filled with floating candles waiting to be lit, idly running her fingers through the cool water. The sky had warmed to a startling shade of cornflower blue and there wasn't a single cloud to interrupt the view. Everything seemed sharper, more focused here. The foliage was a vivid shade of green, lush and vital. Smells and tastes were amplified, at least to her human taste buds. Even the birdsong was more beautiful than any she had heard at home.

It felt like a trap. Constructed to lure people in and keep them from ever leaving. Like that poem about the goblin market they'd studied in English. Suddenly, she wished she hadn't eaten or drunk anything since setting foot in the Fair Realm.

She had to get away.

From her position on the fountain's edge, she watched Rainer helping a couple of local boys stack barrels of mead and wine for the party. He towered over them, a foot taller than the tallest and easily twice as broad as the biggest. His pristine clothes marked him out as wealthy. The villagers were not shabbily dressed by any means, it was clear they took pride in their appearances. But, the knees of trousers were thin with wear, and leather shoes showed signs of having been mended several times.

Looking around, Aria noticed that there were fewer men than women in the town. A few elderly gentlemen, several teenage boys, but no men. Another reminder of the war that had devastated the realm— no wonder Kiefer and Coulter had been so popular with the local girls.

The sun was high in the sky now, and Audrey and Bonnie were handing out mugs of water. There was laughter and shouting, banging and clattering as barrels and pallets were lugged about. If the noise and commotion of the preparations was anything to go by, the party would be a raucous affair.

A perfect cover for her midnight flit.

She pushed up from the fountain's edge and made her way over to where Rainer was hefting the last barrel. "Need a hand?" She had deliberately waited until they were almost finished, hoping to find an excuse to wander off on her own and put her plans in motion. Up close, she realised the two boys helping Rainer were the stable hands who had taken their horses the previous night. One was tall and skinny, with light brown skin and curly black hair, like Bonnie's. The other was also skinny—there wasn't a single overweight person in the village, it seemed to Aria—with sandy hair and a ruddy face.

Rainer hadn't even broken a sweat, and it was a warm day. "We're about done here. You could help Quade with the stalls, I'm sure he'd appreciate the assistance," They both looked over to the village green, where Quade wrestled with a canvas tent and a pile of wooden pegs. He managed to make it look like a particularly complicated jigsaw puzzle. Aria laughed and Rainer shook his head, chuckling under his breath.

Xander appeared at the door to the inn, limping across the square towards the village.

"Where's he going?"

"To see Bonnie's grandmother, she's the village healer. For his leg."

"Bonnie's grandmother?"

"Yes. Why?" Rainer's tone was curious, but his expression was clear. He wasn't suspicious then.

"No reason. I might see if he needs a hand." She jogged in the direction Xander had been heading before Rainer could say another word.

Ever since her conversation with Bonnie that morning, she had been desperate to get the girl alone and quiz her about the prophecy. Perhaps her grandmother would know more.

Xander opened the gate to a small cottage with a tidy and well-tended garden in front. Aria caught up with him at the door. "Aria? What's wrong?"

She slipped an arm under his elbow just as the door opened to reveal a short, wizened old woman with salt-and-pepper hair and deep wrinkles around her eyes and mouth. Aria turned a her brightest smile on the woman. "Hi, my friend Xander here has an injured leg. We were told you're the village healer, is that right?" She could see Xander watching her out of the corner of her eye with an incredulous look on his face. She focused on the woman.

"Yes, dear. Come in, come in. I've been expecting you." She turned and slowly hobbled into the house, leaving the door open so they could follow.

Aria was surprised. "Are you psychic, too?"

The woman laughed, a rattling, phlegmy sound that made Aria want to clear her own throat. "No, dear. My granddaughter, Bonnie, she told me you'd be coming along."

Aria's cheeks burned. "Oh, of course." She could feel Xander shaking gently with silent laughter, and refused to turn her head.

"Hop up on here, Your Royal Highness." She patted a wooden table in the centre of the room and Xander eased himself onto it. They were in a small kitchen, a large window in one wall let in warm, yellow light, and looked out onto another patch of garden with neatly planted rows of flowers and herbs.

"Please, call me Xander." The old woman nodded vaguely as she bustled around the kitchen, picking up pots and bowls and bringing them to the table. She placed a pile of cotton strips next to Xander and started to crush a fistful of white flowers with a pestle and mortar.

"Which leg?" She poured a little warm water from a copper kettle into the bowl, added a drop of two different essential oils, and continued her mixing. Aria recognised the scent of lavender and tea tree, but she couldn't identify the flowers.

Xander rolled up his trouser leg, exposing the long pink wound, sewn shut with black thread. It wasn't bleeding anymore, but it was far from healed. Bonnie's grandmother tutted, shaking her head and fishing a pair of scissors from a hook on the wall. She placed the kettle back over the fire to boil some water.

Aria wanted to ask about the prophecy, but she didn't want Xander to hear. She needed to get the woman alone. "Is there anything you need from the garden? Would you like me to collect more flowers?"

The woman eyed her. "How kind. Come, I will show you which ones to pick." She picked up a basket and gestured for Aria to follow into the back garden. She closed the kitchen door behind them, calling to Xander to shout if the kettle boiled. They walked to the furthest edge of the garden, a corner behind tall bushes, out of view of the kitchen window. The woman stopped, turning to Aria. "Ask me what you came here to ask."

Aria stammered, taken aback. "Mrs—"

She realised she didn't know the woman's name.

"Saffi," said Bonnie's grandmother.

"I'm Aria."

"The human girl. My granddaughter spoke about you."

"Yes. Well, maybe. Bonnie mentioned a prophecy, and I thought you might know…something." She felt stupid. It was probably just a story kids told each other, why would Saffi be interested in something so silly? She was a healer, a scientist. What Aria had seen since arriving at the little cottage hadn't been mysticism or superstition, Saffi was not a witch doctor, but a genuine medic with scientific knowledge of plants and their healing properties.

Aria was about to apologise when Saffi reached out and took both of her hands, clasping them between her own. She studied Aria's face with a gaze that made Aria's skin prickle, like she could see into her soul. She must have been satisfied with what she saw, because she nodded and let Aria's hands go.

"Around twenty years ago, a prophetess had a vision of a child. A child who would end the war and bring peace to the Five Kingdoms."

Aria tried to take this in. She was weeks away from her eighteenth birthday, if the prophecy was made twenty years earlier, it could have foretold her birth.

She couldn't believe she was entertaining the idea that she was the subject of a prophecy.

"What did the prophetess see?"

Saffi shook her head, sadness in her watery eyes. "No one knows. The prophetess died long ago. There are rumours, there have been many over the years, but it is impossible to know which are true. If any."

Aria's shoulders slumped. If no one knew what the prophecy said, how would she discover the truth? She couldn't disprove a prophecy she didn't even know. But, Saffi had spoken of rumours. "Which do you believe?"

Saffi scanned Aria's face, taking in her dull brown eyes, her rounded ears and human features. After several seconds of scrutiny, she said in a strange voice, "A daughter of flame and aether will one day unite the kingdoms and bring peace to the realm. A child born of the Fair and raised by humans, the Fair Queen will return when the sun takes its longest path across the sky. And she will be the one to unseat the usurper and end the war."

The temperature seemed to drop and goose bumps rippled over Aria's flesh. The first part she'd heard before, but the second part…

A child born of the Fair and raised by humans.

And she had been taken by the Gnomes on the Summer Solstice.

She struggled to get her head around what she was hearing. Could she really be the one the prophecy referred to? No, it wasn't possible. She was just a normal girl from Hartwood, this was all a mistake. It had to be.

But, if Xander and Rainer and the other Gnome's truly believed she was this Fair Queen, they wouldn't be alone.

Unseat the usurper…was this the Celeste King she kept hearing about? The one who wanted her dead. Had sent the barghests to attack them. He clearly believed the prophecy was about her, why else would he care about some random human girl?

Aria was staring into the distance, eyes wide, the blood draining from her face. Saffi just watched, silent.

The kitchen door opened and Xander called, "The kettle is boiling."

"Come," Saffi said, taking Aria's arm. "I'll make you some tea. A special brew of my own making. Very calming." She ushered Aria back up the garden path and into the cottage. Aria let the old woman drag her along, dazed.

Back inside the house, Xander raised an eyebrow, but didn't ask why the basket was still empty. Saffi spooned a blend of leaves and petals into a large teapot, pouring some of the boiling water on top. She disinfected the scissors and set to work carefully snipping the stitches Aria had put in Xander's leg. He was sitting on the table again, his knuckles whitening as he gripped the edge, teeth gritted against the pain.

She couldn't take it in, her mind still raced with questions.

She was convinced that this was all a case of mistaken identity, but that didn't make her any less of a target for this Celeste King. He didn't seem the sort to think before acting, how exactly would she persuade him that she wasn't the one?

She needed to get away from this place and the danger it held for her as soon as she could.

Saffi poured the now brewed tea into an earthenware mug and handed it to Aria. The heat was comforting, and she held the mug to her nose, inhaling deeply. It smelled of chamomile and lemongrass, a soothing blend from what she remembered. She had never liked herbal tea, preferring coffee, but her mother loved the stuff. She was always trying different blends, extolling their various benefits to anyone who'd listen.

Saffi watched expectantly as Aria took a sip. She smiled, and Saffi nodded, satisfied. The tea was sweet, floral and citrusy. Aria could feel her nerves untangling after the first mouthful. She took another sip.

Saffi pulled the last piece of thread from Xander's shin with a pair of copper tweezers, and used a cotton strip dipped in the boiled water to clean the wound. She used her fingers to slather the area with the mixture she had ground, it was an ugly green-brown colour. Xander winced as it touched his torn flesh. Saffi mumbled soothing words while she worked. She wrapped the wound with several strips of the ripped cotton, tying them off behind his calf. "You should be able to walk on it without pain in a few hours, and remove the bandages in a day."

"Wow. That's fast." Aria was surprised, the wound had been pretty raw, a day seemed soon.

"We heal quickly," Xander explained, rolling his trouser leg back down and accepting a mug of the tea Saffi had made. "Quicker with a little help from a healer. Unfortunately, the war has made Celeste healers rare in Gnome and the other three kingdoms."

"You're a Celeste?" Aria looked at Saffi, aghast. She had opened up to this woman, and all along she had been one them.

Saffi shook her head. "I'm just a keen herbalist. Celeste healers can do far more than I, with their contraptions and concoctions. I'm a Gnome, I work with plants and herbs, not…aether."

Aria was relieved, although she couldn't put her finger on why. She had never met a Celeste, she only had Xander's word for it that the Celeste King wanted her dead, and even if he did, he was just one man. They couldn't all feel the same way.

"Thank you," Xander said, draining his mug and lowering himself to the ground slowly. He tested his leg, which seemed to have improved already. He reached into a pocket and held out a small drawstring bag to Saffi. She took it, pleasant surprise in her expression at its considerable weight.

"My pleasure, Your Royal—Xander." She curtsied, which was almost comical coming from the elderly woman. She was nimble for her age, no doubt owing to her knowledge of herbal remedies. "Get some rest, and your leg should be better in time for the celebrations tomorrow."

As they walked down the short hallway to the front door, Aria spotted a photograph of a smiling couple. It was too recent to be of Saffi herself. "Are these Bonnie's parents?"

Saffi nodded. "My son, Isaac, and his wife, Justine. They were both killed by Celeste soldiers. That was taken ten years ago, I have raised Bonnie and Philip for the last six years,"

She said it matter-of-factly, and that made it all the worse. Aria's heart swelled for her, and the two orphaned teenagers working at the inn, trying to help their grandmother make ends meet after the loss of her son.

Impulsively, Aria threw her arms around Saffi, hugging her.

"Thank you, for everything. Will we see you at the party?" Saffi assured them that she would be there, on hand with her bandages and tea for any revellers who exceeded their limits.

Aria and Xander walked back to the inn in silence, Xander trying not to put too much weight on his injured leg, Aria mulling over Saffi's words about the prophecy. It was pretty vague when she thought about it, it could have meant almost anything. Or nothing at all. It could all be a rumour, and there never was a prophecy. Just a story made up by poor parents in war-torn villages, to give their children hope.

As much as she wanted the part about bringing *peace* and *an end to the war* to be true, she couldn't be the one to bring it about. The Five Kingdoms had been at war for so long, if nobody else had managed it in a hundred and fifty years, how was a seventeen-year-old human girl going to succeed where they had failed?

13

ARIA CHECKED HER REFLECTION in the small mirror on top of the dresser. Bonnie had given her a white shift dress to wear to the festival. White was customary for the Festival of the Fair Queen, apparently it symbolised purity, and peace.

Ironic, Aria thought as she straightened the straps.

After her visit to Saffi's cottage the previous day, she'd drifted around barely noticing her surroundings, the medicine woman's words ringing in her ears. She'd had to reconnoitre the village properly this morning, putting her plans into place as she went. At least her trance-like state the day before seemed to have convinced the boys she wasn't a flight risk anymore.

She combed her hair through and twisted it into a bun at the nape of her neck, A few short strands sprang free, framing her face with wavy ribbons of rose gold. A scattering of freckles had appeared across her cheeks and nose, the result of a few days spent outdoors with no sunscreen.

She pulled on her boots. She had no other shoes and Bonnie's feet were smaller. Aria didn't mind, she thought the boots were a fun juxtaposition to the feminine dress. A glimpse of her personality.

She gave herself one last cursory glance in the mirror before leaving the room. She paused, peering closer. For a moment, she thought she'd seen a glint in her eye, a bronze glimmer that hadn't been there before.

It had only been a trick of the light, there was nothing different about her muddy brown irises. She shook it off and opened the bedroom door, stepping out into the hallway, and almost walked straight into Xander, who was lifting a knuckle to rap on the door.

They both took a step backwards, apologising in unison. Xander froze, he took in Aria's appearance, eyes gliding over her face, the borrowed dress, and coming to rest on her boots. He raised an eyebrow, eyes flicking back to her face. "You look…" He stumbled over his words before recovering. "I particularly like the boots."

Aria grinned and stuck out a leg as though she were a footwear model. "Thanks. You don't look bad yourself."

It was true. He wore a white linen tunic, with forest green leaves embroidered around the neckline, and dark green trousers. He had bathed and he smelled like lavender, his hair was slicked back, exposing his pointed ears and emphasising his sharp jaw and cheekbones. He was all angles and hollows, pale skin and jet-black hair. Thick brows hid his eyes in shadow. It made him difficult to read. Except when he smiled, as he did now. His thin lips curved upwards at the corners, almost reluctantly, and he bowed his head as if to hide it.

It was so rare to see anything other than a scowl on his face, Aria felt a small swell of pride that she had caused it.

"Did you need something?" She asked, stepping back to allow him past her into the room.

He opened his mouth and shut it again. He ran a hand over his slicked back hair, "I was just coming to see if you were ready. Shall we?" He gestured for her to take the lead and head downstairs.

In the den, the other boys had gathered at the same corner table as the previous night. They were all dressed in white tunics, all clean and fresh smelling.

"Aria!" Quade called out as she entered, and she found herself smiling. He had a disarming way about him, no matter how much she wanted to she couldn't dislike him. "You look nice." He plucked a white anemone from a vase on the window ledge. "Just, one last thing." He tucked the tiny flower in her hair behind her ear and leant back, admiring his work. "There." Aria curtsied for him.

Music drifted in through the open windows, it sounded like a reed pipe accompanied by some kind of drum.

"Come on, let's see what a Gnome party is like then." The boys followed her out to the village square, where a duo performed on the stage and a handful of people were already dancing. It was still light, but as soon as the sun went down and the candles and lanterns were lit this place would look magical.

Audrey and Bonnie weaved through the crowds with trays of mead and wine, and the two young stable boys, Bonnie's brother Philip, and Stoddard, were manning the stack of barrels outside the inn.

Earlier in the day, Aria had snuck out to the stables and stashed a bag containing her jeans and t-shirt, a bundle of bread and cheese that she had stolen from the kitchen, a flask of water, and a few apples for Xander's stallion. He knew her, and therefore made the most sense to take. She only hoped she could handle him alone. She'd hidden the bag under the hay in his stall, hoping the stable boys would be too busy today to muck out the horses, and she would be long gone by tomorrow morning.

She planned to slip away later, when the party was in full swing, hoping by then her guards would be having too much fun—or have drunk too much mead—to accompany her to the bathroom. She'd push the horse as hard as she could for as long as it would let her, hoping to make it to dawn before they had to slow their pace. She'd stolen a small sharp knife from the kitchen at the inn and wrapped it up in a napkin, just in case she came across any creatures.

She'd figure the rest out when she got to the crossing.

A hog was roasting on a spit, being turned every so often by a large, ruddy-faced woman with a cloth in one hand and a big fork in the other. The white-clothed tables that lined two sides of the square were beginning to fill with all kinds of food that had been kindly prepared for the festival by the villagers. Aria got the impression this was all the food some of them had, as she saw large bowls of fruit and small dishes of nuts being set down on the table. The feast was clearly an integral part of the celebration, a tribute to the first Fair Queen in remembrance and gratitude for creating the realm that kept them safe.

Kiefer spotted the girl he had met the night before, Charlotte he'd called her, and immediately made a bee-line for her, tossing a wink over his shoulder at the rest of them. Aria laughed.

"He's trouble, that one," she muttered under her breath. Xander, at her side, huffed a laugh. She flicked her eyes to his face and saw him watching his younger brother with fondness, his sharp features softened by affection. It was a moment of vulnerability that she hadn't expected to see. A strange feeling came over her as she looked at him, almost like nausea, but altogether more pleasant.

Quade appeared in front of her then, he bowed slightly and held out a hand. "Would you like to dance, Aria?"

She glanced at the dancers, a line forming between her eyebrows. "I don't know the steps." They were performing some kind of line dance, they stood in a circle holding hands and took two steps to the left, then the right. They raised their clasped hands above their heads and stepped forwards, the circle shrank and then expanded again as they stepped backwards.

"This one is quite simple. I'll teach you, come on."

She considered refusing, but if she appeared to be enjoying herself and embracing the festivities, perhaps they'd let their guards down.

Quade led her to the centre of the square and the group of dancing villagers, who all smiled and made a space for them to join the circle. Aria took Quade's left hand, and the right hand of Stoddard, the stable boy. He had sandy hair and a round face with chubby cheeks. He couldn't be older than fourteen, still carrying the softness of youth. He smiled warmly at Aria, a real smile that reached his large hazel eyes. To his left was a very pretty, dark-haired girl with dimples in her cheeks. He kept sneaking glances at her under his long, blonde lashes when he thought she wasn't looking.

The dance started again from the beginning, everyone took two steps to the left and two to the right. Aria looked at her feet as she copied the movements, tripped over herself and almost pulled Stoddard down with her. He gave her a sharp look, embarrassed in front of the pretty girl, but his features smoothed quickly as he caught himself. Aria apologised, and Stoddard joined in with Quade's chants of *left, left, right, right*.

Within minutes, Aria found she was enjoying herself. She had almost perfected the steps and was now listening to the music and trying to learn the lyrics to the song. She looked across the square and caught a glimpse of Xander through a gap in the crowd. He stood by the stage with a frothy mug of mead in his hand, watching her with the same intensity she had seen in his face before, back in the woods. It sent a tingle down her spine.

She stumbled again as the circle of dancers stepped backwards, pulling her along with it like a receding tide. She apologised, thanked the dancers and broke the circle.

Quade followed her. "Did you enjoy that?" Concern clouded his shimmering blue eyes.

She nodded and his brow smoothed. "I'm just thirsty." She caught Bonnie's attention as she passed with a tray of glasses filled to the brim with jostaberry wine. She took a glass and sipped tentatively, her eyes closed as she savoured the sweet, fruity wine.

Bonnie beamed. "Good, right?"

Aria had a sudden spark of inspiration. Maybe it was the wine, but she glanced between Bonnie and Quade and couldn't help herself. "Bonnie, do you like to dance?"

Bonnie's face broke into a wide grin. "I love dancing! This is one of my favourites." She gestured towards the circle of dancers, which had almost doubled in size since Aria had joined in. They were facing each other in two rows now, stamping towards each other and then clasping hands with the person opposite to create an archway for the couple at the far end to run through.

"Quade likes to dance, too, don't you Quade? Why don't you show him how it's done?" She elbowed Quade in the ribs.

"Oh, I don't—" He stammered, blushing. Aria gave him a pleading look and took the tray of glasses out of the maid's hands. Quade looked at Bonnie who was studying her feet and chewing her full bottom lip. "It would be my pleasure."

Bonnie grinned and took the arm Quade proffered. They joined the other merrymakers, taking their place at the end of the line, hands clasped above their heads.

Aria watched them for a moment, smiling to herself and sipping her wine. She could feel the alcohol warming her bones and loosening her joints. She would have to be careful, she didn't want to be tipsy when she slipped away later, she needed to keep her wits about her.

Kiefer and Charlotte had now joined Quade and Bonnie in the dance, they were laughing together, completely at ease as they performed the steps. Aria walked along the edge of the square, watching them and sipping from her wine glass. She reached the path that separated the square from the village green and made for the row of tents that housed the games. Behind the tents, the pile of wood for the bonfire had grown tenfold since the day before, and a couple of young men Aria recognised as the guards from the guard post were throwing more wood on and attempting to light fires in various places around its base.

Good, her escape was falling into place. All she needed to do now was choose her moment.

Rainer and Coulter were throwing balls at coconuts on stilts. Coulter's accuracy was phenomenal—his talent for archery lent itself well to the test of hand-eye coordination.

Rainer took his turn, throwing the ball so hard and fast that it hit the back of the tent and pulled out three of the pegs holding it down. The coconut was still standing. He threw his hands up, cursing imaginatively.

"It doesn't matter," Coulter said, putting a hand on his arm. "If the ball had been an axe, that coconut wouldn't have stood a chance." Rainer looked down at the other boy, placed one hand on Coulter's cheek and drew his face towards him. He kissed Coulter on the lips, stroking his thumb along his cheekbone. Breaking apart, they smiled at each other, and Aria looked away, not wanting to intrude on the tender moment. "Maybe we should try something safe like skittles next?" Coulter said, and Rainer laughed. They moved along to the next tent.

"Having fun?" Aria jumped, spinning around to find Xander standing behind her. She almost fell into him and he caught her by the elbow, holding her steady.

Her face warmed. "It's a great party." She looked around at the faces of the villagers who were all laughing and smiling with one another, sharing a drink, dancing and playing games. It reminded her of home, of Hartwood, where everybody knew everybody else. Long summer evenings meant pub beer gardens and street parties, summer fayres and late-night strolls back to the bungalow under the stars. It was easy to forget that a war burned cold as ice here, that life wasn't always festivals and feasts.

"Would you like to play?" They stood in front of the ring toss, three tall milk pails were arranged several feet away, a white chalk line demarking where contestants stood to throw the metal rings. Aria had been terrible at sports at school. She could break a window playing badminton. But, there were no windows nearby, and she didn't have Rainer's brute strength, so it couldn't do any harm.

She stepped forward and picked up the metal rings. "Loser buys the next round."

"The drinks are free, Aria," Xander said, frowning. She laughed, high and musical, and a small smile broke out on Xander's face, barely more than a smirk, but she'd take it.

Aria lined the toe of her boot up with the chalk and swung her arm back and forth, testing the ring's weight. She'd seen people do it on TV before and wanted to look like she at least had some sporting acumen in front of the prince. She tossed the ring and it landed a foot in front of the nearest pail. The second hit a pail and bounced off, rolling across the grass. She swore under her breath. The third went long, disappearing into the tent behind. Aria collected the rings and handed them to Xander, shrugging.

He stepped up to the line and tossed the three rings in quick succession, leaving them ringing around the three metal pails with ease.

"Show off," Aria muttered under her breath as he collected the rings and left them next to the chalk line for the next participant.

He strode back to her with a grin on his face. "I guess you owe me a drink."

They walked back across the cobblestone path to the square and Xander picked up two mugs of mead from a passing tray. He handed one to Aria, watching with curiosity as she looked at it for a long moment. Refusing would arouse suspicion. She took a sip, deciding that she could handle one more drink, and if it came to it she could always spill it on the floor when he looked the other way.

"Your leg seems better."

He bent his knee, testing it out. "It feels almost good as new. Whatever Saffi put in that poultice clearly did the trick."

The sun had begun to set and someone had lit the candles that floated in the fountain and hung from branches in glass lanterns. It had a softening effect on the village, the crumbling buildings looked charming, the cracks in the fountain and cobbles less noticeable in the advancing dusk. Even the villagers looked more attractive. Like something out of a painting of a party, rather than the real thing.

Or maybe that was just the wine.

The music the band played lilted pleasantly, and Aria was captivated by the dancers, their smiling faces and the sound of their laughter and singing. She felt happy for the first time in days.

"Let's dance," she said suddenly, grabbing Xander's hand and pulling him towards the centre of the square. Bonnie and Quade were still in the thick of it, she appeared to be teaching him a new dance, demonstrating the steps and nodding effusively when he mimicked her. Aria and Xander joined Quade, copying the dance steps Bonnie showed them until they were ready to join the rest of the crowd. They twirled, hands on hips, before turning back the other way and slapping hands with the person to their left. It was a jolly tune, and they danced the steps with enthusiasm, even Xander grinned and appeared to be enjoying the festivities.

The song ended and another began, this one slower. The dancers paired off, some remaining on the dance floor, others taking up positions around the edge while they caught their breath. Bonnie and Quade smiled shyly, arms around each other.

Xander offered Aria a hand. She looked at it, nerves crackling like electricity. "I don't know it," she breathed.

"I do. I'll teach you," The mead had made him bold, he took her hands and placed them on his shoulders, resting his own on her waist. He began to chant the steps as his feet moved, backwards then forwards, left then right.

Bonnie and Quade were dancing with grace and ease, both of them familiar with the steps. Seeing the way they looked into each other's eyes, Aria felt a sort of pride for having encouraged them together. She glanced back at Xander and saw that the intensity was back in his eyes.

"What are you thinking?" She asked before she could stop herself.

14

IS FEATURES SMOOTHED, but his eyes were just as fierce. "I'm just enjoying the festival." He stepped backwards and held her hand high between them so she could twirl, like the other girls around them. She spun under his arm and back into his embrace. He held her closer now, and she could smell leather and soap, the slightest hint of horse underneath, and the sweet scent of jostaberries on his breath. She felt tipsy and light, the cool evening breeze doing nothing to lessen the heat in her skin, in her veins.

She felt brave. "Liar," she teased. His hands were back on her waist and they swayed in time to the music, stepping left and right, forwards and backwards. She stepped on his toes frequently, but he didn't show any signs of pain or annoyance. He didn't show any emotion at all, he was looking at her face with a carefully controlled expression that was impossible to read.

"Xander, tell me the truth." She tried to appeal to the boy she saw underneath. Not the crown prince, not the soldier, the boy who looked at her with such intensity it felt like a caress. Or a blow.

Something flickered in those glistering silver eyes, his lips parted. For a moment she thought she'd won. But then the shutters came down.

"I'm concerned about the delay, that's all. I need to deliver you to your father in time. If he succumbs to the sickness before we reach the Salamander Kingdom…" He shook his head.

Aria's chest tightened, she'd forgotten about her alleged sick father, the reason for Xander's mission. He was doing what he thought was right, reconnecting a dying man with his long-lost child.

She still wasn't sure what she believed, but looking into Xander's eyes she could see he believed he was doing the right thing.

The song ended and another, faster one began. Bonnie and Quade broke apart reluctantly and linked elbows, spinning in a circle before swapping arms and twirling back the other way. They clapped their hands in the air, hopping from left to right and touching their heels before linking arms once more.

Aria pulled away from Xander, her cheeks heating as she felt the rush of cool night air against her skin and realised how close they had been just moments before. She watched the new, fast-paced dance, convinced she would never pick up the steps before the song changed. She looked at Xander and laughed, shaking her head. They moved to the side of the dancefloor.

She should excuse herself now, while everyone was enjoying themselves, distracted by the music and lightheaded from the drink.

"I just need to…"

Over Xander's shoulder, she saw a woman stepping onto the platform where the band were still playing. A singer, taking over for the next song perhaps—a traditional Gnome song to celebrate the festivities.

The woman wore a flowing white gown that drifted about her legs in the evening breeze. A cowl was draped over her head, so Aria couldn't see her face as she approached the edge of the stage, facing the dancing villagers. Long, black hair spilled out of her hood, contrasting with the pale dress like squares on a chessboard. The villagers continued to clap and stamp along to the music, cheering and laughing, even as the band faltered. They stared at the woman, consternation on their faces.

Xander raised his eyebrows in question and turned to see what had caught Aria's eye and made her pause mid-sentence. Bonnie was still twirling, clapping her hands above her head and stamping her feet. When the music stopped, she spun to face the stage and froze, hands still up by her face,

The woman reached up to take her cowl down, pulling the gauzy material back from her face and looking out at the sea of people before her. Aria gaped. The woman's face and hands were as pale as the dress in the moonlight. But it was her eyes that stole Aria's breath and stopped her heart dead in her chest.

Where the woman's eyes should have been were black pits from which blood as dark as tar seemed to pour. She opened her mouth wider than humanly possible, jaw dislocating to expose a gaping hole rimmed with sharp, broken teeth, like shards of glass.

Xander spun and lunged for Aria, hands out-stretched. But Bonnie got there first. She clapped her hands over Aria's ears, just as the woman started screaming.

15

ANDER HAD QUICKLY COVERED HIS OWN EARS, and was now yelling at Aria, mouth moving angrily, eyes never leaving her face.

But Aria wasn't looking at him. She was looking at Bonnie.

The girl was staring wide-eyed, her lips forming a small O. Aria watched in horror as tears formed in the corners of her eyes, spilling over her dark lashes and streaming down her cheeks. Tears the colour of blood. The whites of her eyes turned red, and blood ran down from each nostril in a constant stream. Her skin paled, turning ashen, her cheeks caving in on themselves.

Aria's stomach turned and an acrid taste filled her mouth. She tore her eyes away from Bonnie's face and finally looked at Xander, who was still trying to signal to her. Reading his lips, she placed her own hands over Bonnie's, covering her ears, and saw Xander's shoulders slump in relief.

Aria looked back towards the stage and saw the woman—the creature, whatever it was—still howling. Nobody had moved to stop it. Most of the villagers had their hands pinned tightly over their ears. Many had not.

Bonnie's body started to crumple, her hands slipped down Aria's neck and Aria had to clamp her own hands over her ears as tightly as she could or risk Bonnie uncovering them. Xander's eyes were wide, he didn't appear to be breathing as Aria replaced Bonnie's hands with her own, body quivering in shock at what she was seeing.

Xander scanned Aria's face for any sign that she had heard the creature's deadly scream. Satisfied she was unharmed, he turned to scan the crowd for the others.

Rainer and Coulter were nearby, standing close together. They were both looking around the square at the bodies falling one by one. Both covering their ears. Aria looked around. Kiefer stood closer to the stage, hands over his ears, mouthing something over and over to Charlotte. She was covering her own ears, but her tanned face had blanched and tears streamed down her cheeks. With a rush of relief, Aria saw they were clear, not blood-stained.

Kiefer turned to look for Xander, Quade and the others. Finding them safe he nodded in acknowledgement and turned back to his dance partner.

Bodies had begun to drop to the floor like some sickening Mexican wave. Aria couldn't bear it, she had to make it stop somehow.

She wasn't sure what made her do it, but she started to make her way towards the stage, unable to look down as she stepped over Bonnie's lifeless body. She felt like somebody else was controlling her body, like her limbs weren't her own.

Xander tried to stop her, but with no hands he could only mouth *stop* and try to block her with his own body. She stepped around him and kept moving forward, approaching the stage and the hideous screaming creature.

She passed Kiefer and kept moving. He watched her go, a look of confusion on his face.

The wraith-like creature was still screaming.

Aria finally reached the stage, but the thing didn't look at her, just kept staring straight ahead and screaming that terrible scream. The scream that had killed Bonnie.

Bonnie.

Aria looked into the creature's ruined eyes, took a deep, shuddering breath, and shouted at the top of her voice. "STOP!"

Nothing happened.

Then the creature slowly lowered its eyes to look at Aria. The scream ended and silence filled Aria's mind and body. A silence so complete she thought she might never hear another sound again.

An explosion of light and heat roared over on the green, behind the games tents.

The bonfire. The soldier's must have thrown some kind of accelerant on it, because the flames lashed up at the navy sky and licked the canvas tents, threatening to spread to the rest of the village.

At the sight of the fire, the creature whirled and, in a maelstrom of white gauze, ran from the stage into the night. The way it moved was not human. It was like floating. A grace that contradicted the vicious massacre it had just inflicted on the villagers.

Somebody touched Aria's shoulder, turning her gently to face him. Xander. He was mouthing something—speaking to her—but she couldn't hear him. Her hands were still pinned over her ears. Slowly, cautiously, he reached up and tried to pull Aria's hands away from her ears. She jerked away and shouted *no*. She fell to her knees in front of the stage and started to sob. She gasped for air, her breath catching painfully in her chest. She pictured Bonnie's face as it crumpled, blood streaming from every orifice. Tears came in a hot flood, her chest heaving.

Xander crouched in front of her. He reached for her hands again, nodding, and murmured something she couldn't hear. She let him take her hands this time, and when he put his arms around her she fell against him, sobs racking her body as he held her tight.

16

ODIES LITTERED THE SQUARE. Blood ran in rivulets between the cobble stones, dark pools forming in the cracks. The sky was pitch black now, and the soft glow from the candles only emphasised the macabre scene.

Aria sat with her arms wrapped tightly around her knees, staring at the lifeless forms around her. People ran across the square, looking for friends or family members. Some were screaming.

Aria wished they would all stop screaming.

She stared through the legs of the villagers, over the tangle of limbs and ruined faces of the dead, to where Bonnie lay. She couldn't take her eyes off the girl.

Xander crouched beside Aria. He was speaking, repeating meaningless platitudes that she couldn't hear, couldn't take in. Nothing was going to be OK, no matter how many times he said it. Nothing would ever be OK again.

They had fought off the barghests with barely a scratch. No one had died. Now this. That thing had massacred dozens of innocent people with only its voice. How did you fight something like that?

Rainer appeared in Aria's peripheral vision. He spoke to Xander in a low voice, but nothing could cut through the wall of ice that surrounded Aria, blocking out all sound but that horrific scream. It ricocheted around the inside of her head, she wanted to claw it out with her fingernails, open her mouth and let it out until her throat was raw.

Coulter knelt in front of her, a steaming mug of coffee in his hands. She took it without a word, the heat from the mug doing little to warm her bones. She shivered continuously, despite the warm summer evening. Coulter stood and spoke quietly with the others, their voices washing over her.

One word stood out. *Banshee.*

So that's what the creature had been.

Aria watched as the surviving villagers huddled together in small clusters, weeping and hugging each other. By the looks of the crowd, the population of the village had been reduced to a third of its former size. Those who hadn't been at the festival had left their homes on hearing the disturbance in the square, the screams of their neighbours. They were now draping blankets round the shoulders of those who were suffering from shock. Aria's own shoulders were shrouded in a heavy horse blanket Rainer had fetched from the stables.

Audrey and Stoddard carried trays of mugs containing the same hot, sweetened coffee Aria held, offering them to the remaining villagers. Philip was helping Saffi to drape bed sheets over the bodies of the fallen. Bonnie was obscured from Aria's view as her grandmother draped an off-white sheet over her small, dark form, shoulders shaking gently as she did.

Aria could hear the boys talking, but it was like she was underwater. Their voices were muffled and distant. Distorted by her state of shock and the ringing in her ears. She felt like she could still hear the banshee screaming, it made every other sound seem like silence. Every time she blinked, that pale face with the hideous black pits instead of eyes and the unnaturally gaping mouth flashed inside her head. Staring unblinking into space was easier than having to see that face again.

"We need to leave as soon as we can get the horses loaded. We have to go before—"

"No."

Xander's head snapped to face her. "Aria—"

She stood, letting the blanket fall from her shoulders, and looked him in the eye. "I said no. We are not leaving." Her chest rose and fell sharply, her fists were clenched at her sides, knuckles white as bone.

"It's not safe here, Aria. We need to get you to safety." He reached for her hands, but she flinched away.

"And what about everyone else? What about their safety? Are you just going to leave them all in danger *for me*? I'm just one girl, I can't possibly be that special. And you can't be that selfish."

Xander looked like she'd slapped him. His expression hardened. "Aria, I know this is difficult to understand, and what happened here is terrible—" He held a hand up to silence her as she opened her mouth to cut in. "But, if we leave here, they will no longer be in danger."

She studied his face, understanding just out of reach.

His tone softened. "It is you the Celeste King wants. He sent the banshee here for you."

Aria's anger dissolved. Her knees buckled and tears sprang to her eyes. Xander reached for her again, but she steadied herself, stumbling backwards to keep him at arm's length.

It was her fault. They had died—Bonnie had died—because of her.

"Hell, no, we are not leaving!" Kiefer appeared behind Aria. It was his voice that finally broke through the screaming inside Aria's head. "By the Elements, Xander, what is wrong with you? Leaving these people—*our* people—after what just happened?" His voice shook with rage, eyes flashing dangerously at his older brother.

"Kiefer," Xander said quietly, trying to diffuse the situation. "These people are still in danger. As long as we stay, they are at risk of another attack."

Kiefer struggled to control his voice. "We need to stay and help them. We cannot leave them like this. We need to send for support, defend them from further attacks, not abandon them. They didn't ask for this, they are innocent."

"I understand, Kiefer, but it will be safer for everyone if we leave immediately."

Kiefer's expression was incredulous. "What about Charlotte?" His voice dropped dangerously low and took on an odd tone. "How is it *safer* for her to be left alone, at the mercy of Auberon? She didn't volunteer for this. This isn't her war."

The air seemed to vibrate between the two men as they stared at each other in tense silence.

"She's Fair. This is just as much her war as ours."

Aria was still shaking, only now she wasn't sure if it was a symptom of shock or a physical reaction to the horror she felt. Her throat was thick with unshed tears. She wanted desperately for her mother to be here right now, to stroke her hair and sing softly to her as she fell to sleep.

Blinking away the image of the banshee's hideous face, she didn't think she'd ever sleep again. At least not without waking in a cold sweat, a scream trying to claw its way up her throat.

Xander was losing his patience with his younger brother, his steel gaze was a knife's edge and his tone brooked no argument. "Kiefer, I suggest you take a walk and calm down. We will—"

Kiefer swore and stormed off in the direction of the huddled villagers. Xander watched him go, and Aria could see what it cost him to argue with Kiefer about this. His eyes were hard as flint, a muscle ticking in his jaw.

Rainer put a hand on his back. "I'll get the horses saddled and ready to go in an hour." He gave Coulter a meaningful look before striding towards the stables. Aria watched him go, trying to order her thoughts. She didn't want to leave these people to pick up the pieces of their lives alone, knowing the attack had been her fault. But, if she stayed, she knew the banshee might return, or some other, worse creature would come, and finish what it had started.

Coulter rubbed his jaw, taking in the scene in the square, before looking over to where Kiefer crouched with Charlotte and a younger girl with the same dark hair and tanned skin. Her sister, Aria surmised. "I'll speak to Kiefer."

"Thank you," Xander said, tearing his eyes away from his brother and running his hands over his slicked back hair. He turned away from the square, facing Aria, his back to the bodies of the dead villagers. "Come. We need to prepare to leave."

She looked into those steel-grey eyes, and shook her head. "I'm not leaving, Xander."

His jaw clenched again, unwilling to argue with anyone else on the subject. But she had to try. "This is my fault. I'm going to stay with Kiefer and help these people. Do what I can to—to make up for the pain I've caused. I'll stay at the inn with Audrey, take on Bonnie's work—"

"No." He said it with such finality that she was lost for words for a moment.

"No?"

"No," he repeated. "I can't—I won't allow you to endanger yourself and the rest of the villagers by staying here, Aria. We have to keep moving. The Celeste King already knows where we are, he'll send others." He held out a hand and she stared at it, warring emotions on her face and in her heart.

"If you don't want Bonnie's death to have been for nothing, come with us."

17

BEFORE LEAVING HITHERHAM, Aria had felt compelled to seek out Saffi and—she wasn't sure what. Offer her condolences? Apologise for getting Bonnie killed? Anything she could think of to say felt hollow and insincere, a drop in the ocean compared to the sacrifice Bonnie had made in saving Aria's life instead of her own.

In the end, she hadn't needed to say anything at all. Saffi had said it all for her.

"What Bonnie gave you was a gift. The gift of time, the gift of *life*. Don't you waste it, Fair Queen," she'd said sternly, jabbing Aria in the chest with a bony finger, eyes swimming. "Don't you dare waste it."

Philip had draped an arm around his grandmother's shoulders and led her away, casting Aria a bleak look, and she had promised she wouldn't, tears rolling down her cheeks as she sobbed the words.

She thought about the exchange now, as the horses picked their way through the undergrowth in the dim light of the early morning. Saffi had called her the Fair Queen. Not Aria.

And she had responded without a second thought.

"So," Xander said, breaking through her reverie. "You were going to run."

It wasn't a question, and Aria hadn't been expecting it. Her heart leaped painfully against her rib cage.

"No. I wasn't. I—"

"There's no point denying it. Rainer found a bag full of your belongings in Smith's stall." He flicked his gaze to her briefly before looking back at the trail ahead. She'd changed into the woollen trousers and linen tunic Bonnie had lent her, leaving the white shift dress folded neatly on the bed for Audrey. Or Saffi. "When were you planning to leave?"

"You named your horse Smith?" It was pretty unimaginative, even for him. Ordinarily, she would have teased him, but she didn't have a drop of humour left in her. Only a few hours earlier she had watched Bonnie die, and then she'd left the surviving villagers to fend for themselves.

She still wasn't sure they had made the right decision in leaving. She could feel the guilt hardening into a ball in the pit of her stomach, weighing her down.

"Don't change the subject. When did you plan on making your getaway? I presume you were intending on stealing my horse?"

The horse Aria rode was Kiefer's, a beautiful bay mare called Matilda. When they'd gathered in the stables and she had been handed the mare's reins, she'd looked around for him.

"Where's Kiefer? Is he not coming with us?"

Xander had sighed. "Unfortunately, no." He'd sounded exhausted, physically and mentally. "Kiefer will stay behind to wait for the remainder of the King's Guard, who are on their way to offer aid and assistance to the villagers."

Aria was surprised Xander had conceded after the argument she'd witnessed. She had expected him to dig his heels in, as the senior ranking officer, heir to the throne, and elder brother. Perhaps she didn't understand him quite as well as she thought she did.

"Won't he need his horse?"

"I'm sure the King's Guard will be able to spare a suitable mount for their prince." Aria had raised an eyebrow. It must be nice to be royalty.

It had struck her that she might actually be royalty too, if the stories were true. And she was beginning to realise that *all* of the stories may be true. It was an unsettling thought.

Xander had looked at her quickly. "Take good care of Matilda, though. If anything were to happen to that mare, Kiefer would never forgive me."

Now, as the horses picked their way through the maze of tree roots and underbrush, he wanted an explanation. "Out with it then. Were you intending to steal my horse and disappear into the night without a word?"

"Saying goodbye would have ruined the surprise, don't you think?" She grumbled.

It was the wrong thing to say. Xander reached over and grabbed her reins, pulling both horses to a sudden stop. "Aria, this isn't a joke. Has it still not sunk in how dangerous this place is? Especially for you. Running off on your own would be a really stupid way to die."

Aria stared at him, speechless. She hadn't seen this much emotion from him at any other moment, not even during his fight with Kiefer.

She snatched her reins back from him. "Don't take your frustration at your brother out on me. I didn't choose to come here, you kidnapped me. Or have you forgotten?"

She nudged the horse on, satisfaction blooming inside her chest when he didn't follow immediately. She could have kicked herself for dancing with him at the party. The wine must have gone straight to her head, there was no other explanation. She'd been right to hate him from the beginning.

The sky had barely begun to lighten, but her eyes had adjusted to the dimness and she could make out Rainer and Coulter's horses a few feet ahead, tails swishing side to side as their riders bent their heads together, talking quietly. Quade brought up the rear, and Aria wouldn't have been surprised to look behind and find him asleep in the saddle.

Then Xander was beside her again, and his expression held nothing but cold fury. "You know what, you're right. You've got your own horse now, why not just leave? Take your chances in these woods alone, because I won't be there to save your pathetic life next time." His voice was low and dangerous. "Just waste the sacrifice Bonnie made for you and go try your luck against the barghests and the banshees, and all the other Solitary creatures. Good fucking luck."

The mention of Bonnie's name sent Aria's mind back to the scene in the village square, and tears stung her eyes. She forced them back. She wouldn't give him the pleasure of seeing her cry again.

"That was before Bonnie," she said, her voice measured, and urged her horse forward, leaving him behind.

She couldn't leave now. She'd made a promise to Saffi and she intended to keep it. Bonnie wouldn't have died for nothing, Aria would make sure of that.

They rode in silence for a while. Eventually Coulter pulled back to have a word with Xander, and Aria drew up beside Rainer.

"Where are we headed?" She knew their ultimate destination, but she had no idea how long it would take them to travel to the Salamander Kingdom, or if they'd be camping under the stars for the rest of the journey so they wouldn't endanger any other villages.

Rainer looked up between the gaps in the tree canopy at the quickly paling sky. He took a few seconds to respond. "Aberness, a fishing village on the border of Gnome and Ondine. That's where we cross the River Aspid. There's an understanding between King Lonan and the Ondine Queens, they allow us safe passage through their territory as long as we don't cause any trouble."

He glanced at her then, seemingly taking in her exhaustion. "We'll ride for a couple more hours, then take a short break. We can't afford to waste any more time, we stayed in Hitherham too long and—" He paused, but Aria didn't need him to finish the sentence, she knew why staying had been a bad idea. "Now that we know the Celeste King is ordering the Solitary attacks, we can't stay in any one place for too long. We have to keep moving."

"The Solitary?" Aria realised Xander had used the word earlier, but she'd been too angry to question it at the time.

Rainer's grip on the reins tightened almost imperceptibly and he hesitated. "It's nothing."

Aria raised an eyebrow. "You know I'll just ask one of the others, so you may as well tell me."

"The Solitary," he said, so quietly she had to lean towards him to hear, "are creatures that live in the Fair Realm, but do not belong to the Fair race. Like the barghests, and the banshee. There are many types of Solitary—selkies, trolls, korrigans. Mostly they keep to themselves, but all are incredibly dangerous in their own way. When Queen Oriana created this realm to unite and protect the Fair, she used her aether magic to create an invisible divide between the two realms—the Veil we crossed through."

Aria nodded. She'd been desperate to find out more about the first Fair Queen, ever since her first conversation with Bonnie. She had a feeling that the truth about the prophecy would be tied up in the history of the original Fair Queen.

Maybe the prophecy wasn't referring to her at all, perhaps Oriana would return from the dead somehow…It wouldn't be the strangest thing she'd seen this week.

"Queen Oriana created the Veil to keep everything on the outside, out. But, it also kept everything inside, in. Including any animals that dwelled in the forest—deer, rabbits, birds, wild dogs. Many suffered no adverse effects from the aether magic. But others, well, over the centuries, it became clear that some creatures had been…corrupted."

He paused, letting his words sink in. Aria swallowed, but she found she wasn't entirely surprised. Wasn't it well known that power could corrupt? Magic couldn't be any different. In fact, it was likely worse.

From what she had seen of the Solitary so far, it was definitely worse.

"Wait," she said after a moment. "The barghests are descended from dogs, or wolves or something, right? But, the banshee. It looked so—so human." Her voice faded to a whisper at the end. That ruined face flashed behind her eyes again and she had to shake her head to rid herself of the haunting image.

Rainer took a deep breath, letting it out slowly before replying. When he spoke, his voice held a bitterness that frightened Aria. "Yes. Well, animals are not the only ones who can become corrupted."

After a full night and day of riding with few breaks, Aria was glad when they made camp in an abandoned cabin that night, using the crumbling stone structure for shelter when a summer rain shower blew through. She lay awake for a long time, listening to the rhythmic pitter-patter of rain on the tin roof and smelling the fresh, green scent of the forest.

The backs of her eyelids were emblazoned with the image of Bonnie's blood-stained face, and her ears still rang with the banshee's scream. She hunkered down deeper into her blankets, warding off the chill that had nothing to do with the temperature in the cabin.

She still regretted leaving Kiefer to help the villagers single-handedly. She didn't know how quickly a messenger could get to the Gnome castle and back again with the King's Guard in tow, but she hoped it was no more than a day. They needed all the aid they could get.

The following morning, they unpacked their cooking tins and laid out the remaining supplies that Audrey had packed for them. Apples, cheese-filled bread rolls and mini tarts left over from the party. She had even tucked a bottle of her famous jostaberry wine into the satchel, which was now almost empty.

They rode for hours again, and by the time the sun had crossed the sky and begun to drop Aria didn't think she could go much further. She needed to relieve herself, and she hadn't been able to feel her legs since they stopped for lunch.

They set up their bedrolls and nestled in, Xander took the first watch and it wasn't long before Aria fell into a fitful sleep, plagued by nightmares where Bonnie's face collapsed before transforming into the banshee, blood as black as pitch oozing from her eye sockets.

She woke with a jolt, Rainer's voice right next to her ear, whispering her name. She sat bolt upright in terror, and he clapped a hand over her mouth. Her mind flashed back to the moment she had been taken from her bedroom, and panic rose in her chest. She tried to squash it back down, taking deep breaths through Rainer's fingers, telling herself that he wasn't going to hurt her.

"Don't make a sound," he said in his gravelly tone. "If Xander wakes and catches us, it's over."

Her heart leapt into her throat. What was Rainer playing at? Had he decided to help her escape? Now, after everything that had happened in Hitherham? She wasn't sure she could turn her back on the Fair now.

But if Rainer was going to help her, the decision would be much more difficult. She could go home, see her parents again, and Jasper. She'd be safe from the Solitary, and the Celeste King. And Bazyl.

"I'm going to take my hand away now, stay silent and follow me." Rainer looked into her eyes, searching for comprehension, agreement. He found what he was looking for and took his hand away from Aria's mouth, holding it out to pull her up. She took it and got to her feet without a sound.

Looking across the clearing, she saw Xander and Quade sleeping, and Coulter sitting by the small fire, plucking a wood pigeon. He gave her a quick smile and winked at Rainer, who nodded back before leading Aria into the forest.

Dawn was still an hour or two away, and darkness lay thick between the trees as they picked their way over fallen branches, tree roots and bushes in silence. After several minutes, Rainer stopped and gestured to an uprooted tree. They sat down.

He rubbed his hands over his face before lacing his fingers between his knees, staring at his hands. Aria had never seen him appear anything but perfectly composed, this was a worrying departure from the norm.

Finally, he looked her in the eye. "I'm sorry for waking you, but I wasn't sure when I'd get another chance. Xander and I have argued several times over this, and I've come to see that his mind won't be changed. And whilst he is my senior officer—and will one day be my king—I disagree with him on this one point so fundamentally that I cannot stand by and do nothing."

Aria's confusion became a solid ball of cold fear in the pit of her stomach. "Rainer, you're scaring me. What's going on? Why did you drag me out here?" Her imagination began to conjure images of Xander and Rainer arguing over her life, how best to kill her, where to dispose of her body. Her muscles tensed, ready to run if he lunged, hoping she was faster.

She had no idea where she would go, but back to Hitherham seemed a safe bet. Maybe Kiefer would protect her, help her get back to Hartwood.

Rainer still hadn't answered her questions. "What do you and Xander disagree on?" It came out as a whisper.

"You," he said, and her breath caught in her throat. "And the fact that you deserve to know who—and what—you truly are." He turned his body towards her, fire in his eyes. A determination that made her want to lean backwards, put more distance between them. She resisted the urge.

Who and *what* she truly was? She wasn't sure what he meant. They had already told her that she wasn't who she thought she was, wasn't a normal human girl. She was one of the Fair, and not only that, but the crown princess of a kingdom she had never heard of. Heir to a throne, daughter of a king who may die before they reached him. And, possibly strangest of all, she may be the subject of a decades old prophecy that had foretold her coming before she was even born. What else could there be?

Rainer registered her confusion and reached for her, as though to take her hand. When she flinched away, he dropped his hands onto his knees and sighed. "Aria, as you know, your father is King Ossian, the Salamander King. What you do not know is that your mother was not a Salamander." He scanned her face and took a deep breath, speaking on the exhale. "She was a Celeste. You are a Celeste."

She blinked.

Celeste. The Celeste King, the one who was trying to kill her. Who was he to her? It had seemed odd that a complete stranger would be so desperate to harm her, but perhaps they weren't strangers at all…

"Was? Not is?"

His expression faltered. "I'm sorry, Aria. She died in childbirth."

Aria felt a strange stillness settle over her. Not sadness, or regret, exactly, but an odd absence of emotion.

Rainer ploughed on, needing to get the words off his chest before she interrupted. "Xander doesn't want you to know because—well, he's concerned that you'll try to run again. But, I believe that you need to know the truth, both about your heritage, and your own abilities." He paused as she took in his words. "Aria, you have aether abilities. What you can do—what you did with the barghest, and the banshee, that was aether magic."

Aria's heart beat double time, her breath shallow. She felt light-headed. She was a Celeste. She had abilities. How could that possibly be true? She hadn't done anything that constituted magic.

"What do you mean?" She asked, incredulous. "I didn't do anything." She shook her head, unable to comprehend what he was suggesting. "The barghests attacked us, Xander's leg was injured. You stopped them. And the banshee killed all those people. Bonnie. I did nothing. I couldn't do anything to stop it, I didn't—"

Her voice was choked off by sobs, the words sticking painfully in her throat. Hot tears spilled over her cheeks when she blinked. Rainer inched closer and she didn't move away this time, he put a thick arm around her, pulling her into his side. She was grateful for the comfort, laying her head on his enormous, muscled chest.

"You might think you did nothing, but you're wrong, Aria. I *felt* it. That surge of energy. It's what I do, train the new recruits to use their abilities in battle. But I've never felt anything like that, not even from Xander. It wasn't nothing, you stopped the banshee with just one word."

"I didn't, I—what are you talking about?" She pulled away from him, taking a shuddering breath and letting it out slowly, calming herself. When the pain in her chest eased, she rubbed her hands over her damp face.

"You don't recognise your own power yet. Growing up in the Human Realm, your abilities weren't able to manifest. But they began to develop the second you set foot in the Fair Realm. You used them against the barghests too, you may not have realised it, but you did."

Aria was lost for words. He was being absurd, you could turn anything into evidence of some sort of magic if you tried hard enough.

A thought struck her. "You say I'm half Celeste and have aether magic," she began, "but I'm also half Salamander. So shouldn't I be able to control fire?" She had him there, he couldn't possibly have an explanation for that.

His eyes narrowed. "Can you?" He asked after a beat.

"No! I told you that already."

He held his hands up. "Fair abilities are passed down through the female line. I had to ask, I've never met anyone as powerful as you, and what with the prophecy and all…but it's unlikely that you would have any abilities from your father. It's one of the main reasons that interbreeding is so rare. It's practically forbidden." He said it matter-of-factly, but Aria was appalled.

"*Interbreeding?* That's ridiculous, you can't forbid people from loving each other."

Rainer sighed. "I agree, but we've been at war for so long. One of the first things to happen was the borders closing. Each line of Fair believed itself to be the best, superior to all others. Outsiders were cast out, attacked, killed in some cases. Many cases." He leaned forwards, resting his elbows on his knees, staring off into the distance. Into the past. "Few dared to stay in a kingdom other than that of their birth or lineage after that. It was chaos. Eventually it became clear that closing the borders was a mistake. Magic had already begun to wane after the Fair segregated themselves from humans in this realm—it's against nature to keep ourselves separate, and isolating the five lines accelerated the erosion of magic. But, by that point pride and fear prevented any of the kingdoms from reopening them. No one wanted to be the first and risk opening themselves up to attack. They wouldn't even allow envoys or ambassadors in to negotiate treaties, too afraid of assassination attempts."

Aria watched Rainer's face closely as he spoke. He was far too young to have been there when the war began, or to have experienced most of what he was describing. She could see the ghosts of his ancestors in his eyes. The parents, grandparents, aunts and uncles who had passed on these stories to Rainer. Bedtime tales of prejudice, spite and cruelty that inspired a young boy to fight for what he believed in.

He remembered himself and turned to look at Aria. "What I'm trying to say is that you are a rarity, Aria. An unknown. Your abilities could be unlimited." She scoffed, but he continued. "At the very least you have aether magic, and that is a rare and complicated thing in itself." He looked into her eyes, beseeching. "If you are willing, Aria, I'd like to help you, to train you in your abilities. I could teach you to control your magic and help you discover its limits. If that's what you want."

She didn't know how to respond. She studied his face, trying to figure out his angle. She couldn't think of anything. If she learned to use her abilities, became more powerful, it would only help her to defend herself. She'd be able to keep her promise to Saffi, to honour Bonnie, and when the time was right, she could go home.

"Why?" It wasn't a refusal. It wasn't an acceptance.

Rainer's expression was open and honest. She waited for his answer. When it came, she wasn't prepared for what he had to say.

"Because I believe that you're the one they whisper about, the one we have hoped for. The one the prophecy foretold. I believe you are the Fair Queen, Aria, and that you will bring peace to the Five Kingdoms and end the war. And, when the histories are written, I want to be on the right side."

18

ARIA FINISHED WASHING HER HAIR IN THE STREAM and squeezed out the excess water, humming a tune she had heard at the festival. Her mind wandered back to the party, before the banshee attack. How she and Xander had danced, the way he had looked at her. The feeling of intoxication from the mead and the wine and the masculine, leather-and-soap scent of him.

Her face heated at the memory.

She couldn't work him out, one minute he was hot—well, lukewarm—and the next he was ice cold. He said he wanted to protect her, but he didn't want her to know about her Celeste mother or her abilities. He said they were taking her to her real father, but he wouldn't give her any details. He was so secretive, so guarded.

Their argument still stung and she'd barely spoken to him since.

A few days had passed since Rainer had told her about her true heritage and burgeoning aether abilities, they'd been training for an hour every day while Xander slept and Coulter took watch. Nothing had happened yet, but she was exhausted just from trying. Sacrificing an hour of sleep to work on her abilities, and riding all day were really taking a toll. She hadn't had a good night's sleep or a proper meal in days, and this was her first bath since Hitherham. If you could call an ice-cold stream a bath.

Something moved in the shadows behind the tree line and her heart stopped. She had kept her underwear on while she bathed, just in case, but she still didn't want anyone to see her.

"Quade?" She called out. Maybe he had been sent to fetch her.

It wasn't Quade. A hunched figure appeared, stepping out of the shadow of the trees. Aria's pulse beat a rhythm like a marching band, but she exhaled sharply when she saw it was an old woman, dressed in a tattered cloak and hood, hobbling towards the stream.

"Did I frighten you, my dear?" She chuckled softly, and Aria felt ridiculous for having been afraid.

"Sorry. I thought you were someone else." Aria climbed out of the stream and started to pull on her t-shirt and jeans.

"Oh, but I know exactly who you are," the woman said, taking her hood down. "Princess."

Aria balked. "It's you, from the fayre. The fortune teller."

Her hair was bone white and she looked even older without the heavy makeup, but it was definitely her. Divina. And she had called Aria 'Princess'…

"Wait, how do you know me?"

"I know a lot of things, my dear." Her face crinkled in a wry smile, wrinkles deepening into trenches around her sunken black eyes. She looked to the heavens, turning her palms up. "*When kingdoms unite and flame and aether collide, the Fair Queen shall return. She shall bring forth the fall of a false king and usher in a time of peace."*

The prophecy. In that instant, Aria was back in that colourful tent, warmed by the flames of a dozen candles, goose bumps rising along her arms despite the heat.

"That's right," said Divina, her voice a dry rasp. "I know who you are. You are the one the prophecy speaks of. The one who will bring peace to the Five Kingdoms."

Aria's voice was barely a whisper. "How do you know that?"

The woman smiled enigmatically. "I saw it." She gestured vaguely around her, as though it were written in the wind.

"What do you mean?" A thought occurred to Aria. "Are you the prophetess?"

Divina cackled, a rasping sound that made Aria's skin crawl. "No, dear, no. I was not the first to See. But when I touched your hands in that tent, I knew. I saw you, Princess, taking your rightful place, here in the Fair Realm. Fighting the evil that stalks this realm, protecting the Fair."

Aria stared at her, open mouthed.

The old woman shuffled towards Aria and crouched beside her at the edge of the stream. "Here, let me show you." She cast a hand over the water and the surface shimmered before turning opaque. Images flitted across the dark background.

Aria looked between the strange woman and the images now sharpening into focus on the water's surface. She was surprised that she wasn't more surprised.

Until she saw Jasper's face appear.

She gasped, squatting down next to the woman and peering closer at the images.

Jasper stood in her garden, knocking at her bedroom door. He was wearing the white shirt from his date with the doughnut boy, the night of his birthday. He tried the handle and found it unlocked, so he stepped inside.

The image rippled gently as Jasper entered her bedroom and took in the scene before him. The room had been trashed, her clothes and books were strewn across the bed, picture frames lay shattered on the carpet, photos of Aria smiling in her favourite dress, jumping into the pool on holiday with her parents. Jasper picked up one of the photos that had come out of its broken frame, Aria and Jasper in the school play when they were seven. She'd played Dorothy and he had been the Lion.

Jasper put the picture down on Aria's desk and started to make his way towards the door into the rest of the bungalow. He seemed to be calling out, but Aria couldn't hear a word he said. Could only see his mouth moving as he shouted her name, her parents' names.

He reached the door and opened it, stepping into the lamplit hallway. The house seemed empty, until he reached the living room and came upon Aria's parents sitting on the sofa.

They weren't alone. Two men stood over them, brandishing some kind of blade. Her mother's eyes widened as she spotted Jasper, and she mouthed one word. *Run.*

It was already too late, hands grabbed Jasper's arms from behind and forced him across the room and onto the sofa beside Aria's father. She watched as the men asked Jasper questions and he shook his head in response. She realised they were asking where she was, and neither Jasper or her parents knew.

The men didn't seem to care. They kept asking the same question over and over, waving the knife menacingly, getting closer and closer, spittle flying as they shouted in her parents' faces.

Something moved in the shadowy hallway and a figure stepped into the lamplight. It was Bazyl, auburn hair turned bronze in the low light, blue eyes cold as ice. He nodded once at his companions and leaned casually against the wall as all hell broke loose.

One of the men threw Aria's mother to the floor, kicking her in the stomach, while the others landed blows on her father and Jasper with their fists and the hilts of their blades.

When the first knife-blow fell, a sob ripped from Aria's chest.

"What is this? Why are you showing me this?"

The images faded back to clear water, and Aria turned her gaze on the old woman, who's expression was grave. "You have nothing to go back for now, Princess. Demitree and his men killed your family when they refused to tell him where you were. No matter that they didn't know." Tears streamed down Aria's face, she shook her head, mouthing a silent *no*.

"You'd better run along to daddy now, before the same fate befalls you."

Aria was on her feet and sprinting through the forest before she could stop herself, the mad cackling of the fortune teller ringing in her ears.

19

AZYL AND HIS MEN HAD GONE BACK TO HER HOUSE, they had murdered her parents and Jasper. She couldn't breathe, the pain in her chest was like nothing she had ever felt. Her heart, her lungs, she wasn't sure, but she had to tell the others, had to make them take her back, had to...what? She couldn't save them now, it was too late. The police would assume she had been abducted by the same men who had killed her family.

Or, would they? Did they think she was the murderer? That she had slaughtered her parents and gone on the run? It didn't matter, she had to get back, even if it was only to prove her innocence.

She crashed into the clearing where they had set up camp and collapsed on the ground, breathless and sobbing. Rainer was at her side in a second, scanning her face and body for injuries. "Aria, what's wrong? What happened?"

"They're dead! He killed them!" She croaked between the painful sobs that racked her body. The others gathered round, weapons drawn, their faces tight with concern.

"Who's dead?" Rainer asked, only the slightest note of impatience in his tone.

"Bazyl killed my parents. And Jasper." She gulped down air, trying to calm herself. "He went to my house after you took me. They didn't know where I was, how could they? But he didn't believe them. So he killed them!" Tears spilled from the corners of her eyes, dripping off her nose and chin. She put her face in her hands and shook with the weight of her emotions.

Xander knelt beside her and reached a hand out as though he was going to touch her. He let the hand drop awkwardly. "Aria, who told you this? How do you know he killed them?"

His voice was frustratingly gentle, why weren't they as angry as she was? She looked around at their concerned faces and felt a white-hot rage burn through her. Of course they didn't care if her parents were dead, they had taken her from them in the first place.

"Some old woman in the woods. A seer or something. What does that matter?"

There was a beat of silence while the boys glanced at each other, Aria couldn't read their expressions. Then Xander sent Coulter and Quade to scout the area.

"Aria," Xander said finally, "I don't think that was a seer. I think it was a hag." He said it like it explained everything, but Aria brushed it off.

"Hag, old lady, whatever. Why are we arguing over semantics right now?"

"No, I mean she wasn't Fair. Or human. A hag is one of the Solitary. Like the banshee. It only looked human."

Rainer nodded in agreement. "They often appear as old women to young girls, and as beautiful young women to men. They show you what you want to see—or whatever it takes to get you to go with them. Then they kill you." He gave Xander a nervous look that didn't escape Aria's notice. "You're lucky to be alive."

Aria couldn't take it all in. She grasped desperately onto the only shred of hope she could see. "So, they might not be dead?"

There was a terrifying pause as the boys glanced at each other, unsure how to respond. Xander finally spoke. "No, they may not be dead. What the hag showed you was just a vision, like a dream. It doesn't mean that what you saw has happened, or will happen."

She read between the lines. "But, they still could be dead."

"It's unlikely," Xander said. "The likelihood of Bazyl wasting time killing your family when they didn't know anything is slim." He took in Aria's horrified expression and hastily added, "They would have seen that you were gone and rushed to try and catch us. They wouldn't have bothered asking your family where you were because they would have known where we were taking you."

Aria stared at Xander in disgust. How could he be so blasé about this?

Rainer cut in. "What Xander means is, your family knew nothing of the Fair or our realm, Demitree knew that. There would have been no point in harming your family."

Aria mulled this over, drying her tear stained face on her sleeves. Embarrassment had started to creep under her skin now that she realised she could be wrong, that the hag had been nothing but a malicious trickster. She felt foolish for not seeing the vision for what it was.

"So, Demitree and his men," she began slowly, "are they still following us? Could they ambush us at any moment?"

Xander shrugged, apparently unconcerned. "I don't fancy their chances if they do."

Rainer placed a hand on Xander's shoulder. "We won't let anyone harm you, Aria. But we'll have to stay close to you from now on. No more going off alone."

Back in Matilda's saddle, Aria ran her fingers through the bay horse's silky black mane. Xander and Smith were beside her again, Rainer and Coulter in front, and Quade behind. Aria had been going over and over her encounter with the hag in her mind.

Not the vision she had seen in the water—she tried not to think about that, putting it to the very back of her mind, with the idea that she might never see her family again.

But the prophecy. The hag's threatening words, *run along to daddy now, before the same fate befalls you*. Had the Celeste King sent the hag after her, too? Or had she—it—genuinely been trying to warn Aria?

She asked Xander about the prophecy, quoting it word for word from memory. She hadn't been able to get it out of her mind.

"I have heard several versions of the prophecy over the years," he said. "That is just one of them. All vague, all designed to give hope to the people of the Five Kingdoms. Completely unfounded hope, but hope nonetheless." He managed to make hope sound like a dirty word. He sounded irritated, like the thought of his people believing in something so unempirical and superstitious was a bitter disappointment. "Put it out of your mind, Aria. The prophecy has as much to do with you as it does with my horse."

She was surprised by this. "You don't think the prophecy is about me? You didn't bring me here to try and make it come true?" She wasn't sure she believed him, there had to be more to the story. They couldn't have only brought her here to meet her dying father and take the Salamander throne. Why would a Gnome prince care about the Salamander heir? Surely a kingdom without a king would be easier to overthrow? The Gnomes could have doubled their territory. Won the war, maybe.

"There is no prophecy, Aria!" He said it with a laugh, but it sounded forced, "It's just a silly story invented by bored peasants to give their children something to live for."

Aria's surprise turned to shock, and then anger. She couldn't believe the future king of a war-torn kingdom would be so cruel about his own people. People who were suffering, and had been for over a century.

"So what if the prophecy is just a *nice* story made up by some bored villagers? Or a fantasy dreamed up by a child, playing make-believe with stick princesses and sand castles. You would begrudge them the smallest piece of happiness? Something to wish for and dream about?"

Xander's eyes flashed. "I begrudge that they must hope for a fantastical saviour that may never come!" He barked, startling the horses a little. He carried on as though he hadn't noticed. "I wish that they did not have to hope, or dream, or make believe. I cannot stand the fact that my people suffer and struggle, and their only comfort is an absurd prophecy." He had stopped shouting and now just sounded tired. He ran a hand over his face, composing himself. "I wish that my people believed in me, in my father. Most of all, I wish that we could do something to help them. To take away some of their pain and hunger. To protect them from the cruelty of the Celeste King and the Solitary."

He slumped in his saddle, the mental and emotional exhaustion clear in the set of his shoulders.

Aria heard the shame in his words. He had been forced to watch while his people starved and died, while they were killed by evil things like the banshee. He hadn't been able to stop it. Any of it. And so his people had turned to fairy tales and fantasies to warm them at night, to fill their hungry bellies and soothe their souls.

"I'm sorry," she said quietly. Xander glanced in her direction before focusing his eyes on the road ahead.

"No. I'm sorry. I shouldn't have lost my temper. I just wish there was more I could do to help them."

Aria waited, but he didn't say any more. They rode on in silence for a while, the only sounds the horses' hooves on the forest floor and the cries of birds overhead, black shapes against the cornflower blue sky.

The trees thinned, letting more of the bright sunlight through. Were they nearing the Ondine Queendom already? She was curious about the other Fair, their abilities and customs. The Ondine had command over the water—she tried to imagine what their villages would look like. Maybe they all lived on houseboats, the Ondine Queendom an elaborate network of canals. She was excited to finding out.

But most of all, she looked forward to falling asleep with a full belly in a warm, soft bed. And a real bath! Her mind drifted to steam rising from water, scented bath oil and fluffy towels, clean pyjamas and fresh bed sheets.

Rainer and Coulter had slowed to a stop up ahead, and Matilda did the same, shaking Aria from her imagination. She looked around, inhaling the scent of pine trees and wildflowers. Piles of felled lumber were stacked haphazardly on either side of their path. Mounds of soil and uprooted bushes lay here and there, and tree roots stuck up in the air like the wizened hands of enormous old men, clawing their way out of shallow graves.

Aria realised with a jolt the trees weren't thinning, they had been ripped from the ground and tossed aside by a tornado. Or a giant beast. "What—"

Xander cut her off with a raised hand and a sharp look. He walked Smith forward to join Rainer and Coulter, leaving her behind. She watched them whisper frantically, wondering what could possibly have ravaged the area this way. Quade was quiet behind her, she turned to him, about to ask what was going on.

A roar rumbled through the forest, shaking tree branches and sending a cascade of leaves to the ground. Booming footsteps created tremors that Aria felt ripple through Matilda into her legs, making her teeth chatter,

"Troll!" Xander yelled. Aria was still looking behind her when a hideous giant with greyish skin and long, stringy hair lumbered out of the trees behind Quade. It wore a tattered loincloth that may have once been white, and its mouth was open in a cry that Aria felt reverberate in her bones. She heard Xander yelling, but he sounded far away, she couldn't make out what he was saying.

Quade scrabbled for his weapons. Distantly, Aria wondered what a couple of little knives could do against this goliath. Before anyone had time to react, the troll swung its enormous, meaty fist and lashed out at Quade. His horse skittered sideways and the boy ducked, narrowly avoiding the blow.

But the troll's reflexes were quicker than they looked and it swung again.

Aria could only watch in horror as the creature's massive hand connected with Quade's mount, sending both horse and rider flying. Quade hit a tree with a sickening thud. His grey horse lay broken and bleeding beside him, several ribs protruding gruesomely from its side.

Xander's scream was the most harrowing sound Aria had ever heard.

He charged past her on Smith, making Matilda skitter nervously. He already held his short sword in one hand, the reins in the other, and he struck out at the troll's leg with the blade as he galloped past. He circled back around, thrusting his sword deep into the grey flesh of its calf.

A succession of rapid-fire arrows flew over Aria's head from Coulter's bow, embedding in the troll's skin. The huge beast barely noticed. Until one arrow hit home, right in the creature's eye. It staggered, wailing loudly and swatting at its head. Finally, it fell backwards, crushing several of the uprooted pine trees. Aria held her breath, but it didn't move again.

Xander turned to face them, shoulders slumping, but there was no time to relax. Aria gasped as she saw three more trolls behind Xander, heading towards them. They were swinging gigantic wooden clubs, smashing trees in half as they charged towards the body of their fallen comrade.

Aria screamed Xander's name, but he was already turning to face the oncoming horde. His sword was raised in anticipation, but even Aria could see that he was outmatched. They all were.

She felt like she was watching events unfold in slow motion. First Bonnie and the villagers, and now Quade. Her blood was sluggish in her veins, her vision clouding. She couldn't watch Xander and the others be slaughtered by these monsters.

She had to stop them.

"No!" She screamed. "Please!"

The trolls advanced, getting closer and closer to the enormous body of the dead troll, and the trio of Gnome soldiers surrounding her. She tried again, willing her aether abilities—if she truly did possess them—to command the trolls. "Stop! Please!" Her voice cracked and she was shaking so violently she thought she would fall off her horse. She put everything she had into the want, the need, for the trolls to stop their attack. She felt the last remnants of her energy seep out of her as she watched the trolls descend on them.

A movement in the trees caught her eye. She dared a quick look in case another troll was about to attack them from the side. She couldn't believe her eyes. Some kind of creature seemed to be detaching itself from the trunk of the nearest tree. It looked like a twig, an overgrown stick insect. She saw other movements in her peripheral vision and looked around. There were dozens of the creatures separating themselves from the remaining pine trees, their long limbs like branches, their faces an assortment of knots and notches in the bark of their skin.

At least fifty of the things—more—gathered in a group in front of where Xander sat atop Smith with his sword held high. They barely reached the horse's knees.

The trolls didn't slow.

Rainer and Coulter flanked Aria, one with bow and quiver, the other with a hatchet in hand. She looked at their profiles, the strength and determination in their clenched jaws and furrowed brows, and hoped this wasn't the last time she would see their faces.

"Hold!" Xander cried, as the first troll reached the group of wooden creatures and a chittering cry went up. The troll swung its club, smashing several of them to smithereens. Aria shrieked, shielding her face as splinters rained down on them. When she opened her eyes seconds later, the remaining creatures were climbing the trolls legs. In moments, they covered its entire body from head to toe. Aria couldn't see what was happening, but she heard the bellowing roar that ripped from the troll as it thrashed, trying to dislodge the parasitic creates that crawled over its skin.

It tripped over an uprooted tree and fell, landing in a heap next to the body of its fellow troll. The strange tree creatures continued to crawl over it, chittering to one another as the troll howled and writhed.

The other trolls faltered, watching him squirm. It didn't stall them for long.

"Archers!" Xander called, and Aria felt rather than heard his breath catch, remembering that Kiefer was not with them.

Coulter didn't hesitate, a storm of arrows rained down on the trolls. Aria glanced to her right and saw him moving at an unnatural speed, firing arrow after arrow until his quiver was empty. The trolls batted them away like flies, shaking their heads in an almost bovine motion. They stumbled, but did not fall.

Rainer lashed out and sent his hatchet flying. It keened as it cleaved the air in two, flipping end to end faster than the eye could see. It was nothing but a glint of metal, a silver spark flashing past them as it flew towards its mark. With a crunch it embedded itself in between the eyes of the biggest troll. A bright red line of blood slid down the monster's nose, over its thick grey lips, and dripped off the tip of its chin onto the ground, fifty feet below.

Without uttering a single sound, the troll collapsed to the floor with the others, leaving only one still standing, facing attacks from several fronts. What had seemed a losing battle only moments before, Aria now saw was a decidedly one-sided fight.

Xander slashed at the final troll's legs with his short sword, the remaining tree creatures clambered up its massive body, and Rainer had pulled a length of rope from his saddle bag and begun galloping around the beast in circles, looping the rope around its ankles. They dodged the huge swinging club and giant fists as they fought tirelessly to bring the creature down.

In the same moment, Xander sliced at the troll's ankles and Rainer galloped away, pulling the rope taut. The troll's arms spun like a windmill as it toppled to the ground, sending up a spray of mud and debris. Its cries were soon cut off by the crawling, chittering tree creatures.

As the dust settled, Aria took in the devastation. The surrounding forest had been destroyed. The bodies of the four trolls lay discarded on the ground, surrounded by piles of torn-up trees and bushes, their clubs lying impotent next to them.

The wooden tree creatures had already begun to stream back into the woods, reforming with the trees until it was as though they had never been separated. Aria glanced back at the trolls they had taken down and saw that the creatures' flesh was all but gone, skeletons picked clean by the apparently carnivorous stick insects.

In the aftermath of the battle, she saw Quade lying at the foot of a tree, unmoving. She couldn't breath as she watched Xander dive for his brother. He yelled Quade's name over and over, shaking him by the shoulders. Quade's head lolled awkwardly and Aria knew instantly that his neck was broken.

Quade was dead.

Xander held his brother in his arms, gripping him so tightly his knuckles were white. Aria looked at Xander's face and saw nothing but steel and ice. He didn't shed a single tear. He didn't sob, or rage, or ask why. He only held his youngest brother tight to his chest, and the danger swimming behind his eyes was a living thing.

PART TWO

All is fair in love and war.

— JOHN LYLY, "EUPHUES"

20

THEY WRAPPED QUADE'S BODY IN A BLANKET and Xander lay him over Smith's neck. He looked smaller in death than he had in life. The joy and love and curiosity he had possessed was gone, leaving him an empty shell.

They had been forced to leave Quade's horse behind, the gelding was too heavy to move to a more peaceful resting place. They dug a hole and rolled the horse's broken body in, covering it over with the displaced soil. Luckily the trolls had done them one favour—the uprooted trees meant the job was mostly done for them.

Rainer had said a short blessing, just a few words about returning to the earth to nourish and sustain life, and thanked the horse for his service, and then they rode away, taking Quade with them.

When they reached a spot Xander was happy with, a small clearing with a few pretty wildflowers and the sound of woodlarks singing in the trees, they stopped. They all set about digging again, using the cooking tins from their packs to scoop the earth out. They worked in silence.

When the grave was ready, Xander gently lowered his brother into the ground, and each took a few moments to say goodbye. Aria watched as he untied a leather strap from around his wrist, slide a jade green bead off the bracelet, and tossed it into the open grave.

They covered Quade's body with soil and marked the grave with a smooth pebble Coulter found. Rainer used his hatchet to carve Quade's name into it.

Standing around the grave, Aria felt hot tears slide down her cheeks as she watched the silent devastation on Rainer and Coulter's faces, and the cold rage on Xander's. What would Kiefer say? Who would tell him his younger brother was dead at the hands of a troll?

Aria felt guilt and shame curdle in her belly. She was responsible for yet another death. Another innocent life had been lost because of her. Another attack by another monster that might have been avoided if she had never been there. That could have been stopped if her abilities were stronger.

How had she gotten here? A few days ago she was just a normal girl, wondering what to do with her life after school, hoping she'd still get to spend every weekend hanging out with her best friend. Now she may never see him again. The tears spilling over her cheeks were salty and bitter.

Rainer began to sing quietly, a traditional Gnome dirge by the sound of it, his baritone voice thrumming in Aria's chest. Coulter and Xander joined their voices with his. Aria let the melody wash over her, trying to catch the lyrics. It was similar to the blessing Rainer had said over the horse's grave, giving thanks to the earth and nature, returning Quade to the source, completing the circle of life.

They finished the threnody and fell into a sombre silence. The only sound was Aria's quiet sobbing.

Aria awoke to Rainer's face inches away from her own, a finger to his lips when she opened her mouth to complain. As much as she'd like to roll over and go back to sleep, she was desperate for answers.

He gestured for her to follow him and she slid out of her blankets and pulled on her boots as quietly as she could, catching Coulter's eye as she did. He gave her a sticky thumbs up from where he sat next to the campfire, skinning a rabbit.

Xander was lying on his side, facing away from her, twitching and mumbling in his sleep.

After a few minutes walking, Rainer sat on a flat rock and pointed to another smaller boulder. Aria had barely sat down before the questions started spilling out of her.

"What were those things that helped us fight the trolls? Why were we attacked? Is it the Celeste King? Were they after me?" She took a deep, shuddering breath and closed her eyes. "It's my fault Quade is dead, isn't it?"

Rainer hesitated for a nanosecond, and Aria's heart shattered inside her chest. She had known it was true, that she was the one they had wanted, not Quade. He had died in her place.

"Aria, we're soldiers. Quade knew what he was doing, he knew the dangers—"

"He was sixteen!" She cried, her strangled voice not sounding like her own. "He wasn't a fucking soldier, he was just a kid."

Rainer shook his head, thick brows low over his dark, shimmering eyes. "He was a trained fighter, Aria. Yes, he was young, but he had been training for battle since childhood. He knew exactly what he was doing. This was always a risk."

Aria squeezed her eyes shut, tears threatening to overspill. "He didn't deserve to die."

"No. He didn't."

Aria swiped at her eyes. It was early, the sky just starting to turn lilac through the gaps in the tree canopy. A cool breeze lifted the hair from Aria's neck and she rubbed her bare arms where goose flesh had appeared. "What—what were they? Those twig things?"

"Nats. Tree creatures. They are known to be fiercely protective of their territory, and nature in general. The destruction the trolls were causing to the forest, as well as your call for help, must have caused them to come to our aid."

"You still believe I have aether abilities then? After what happened back here? I couldn't even get a stupid, bloody troll to do what I wanted. I couldn't stop them, I—" She swallowed the sobs that threatened to escape her chest. Rainer waited for her to compose herself. There was nothing but sympathy in his gaze, and Aria couldn't bear it. She wanted him to blame her, needed him to.

The way she blamed herself.

"Yes. I still believe you have aether abilities. The nats didn't come out to defend their habitat until you called to them. The forest was already half demolished when we arrived, they must have been too afraid to take on the trolls until you commanded them." He gave her an earnest look. "You just need training, Aria. You will learn to control your power, to understand it. I promise."

Aria practiced using her abilities for almost an hour with no success. She felt silly speaking to thin air, hoping someone or something would hear her and respond to her call. Rainer watched patiently, encouraging her often, but after so long with no results, even he seemed to doubt her abilities. She could see it in his eyes.

"Take a breath, clear your mind," Rainer instructed. She closed her eyes, inhaling deeply and exhaling slowly. "Visualise your connection to the aether. Remember, it's in everything, all around us. Picture it like invisible strings leading out from your hands, or your heart, wherever works for you."

Aria listened to Rainer's deep, soothing voice and imagined golden, shining threads leaving her chest and expanding outwards, searching for the aether, trying to make a connection. She spoke in her mind as loudly and clearly as she could, announcing herself, inviting the aether to join her.

Nothing happened.

She started to panic. Maybe she didn't have any special abilities, maybe she really wasn't Fair. Somewhere deep down, she'd begun to believe it, that she was different, special. But maybe she was just a normal, average, human girl. She wouldn't be able to fight the Solitary or protect her friends from their vicious attacks. She'd never avenge Bonnie or Quad, or keep her promise to Saffi.

She was nothing—a disappointment, an imposter.

Her heart raced and her breathing hitched. Tears brimmed against her lower lashes once more. What would they do with her when they realised they had the wrong girl?

She had nowhere to go, no home to return to, if the hag's vision had been true.

"Please," she whispered, eyes closed tightly against the fear that now prickled under her skin. In her desperation, she called to the nats, visualising their wooden little bodies and spindly limbs. It was the only concrete thing she could think of, Rainer's invisible thread idea clearly wasn't working.

A creaking sound nearby made her eyes fly open. To her right, a nat was slowly disentangling itself from the bark of the nearest tree. She froze, holding her breath. The nat dropped to the ground and approached her nervously, chittering under its breath. It stopped a few feet from her, hesitating.

"My Queen." The voice that came from the small creature was dry and crackly. It dipped into a low bow, and stood sharply to attention, its movements strangely puppet-like.

"I-uh. Hello," she stuttered, "What's your name?"

"Kiri," the creature responded. "How may I serve your Majesty?"

Aria blushed. "I don't need anything right now, you may return to your…tree. Thank you, Kiri."

The nat bowed again and turned to go back to its home.

"Wait," Rainer said suddenly. He stood and approached the nat, at six foot five he was at least five feet taller than the wooden creature. The nat just stared up at Rainer, waiting for him to speak. "You know who this is?"

The nat nodded, and when Rainer didn't speak, it rasped in that rarely-used voice, "The Fair Queen, returned."

"That's right," Rainer said with a firm nod. "She is the prophesied queen who will bring peace to the Fair Realm and end the tyranny of King Auberon."

"Yes, sir."

Aria listened to the exchange in silence, hardly able to process what was being said, let alone the fact an enormous fairy was currently talking to a twig.

"Who do you and your fellow nats answer to?" Rainer asked the creature.

"To our Queen," the nat answered. It nodded to Aria. She tried to smile but her facial muscles were frozen.

"Remember that. Spread the word, the Fair Queen has come, and she will free us all."

The nat scurried back to its tree, clambered up the trunk and melded with the bark once more, disappearing from sight. Aria stared at Rainer with a blank expression.

He shrugged. "We will need all the help we can get if the Celeste King sends more of his creatures to attack us. If we can convert even a few of the Solitary to our side, we might stand a chance. We might not lose anyone else." He looked down at the ground, thoughts clearly on Quade.

If they had had chance to train sooner, if Aria had been able to control her abilities when the trolls attacked, Quade might still be alive.

She stood and brushed the dirt from her jeans, shaking the thought from her mind. There was no use in wishing now, they had to move forward. "Let's keep training. I want to try again."

Rainer shook his head. "We've already been gone too long, we can't let Xander know what we're doing. If he knew I was training you without his knowledge—"

"Then let's tell him! Why don't you want him to know?" She wasn't sure she believed Rainer's explanation that Xander was just concerned for her safety, or that he considered her a flight risk. "Wouldn't he be glad to know you got the right girl, that I'm Fair? That I can command the Solitary?" She searched Rainer's face, but his expression was giving nothing away. She realised she wouldn't get the truth out him by asking him straight, so she changed tact.

"I can help you now, I can protect you! I'm not just a burden you have to put up with anymore."

"Burden? Aria, you were never a burden." He was standing in front of her now, he towered over her, but it wasn't threatening.

"Then why am I still being treated like the little sister that nobody wanted to tag along? I'm not that fragile."

Rainer sighed and sat back down, gesturing for her to do the same. "That's not…Xander isn't a bad guy. I know he's handled things badly, but he's under a lot of pressure. Losing Quade the way we did. You need to cut him some slack, he's doing what he thinks is right."

Aria had the sudden, unmooring sense of déjà vu. She'd thought almost the exact same thing back at the festival while they had danced.

"For now, it's better that he not know. Just, trust me, OK?"

Aria chewed her lip, torn between wanting to understand and develop her abilities further before revealing them, and the desire to prove herself. After a moment of deliberation, she nodded.

"Come," Rainer said, standing again. "We had better collect some kindling on our way back, or our cover will be blown."

21

"**M**ORTIMER?" Aria drew her horse level with Xander. "Archibald? Randolph?"

Xander had declared that the Ondine border was only a few hours' ride, so after devouring their meagre meal of rabbit and stale bread, washed down with fresh water from a nearby stream, they saddled the horses and continued on their way.

Aria could already hear gulls screeching and she was looking forward to their arrival at the Ondine Queendom. Her body ached from the endless riding, and her clothes were looser than usual, she needed more than the game Coulter caught and the scraps they'd been able to trade for on the journey. The farming communities they'd passed by had made Hitherham look like a sprawling metropolis in comparison.

Xander didn't turn his head. "What are you wittering about?"

"Your name," she said. "It must be something pretty embarrassing if you're this reluctant to share it." She ran a hand through her greasy red hair and tucked it behind her ears. "Is it something girly? Like Agnes? Or Maude?" She probed, looking for a way to relieve her boredom. Teasing Xander until he snapped seemed like a perfect way to kill a few hours. Or minutes, if the look he gave her then was anything to go by. "That's it isn't it? Your parents gave your brothers strong, masculine names, and you got lumbered with a pretty, lady name." She needled him effortlessly, curious to find out his true name, but enjoying the game too much for it to end. "No wonder you go by Xander. Is it especially frilly?" She could have sworn his cheeks were tinged with pink now. Which only served to spur her on. "Or is it just plain hideous? Mildred? Sybil?"

Despite himself, Xander barked a laugh. "Sybil? Even if my name was something feminine—which it isn't—I don't think Sybil would have been my parents' first choice." He shook his head, a reluctant smirk on his mouth. It made a change from his usual irritation. Aria couldn't help but smile as she rode alongside him in comfortable silence.

They crested a hill and the landscape fell away before their eyes. A steep incline led down to a wide, pebbly shore. In the distance, the opposite river bank was lined with pastel coloured buildings, like flavours of ice cream on display in a freezer. Boats bobbed serenely on the surface of the water, tethered to the distant stone embankment.

They rode down to the water's edge, where a couple of fishing boats were beached, drying in the sun. A man with straggly grey hair and a short beard wrestled with a large net. He looked up as they approached.

"Afternoon." He wiped his forehead with a filthy rag and shoved it back in his pocket, squinting up at them. "What can I do for you folk?"

Xander dismounted with the grace of an Olympic gymnast and handed Smith's reins to Rainer. "Good afternoon. We're in need of passage to Aberness. We can pay," he added when the man raised an unruly brow. "Handsomely," He reached into his saddlebag and pulled out a fistful of coins. The man's eyes widened comically. Aria wasn't sure how the currency in the Fair Realm worked, but from the gold glint she thought it was probably more money than the man had ever seen. He threw the net into the hull of one of the boats and stood, wiping his hands on his shorts.

"No problem, friend. I can't take you across myself, but I'll be happy to lend you a vessel to get yourselves there."

"That is very generous, thank you," Xander said, handing the coins to the fisherman. "Which vessel?"

Two boats lay on the pebbles. The man gestured to the one on his left, it was considerably older than the other and its sea-worthiness was questionable. Xander hesitated.

"Are you sure we couldn't take the other one?"

"That's the only one I can spare," shrugged the old fisherman. "She's sturdier than she looks, you'll get across the river fine. Just don't lean over the sides." He laughed raucously to himself while they looked at each other uncertainly. In the end, it was Aria who slid out of her saddle and grasped the rope the old man proffered.

"We haven't got any other options," she hissed. "Come on, where's your sense of adventure?"

Coulter jumped down from his horse and joined her, facing the others who still wore anxious expressions. "She's right. We've taken bigger risks in the past. Now, hands up who can swim." Aria and Coulter's arms shot up into the air. Xander reluctantly raised a hand, and Rainer glared at his friend like he had betrayed him. He pouted, but raised his hand.

"OK!" Aria grinned. "Let's do this."

They would have to leave the horses behind, but Murdoch, the fisherman, offered to take them to a nearby farm where they could be stabled, for a fee. The farmer, his cousin, regularly purchased fish from Murdoch, and he had thrown in a few freebies over the years, so the cousin owed him a favour. They could pay for the horses' keep on their return, on the condition that if they did not return the farmer would keep the horses. Xander's expression turned nervous at that.

Murdoch also recommended a Gnome-friendly inn on the waterfront, owned and run by his sister, Dorit. "Try the clam chowder, I dig the clams myself," he told them proudly.

The boat only had two paddles, so Xander sat in the front, acting as coxswain while Rainer and Coulter rowed, leaving Aria to sit back and enjoy the short cruise across the river.

There was a delicious breeze over the water, Aria closed her eyes, relishing the cool air and fine sea spray on her bare skin. Hearing a cacophony of screeches and caws, she opened her eyes and spotted a small island in the middle of the river, home to a variety of birds, some she recognised, some she didn't. She could make out herons, mallards, swans and coots, all living together in relative harmony on the twenty-foot-long islet.

Why couldn't the people of the Five Kingdoms be more like those birds, sharing a small patch of land without the perpetual power struggle? She'd heard about the animosity between the different lines of Fair, but her first experience with an Ondine had been pleasant enough. Unless he'd refused them the sea-worthy boat on purpose.

She wasn't sure what to expect when they landed on the far side of the river. Would everyone be as genial as Murdoch had been—as long as they paid well—or would they face dark looks and derogatory comments?

As she gazed across the water, an enormous heron with a long, sharp beak attacked a mallard duck, sending a cloud of feathers into the air. They drifted down slowly, settling on the water's surface. Aria turned away.

She leaned over the side and reached down to run her hand through the boat's wake, the foamy, white water spilling through her open fingers.

A shadow moved under the surface. Aria leaned forwards, squinting to make out the fish that swam beneath them. The sun glinted off the surface of the river, turning it to silver, a mirror reflecting the azure sky with wisps of white scudding across it.

Xander's voice broke through her reverie. "Don't, Aria—"

Something cold and clammy gripped Aria's fingers, and pulled.

22

S HE DIDN'T EVEN HAVE TIME TO SCREAM before she was yanked
out of the boat, hitting the water with a loud slap. More icy
hands joined the first, their steel grip pulling Aria steadily
downwards.

She opened her eyes and saw that she was surrounded by eerie
glowing lights. She couldn't make out much in the murky depths, the
lights turned everything else to shadow, but she thought she caught a
glimpse of a fish-like tail, a wisp of long hair. Mermaids?

Her chest felt like it was wrapped in iron chains. She hadn't been in
the water for more than a few seconds, but she hadn't been prepared,
hadn't filled her lungs with enough air. She couldn't hold her breath any
longer, a stream of bubbles escaped her lips as she thrashed against her
attackers.

She couldn't see the surface now, she was surrounded by the
strange glowing things and the water beyond seemed pitch black. She

wasn't even sure which direction the surface was. Panic began to creep in at the edges of her mind, she needed to take a breath, the pain in her lungs was excruciating.

The creatures were shrieking now, a high-pitched sound that hurt Aria's ears. She wanted to scream at them, command them to let her go, use her ability, but she couldn't open her mouth or risk inhaling the river water. The pressure on her skull and the lack of oxygen were making her light-headed. She closed her eyes, the last of her breath escaping from her mouth as unconsciousness called to her from the blackness.

An arrow sailed through the water right by her head, embedding itself in one of the creatures that gripped her arm. The thing emitted an ear-piercing screech and let go of Aria. Another arrow shot past her, sinking into the torso of one of the creatures. The glowing lights dimmed as several of the mer-monsters were struck and killed by the volley of arrows. In the weak light, Aria got a better look at their features, they were nothing like the fairy tale mermaids she was used to. They were more fish than man, luminous scales covered their entire bodies and gills flapped in their muscular necks.

A shadow approached at high speed, but Aria couldn't tell which direction it was coming from. Was that the surface? The depths? A warm hand gripped her ankle and pulled, but the creatures' grip on her wrists was still strong. She saw a flash of silver in the dull light and heard the monsters shriek again as the blade slashed at them. Xander's face swam in her vision before darkness crept in at the edges and consciousness slipped from her grasp.

Someone was knocking on Aria's bedroom door, she could hear the sound through the fog of sleep.

Now they were shaking her, trying to wake her. She groaned and tried to open her eyes, but they were glued shut. She tried to breath, but there was no air.

The knocking was louder now, the shaking more violent. Someone pressed their mouth to hers, filling her lungs with air.

Water erupted from her mouth and she turned to the side, vomiting onto the floor.

She wasn't in her bed, she was lying on the stony ground. Rolling onto her back she saw blue sky, and in front of that, Xander. Concern was etched into the lines of his face.

"Aria." The relief in his voice made her heart squeeze painfully. He reached forward and brushed the damp hair from her forehead with unexpected gentleness, letting his hand stroke down her face to cup her cheek. Aria closed her eyes at the touch. "Are you alright? How do you feel?"

Her chest heaved as she took in deep breaths, trying to replenish the oxygen she had lost. Her mouth was surprisingly dry. She swallowed. "I'm OK. I think."

Xander seemed to come back to himself then and sat back on his heels, putting some distance between them. Aria pushed up onto her elbows. "What happened?"

Rainer and Coulter were standing over her with worried expressions, their arms touching all the way down from Coulter's shoulder, which was two inches lower than Rainer's, to the backs of their hands.

Xander stood and held a hand out to help her up. "You were pulled in by the dracae. Water demons. Aria, I apologise, that should never have happened. That bastard Murdoch must have known there were dracae in the river, I'll be having a word with him on our return." Now he knew Aria was going to be OK, his concern had vanished and been replaced by anger.

"No, Xander, it's not his fault, I shouldn't—"

He cut her words dead. "You're right, it's not Murdoch's fault. It's mine. I should have been keeping an eye on you, I should have gotten to you faster." He turned away, looking across the water. His fists clenched, the skin over his knuckles bone-white.

Rainer placed a hand on his shoulder. "Xand, we need to get to the inn, and get you two dried off." Aria hadn't noticed that Xander was soaking wet too. She remembered now seeing his face in the dark water as he fought off the dracae.

"Xander, thank you. I—I think you saved my life."

He turned back to her, eyes momentarily unguarded. In them, she saw the bottomless grief that he felt for Quade, mingled with the fear he'd faced of losing her. It only lasted a moment before the shutters came down again. "Yes, well. I'm sorry it was necessary."

"Come on, we can discuss this once we've all got a hot meal in our bellies," Rainer said gently, clapping Xander on the shoulder and heading up the embankment towards the row of waterfront buildings in every shade of pastel. Xander followed without a word.

Coulter offered Aria an arm and a cheeky grin, both of which she gratefully accepted.

"Do you think we'll be safe in Murdoch's sister's inn? I don't want to be attacked in my bed by some amphibious Solitary creature," Aria whispered, only half joking.

"It's the only recommendation we have, and the inn is right there," Coulter replied, pointing up the shore to a narrow, duck egg blue building with a wooden sign that read 'The Crappie Inn'.

"The name doesn't fill me with confidence," Aria muttered. Coulter laughed and it was like music to her ears.

23

ARIA BRUSHED HER CLEAN, DAMP HAIR and tugged at the hem of the pale-blue tea dress Dorit, the landlady, had given her.

Her clothes had been taken away to be washed, and Dorit had sworn her daughter had been about Aria's size. The dress was a little snug on the hips, but the cut was flattering and she liked the tiny seahorse print.

She'd been given her own room this time. Whether it was because of their dwindling number, or that they now trusted her not to run in the middle of the night, she wasn't sure. But the privacy was nice after weeks of no personal space.

She pulled on her boots and reached for the door handle just as a knock sounded from the other side. She shook it off and opened the door.

Xander stood in the hall looking just as surprised. "Oh, Aria. Hello. Um…"

"Xander?" He had also bathed and changed into clean clothes, he smelled like citrus and sea salt. His eyes were bloodshot, whether from tears or exhaustion, she wasn't sure.

"I was wondering if we could speak. I wanted to make sure you're alright after…" When he couldn't find a suitable description for everything they had been through he stood there looking at her face for so long that she felt heat creep up her neck.

She gave in and held the door open to let him step inside. She sat on the edge of the bed and gestured for him to take a seat at the white-washed dressing table, but instead he hovered in the middle of the room looking out of place.

"Xander, are you alright?" She was starting to worry he had some terrible news to tell her. That her father had passed away before they could reach him, or her parents had truly been killed by Bazyl and his men.

Finally, he sat down, looking as uncomfortable as he had standing. "I'm fine. Are you fine?" She nodded, still confused. He cleared his throat. "I wanted to say how sorry I am about today's…events. I will be speaking with that fisherman, he will be held accountable—"

"No, please don't blame Murdoch. It was my own fault." She couldn't let him punish someone else for her mistake. Not after what had happened to Quade. These attacks were all because of her. "I let my guard down. I shouldn't have leant over the edge of the boat, I saw something in the water and I forgot for a second where I was. I forgot *who* I was." She looked down at her hands, fingers threaded together, palms raw and blistered from the reins, nails chipped and cracked. They were not the hands of a princess.

"Aria, none of this is your fault." When she didn't look up he crossed the room and knelt in front of her, taking her hands in his.

They were warm and rough against her skin, scarred and calloused. A soldier's hands, not a prince's.

"You didn't ask to be brought to the Fair Realm, subjected to vicious attacks. If we had not found you and brought you here this may never have happened." He dropped her hands and stood, fists opening and closing at his sides. "It's my fault, I brought all of this upon you. All of you. I'm to blame for Quade's death."

He turned away, hands on the back of his neck as he hunched over, his body forming a protective barrier against his pain and grief.

Aria stood and hesitantly placed a hand on his back. "You're not to blame, Xander." She let out a slow breath, steeling herself. "And neither am I."

He turned to face her then, a question in his eyes, a plea for her to make some sense of this string of horrific events that had taken his brother and dozens of his people. "It's the Celeste King we should be blaming. He's the one sending these creatures after me. Why does he want me dead? What could I possibly have done to offend a man I've never even met?" She shook her head, feeling the prickle of tears at the backs of her eyes.

Xander gripped her by the elbows and forced her to look him in the eyes. His were like steel, cold and sharp enough to cut men down. "Nothing, Aria. You have done absolutely nothing wrong." He scanned her face, searching for something she wasn't sure he would find.

They were mere inches apart. Aria realised they were alone for the first time, standing almost as close as they had when they had danced at the festival. The air was suddenly heavy, pressing down on Aria, making her feel rooted to the spot. She couldn't tear her eyes away from Xander's, which had turned from cool steel to molten silver, equally deadly but infinitely more beautiful. The distance between them felt too small and too large. Aria felt an invisible string joining them, pulling them inexorably towards one other.

She tore her gaze away from his eyes to look at his lips, soft and slightly parted. Her breath hitched in her chest.

A knock came at the door and Xander let go of her arms and leaped backwards almost comically. Aria turned to face the window, hiding the colour that had risen to her cheeks. The cool breeze that drifted in was soothing on her burning skin, bringing with it the scent of fish cooking on a barbecue. The knock came again and Xander moved to answer it, having regained some composure. Rainer was standing on the other side of the door.

"I—Xander? Sorry, I didn't mean to interrupt." He bowed and was about to leave when Xander stopped him.

"You're not interrupting anything." Aria flinched at his tone. Had she misread the signals? Had he not been about to kiss her? She felt embarrassed then, silly for feeling so flustered when Xander clearly felt nothing.

"I just wanted to speak with Aria. About earlier. To make sure she's OK." Rainer stumbled over the obvious lie.

She turned then, smiling at Rainer and deliberately avoiding Xander's eyes.

"Then I shall leave you to it," Xander said, bowing to the room and slipping out the door without so much as a glance in Aria's direction. She watched him go with a blank expression, emotions clashing under the surface.

Rainer turned to her with a grimace. "Did I cover that well?"

"No. Not at all. What did you want?"

"To see if you wanted to train for an hour before dinner, but I think that plan's ruined." He furrowed his brow. "Are you alright? You gave us quite a fright back there."

She nodded slowly, remembering the feeling of the air being squeezed from her lungs, the blackness encroaching on her vision. She shivered at the memory. "I'm OK. I'll be better after some food."

Rainer chuckled. "Is your stomach all you think about?"

"It's definitely top three. You go, I'll just be a minute."

After Rainer had left, Aria stood in front of the mirror and gave herself a final onceover. Her hair was almost dry now, curling slightly around her face, and her freckled cheeks were rosy from the strange, heated moment with Xander.

She really couldn't work him out. Just when she thought she was getting somewhere with him, he pulled the rug out from under her again.

Something caught her eye and she leaned closer, studying her reflection. Something sparkled in the evening light from the window.

Her eyes.

The dull brown was now a shimmering metallic bronze. Her irises looked as though they were lit from within. They shone and sparkled, just like Xander's and the others'.

Like one of the Fair.

She was one of them, this was her proof.

She ran from her room and down the hall towards the rooms Xander and the other boys occupied. In the back of her mind, she wondered at the fact that her first instinct was to go to Xander, but she would worry about that later.

His door was open a crack, and as she approached she could hear him speaking with someone in low voices. Not wanting to interrupt she hovered for a moment, unsure whether to go back to her room or try and find the others so she could share her news with someone.

She thought about finding Rainer, before realising that the other voice coming through Xander's door was his.

"Xander, I understand, but I don't—"

"She needs to focus. She needs to go into this with a clear head."

Were they talking about her? She crept closer to the door, feeling guilty for eavesdropping, but too curious to stop herself. She held her breath.

"We've lied to her long enough, Xander. We have kept too much to ourselves in our efforts to protect her. She deserves to know. If she discovers this from someone else, another hag or some other Elements forsaken creature, she will not forgive us. We'll lose her, Xander."

What was he talking about? What else could they be keeping from her? She felt her stomach plummet as she listened to their conversation, but she couldn't walk away now, she was rooted to the spot.

"I know, I know. But—"

"No, Xander, no buts." Aria was surprised by how firm Rainer was being. "If we do not tell Aria now, she *will* find out and she will never forgive us. We need her, Xander. She's the one. I've seen her abilities, she's the one who will bring the war to an end. But only if we tell her the whole truth. Now."

Aria was proud of Rainer for standing his ground. She wanted to hear the truth, whatever it was.

But Xander's next words made her question that desire.

"Rainer, if Aria finds out we've been keeping the fact she's a changeling from her—that her father killed the real child and left her in its place, she will break. She will not—"

Aria pushed the door open and the two men froze. She wasn't sure which of them looked guiltier. "What did you just say?" Her voice was brittle and cold, like ice cracking under foot.

24

"ARIA, WE WERE JUST—" Xander stopped dead when he saw her expression. There would be no talking his way out of this.

"My *real* father," she said in a lethal voice, "who asked you to drag me away from my parents—the man who insisted I be brought to him so I could take the throne when he dies—he killed my parents' child? *Murdered a baby*?" A shard of ice pierced her heart and stole her breath, she doubled over, curling around the pain. Rainer moved towards her and she held out a hand, stopping him short.

"My parents raised me believing I was the daughter they had created, their flesh and blood, and all along she was dead, and I…" She clutched her stomach, unable to find the words. "I was just some *thing* that had been planted in their home?"

She was an imposter, a fraud. Her breath came in heaving gasps, almost sobs. She felt bile rising up her throat, burning her from the inside. *A changeling*. What did that even mean? Was she the reason for yet *another* death?

Rainer and Xander both stepped closer, but she held them at bay. She didn't want either of them touching her. She couldn't handle this right now, she had to get out of this room, the walls were closing in on her, she needed air.

Even as she sprinted from the room and down the stairs of the inn, she knew they would follow her. They couldn't possibly let such a valuable asset escape their clutches. She ran through the tap room, where several patrons were sipping from tankards of ale, and burst out the door onto the street.

She only stopped when she reached the shoreline, remembering the dracae that had almost drowned her. She took a step back from the water's edge. The cool mist off the water caressed her burning cheeks and stinging eyes. She had never gotten to tell them about her eyes. Not that it mattered now—they'd known she was Fair all along, she was the only one who hadn't known, hadn't believed what she truly was.

She walked along the embankment, looking out over the water and listening to the gulls screeching. She hadn't gone more than a hundred metres before Xander jogged to catch up to her.

"I don't want to hear your excuses, Xander," she said without looking over her shoulder.

"Aria, I'm sorry for what you heard."

She spun to face him. *"You're sorry for what I heard?"* She hissed, incredulous. "How about you're sorry for lying to me? How about you're sorry I'm the daughter of a child murderer? How about—"

"Aria, what your father did, he did to protect you." She opened her mouth to reply but he spoke first. "He did what he thought was right. He did it to protect his people."

"He killed a baby!" She roared, her anger writhing like a living thing inside her. "There is no excuse for that! Oh god, I'm a changeling, I'm a monster." She gasped, the reality of what she had learned dawning on her. She stumbled away from Xander, retching onto the stone floor.

When her stomach was empty, she wiped her mouth and stood, facing the water. The anger had leeched out of her, leaving her bone tired and hollow.

"I don't want to hear your explanations and excuses, they're not enough. Not even close. My parents' child is dead and I'm just a... an uninvited, unwanted imposter. My real parents didn't want me, and my Mum and Dad have no idea I'm not even their real daughter. I don't belong here, and I don't belong with them anymore either. If they're even still alive." She closed her eyes, struggling to sift through her feelings as they hit her one after the other, like waves crashing on a beach, threatening to drag her under.

"I'm sorry," Xander said finally. He didn't move any closer or attempt to comfort her, and she was grateful for that. For once, his stoic demeanour was a welcome barrier between them, she thought she might burst into tears and never stop crying if he showed her the slightest kindness right now.

The silence stretched out between them, becoming more palpable by the second. Aria could feel it on her skin like electricity, lifting the hairs on her neck and raising goose bumps along her arms. She was about to turn around just to break the tension when Xander cleared his throat.

"Balthasar."

"Bless you," she replied automatically.

"Pardon?" He sounded confused. She turned to look at him finally.

"You sneezed. I said 'bless you'," she shrugged. "It's probably a human thing. Not that I'm even human…"

He ignored her last comment. "I didn't sneeze." She raised an eyebrow and he sighed, closing his eyes. "That is my real name. Balthasar."

Aria stared at him for a moment, a blank expression on her face. And then she burst out laughing.

"I'm like that bird that kicks the mother's real eggs out of the nest and pretends to be her chick—which bird is that?" Aria tore a hunk of bread off and dipped it into her steaming bowl of clam chowder before popping it into her mouth.

"Cuckoos are actually quite misunderstood creatures," Xander said, a forkful of baked trout inches from his lips.

"That's the one, a cuckoo. I'm a big, fat cuckoo."

"They really are very intelligent birds. And beautiful. Sadly, their population is in decline—"

"Then why is that film about a mental institution named after them? Hm?"

"I…don't know what you're talking about." He furrowed his brow and Aria huffed a sigh, stirring her chowder idly.

"Oh, forget it. I don't even know why I'm talking to you, you knew this entire time and you didn't tell me."

They were back at the inn sitting in the tap room, two bowls of clam chowder and a whole baked trout between them on the table, and two frothy tankards of ale. It had taken Aria several minutes to stop laughing and catch her breath. With the tension broken, she had listened to what Xander had to say. She hadn't accepted his explanation that her father had done what he did for the greater good. There was never any excuse for killing an innocent. She was glad she had been spared having to grow up under the care of a man who could justify cold blooded murder to himself.

She missed her parents so much it physically hurt.

"What is that divine scent?" Coulter appeared next to the table and slid into the seat next to Aria, peering into her bowl. "Are you finished with that?"

She pushed her half-eaten chowder towards him and he tucked in greedily, tearing off chunks of bread and shovelling trout into his mouth like he hadn't eaten in weeks.

"What are we talking about?" He dribbled chowder down his chin and wiped it with the back of his hand.

"Oh, nothing," Aria said airily. "Just the fact that I'm a changeling."

Coulter froze with the spoon halfway to his lips and looked at Xander, eyes wide with panic. "Oh. You, er, you know?"

"Yep."

He held up his hands, spoon dripping globs of chowder onto the table. "It is a barbaric practice, I completely agree. It's not very common nowadays, but back then, yes. Sometimes the Fair took healthy human children and swapped them with sickly Fair children." He spooned chowder into his mouth and spoke around it.

"But, King Ossian did what he did to protect you, not because you were sick. Most Fair infants who were left with humans died soon after." He continued eating his weight in fish.

Aria was aghast. "You mean to tell me changelings were usually left with humans because they weren't expected to survive? That's…"

"Barbaric, I know!" He finished Aria's bowl of chowder and Xander pushed his own towards him with a shake of the head. Coulter dug in. "With the war and everything else going on, not many Fair can afford to have children at all, so it's pretty unheard of now."

Aria barely heard him, she had spotted Rainer in the entrance hall, handing a piece of paper to one of the inn's maids. His expression was grave. Catching Aria's eye, he forced a smile to his face. He exchanged a few more words with the maid and she turned to leave, clutching the note tightly.

He approached their table, the false smile back on his face. Coulter offered him the spoon and almost empty bowl, but he shook his head. "Aria, would you like to take a walk and explore the town? The Ondine Queendom has some fascinating architecture and interesting historical—"

"It's alright, Rainer," Xander interrupted. "I know you're training Aria in her abilities. I've known for weeks. You really aren't a very good liar. I'd like to join you, if you don't mind?" He aimed the question at Aria, but he pushed back from the table and stood before she could answer. Clearly this was not a request.

25

"I THOUGHT WE COULD TRY SUMMONING A SELKIE TODAY." He looked at Aria quickly. "That is, if you're comfortable being near the water."

She hesitated. She certainly wasn't keen on the idea, but as long as she didn't have to actually go in the water, or set foot on a boat, she would be fine. Probably.

"OK, but I'm staying on the shore. I don't care what they say, everything is *not* better under the sea."

On the walk down to the river, Rainer explained that selkies were water creatures that took human form when they set foot on dry land.

"No one knows what they look like under the water, anyone who has ever seen them has not returned." Aria balked. She was starting to regret agreeing to this training session. "They can be quite…charming. They're well known for seducing lonely travellers and then dragging them down to their underwater cities to live forever. Or die, as the case may be."

Aria snorted. "After what happened with the dracae, I don't think I'm in any danger of being seduced by a sea monster."

"Just be careful. I'll be right behind you."

They stopped at a secluded spot on the embankment and stood a few feet from the edge where dark water lapped onto the stone. Xander observed Aria and Rainer with quiet consideration. It made Aria nervous.

"Go ahead," Rainer said under his breath so only she could hear. "Take your time. I'm right here if you need me."

She turned to face the water. It sparkled in the late afternoon light, it would have been inviting if it weren't for the various creatures she knew resided beneath the gentle waves. The woods they had ridden through were visible across the river, the small pontoon where Murdoch's boat bobbed. Above them, the sky was a pale cornflower blue, gulls hovered here and there, casting shadows on the surface of the river, filling the air with their high-pitched calls.

Aria closed her eyes, took a deep breath, and began to picture a selkie in her mind's eye. She didn't have the first clue what they actually looked like, but she conjured an image of a man slipping under the waves, transforming as he did, disappearing into the dark depths, and resurfacing, human once more. With that image held in her mind, she opened her mouth to call to the selkies, but a splashing sound close by made her leap backwards, her eyes snapping open.

Something crawled out of the water onto the stone embankment. A man. A human.

Well, his top half was human. The part still under the water was a dark grey shape, something like a dolphin or a seal. As the selkie dragged himself onto the stone his body became entirely human. Aria was amazed to see the transformation that took place at the surface of the water, although she couldn't see how it happened exactly, the instant the selkie's body broke the surface it became flesh and bone, casting off the blubber and gills of his other form.

He stood before them on newly formed legs and bowed deeply to Aria.

"My Queen." When he stood up straight Aria looked away, blushing. He was completely naked. And apparently unconcerned about that fact. "A little fishy told me you were beautiful, but they did not do you justice, Your Majesty. You are exquisite." His eyes sparkled with mischief. Aria tried her hardest to focus on them. Brown. They were brown, and his lashes were long and black. He had a straight nose, and a strong, square jaw. His skin was pale, almost silvery, and he had broad shoulders and a muscular chest. His stomach was flat and toned. Eyes! His eyes. They shone with silent laughter at her embarrassment.

"Erm, thank you, er—"

"Sid," he replied. "My name is Sid, my illustrious ruler."

Aria could practically hear Xander rolling his eyes. "Thank you, Sid. I'm Aria. Er, are there many of you?" She wasn't used to meeting such chatty members of the Solitary, she hadn't been prepared for small talk. The selkie smiled.

"Yes, my lady, there are a great many of us."

"Good. And, erm, do you all answer to me?" She felt embarrassed asking, but Rainer had had a similar conversation with the nat. She thought she had better ask, just to be sure.

"Of course, my majestic queen. We are but your humble servants," he said, bowing low again. Aria thought she heard Rainer snort behind her.

"And will you come to my aid when I need you?"

"Indeed, my lady. Wherever possible, we will answer your call."

Aria smiled, selkies weren't so bad, Rainer had obviously been exaggerating. She had nothing to worry about with this one at least.

He cast a glance at Rainer and Xander, eyes narrowing, before looking back to Aria. "Would my queen like to join me for dinner and meet some of her other subjects?"

There it was.

"I'm afraid I can't on this occasion, Sid, but thank you very much for the kind invitation."

His lips curved in a sensuous smile and his eyes found Rainer over her shoulder. "How about you, handsome?"

Rainer coughed and spluttered. "I'm taken. Sorry."

Aria turned back to the selkie. "That will be all, thank you, Sid," she said firmly, forcing a smile back.

"I believe this belongs to you, Gnome Prince." Sid opened his hand and sitting on his palm was a black string with two jade green beads. Aria saw Xander's hand go to his bare wrist, and then he stepped forward cautiously and took the bracelet from the selkie's palm.

"Thank you. Where did you find it?"

"The river takes many things. I'm glad to be able to return it to you." The selkie bowed one last time, winked at Aria and dove into the water, transforming into the slippery grey creature on contact.

"Well, that was interesting," Rainer said, once the splashing had subsided. "He was certainly very…loyal." Aria was surprised to see Rainer blushing.

"I thought gentlemen preferred blondes," she teased.

"He wasn't blonde?"

Aria laughed, swatting Rainer's arm. Xander coughed loudly, drawing their attention to his presence. "That was impressive, Aria.

You summoned the selkie with your mind. I wasn't aware your training had been quite so successful."

"That's the first time I've ever done it. It's weird, I was just about to speak and he appeared. It's like he heard my thoughts or something." A shiver chased down her spine, she hoped he couldn't hear her thoughts right now. Did she have a mental connection to all the Solitary?

"Your abilities have developed further than I had hoped," Rainer said. "Commanding the Solitary by projecting your thoughts is an incredibly advanced technique. You should be proud of what you've achieved, Aria."

Rainer smiled, but Xander's expression was as unreadable as ever.

Aria lay on top of the bed staring at the white washed ceiling. She'd kicked off the blankets, despite the open window there was no breeze to speak of, just the pungent scent of fish wafting in and permeating her hair and clothes. She'd never be able to scrub the smell out.

The sky had begun to lighten, they would be leaving Aberness as soon as the others woke, and she was glad. It was a pretty little town, and Dorit had certainly made them welcome at the inn, despite some of the dark looks and muttered comments they had received from other patrons. Aria doubted anyone would dare speak up about the presence of Gnomes in the Ondine Queendom within earshot of Rainer. He stood a head taller than most men, and almost twice as broad.

But Aria was anxious to continue their journey and finally reach the Salamander Kingdom. After everything she'd learned, she felt torn between wanting to know the truth about herself and her destiny, and the anger she felt for the man who was supposedly her father.

Dorit had looked surprised to hear there were dracae in the river, she said there hadn't been a sighting for miles in the last thirty years. Aria knew why they were here. The Celeste King had sent them for her. She hoped when they left Aberness the dracae would crawl back to whichever dark hole they had come from, back to their master, and leave the little town in peace for another thirty years.

At some point in the night, Aria had begun to think about everything she'd been through since that day at the fayre with Jasper. How much she'd changed. If she went home now, she'd be a completely different person to the girl who crossed through the Veil that night.

And she couldn't abandon the Fair to their fate if there was anything she could do to help them, anything at all. She couldn't let Quade's death count for nothing. Or Bonnie's. Or her parents' child's. Or any of the other innocent people who had been killed in the war, or at the hands of the Celeste King.

Lying there in the half-light, she had decided to stay and fight. She would do whatever she could to help in the battle against the Solitary and the Celeste King, and when the war was over she would return to Hartwood and her family. She couldn't stay and rule the Salamander Kingdom, but she would ensure that whoever took over the throne from her father was fit for the job. She would leave this place a little better than she had found it, and that was the best she could do.

She hoped it would be enough.

The sound of movement in the hallway reminded her that daybreak was almost here, and she pushed herself up on her elbows. Her old jeans and t shirt were folded on the stool, having been cleaned and pressed by Dorit's maids. Her brown boots lay on the floor next to the bed, where she had stepped out of them the night before, Dorit's daughter's dress in a heap next to them. She picked it up and smoothed out the creases, folding it neatly and setting it on the dressing table. It was a pretty dress, and Aria felt that it held some memories for Dorit.

She hadn't asked where Dorit's daughter was or what had happened to her, she hadn't wanted to pry. Photos lining the stairs of the inn showed a smiling young woman with honey blonde hair wearing the blue tea dress, sitting on the embankment wall in the sunshine with an ice cream, and dancing at a festival celebration like the one they had attended in Hitherham. Aria hoped that wherever the girl was she was alive and well, perhaps with a handsome fisherman husband and a handful of blonde children.

Somehow, she did quite believe it.

She pulled on her clean clothes, they smelled fresh, like lemon and saltwater, and laced her boots, checking her reflection before leaving the room. In all the kerfuffle of the previous day, she had never told anyone about her eyes, and no one had mentioned it either. They shimmered now in the soft dawn light coming through the window. Pushing her hair behind her ears, she stroked the tops. Still rounded.

She was the first one in the den, and one of the maids brought her a strong mug of coffee. She was beginning to like it that way. After a hearty breakfast of toast with smoked salmon and cream cheese, muesli with dried fruits, and more coffee, they packed their satchels with parcels of salted cod and fresh bread, filled their water skins, and set out on foot.

Aria gave Aberness one last look as they walked away from the town and its pastel painted buildings with white wooden shutters, and rows of fishing boats rising and falling with the ebb and flow of the water. She was starting to understand that this whole realm was like this town, seductive and appealing at first glance, but danger lurked around every corner and could bare its teeth at any moment.

26

ACCORDING TO RAINER'S MAPS the Salamander Kingdom was just a few days' hike from Aberness. On the downside, it would be largely uphill until they reached the Caelum mountain range and began the descent towards Penny Crag and the Salamander Stronghold.

Aria found the walk a pleasant change from riding for the first few miles, and then she began to miss Matilda's gentle rocking motion and the comfort of knowing she could escape at speed if needed.

Although, there was nowhere for the Solitary to hide in this part of the Ondine Queendom, Aria noticed with no small amount of relief. The terrain consisted predominantly of lush, green meadows, populated by herds of grazing cattle, with only the occasional small cluster of trees to break up the vista.

Unless the cows here were actually aether-corrupted, bloodthirsty monsters, she reckoned they'd be fine.

"So, what do the beads mean?" She asked Xander, indicating the bracelet the selkie had returned to him.

Xander glanced down at his wrist briefly before returning his gaze to the path ahead. "They're alexandrite. It's our family jewel."

"And each bead represents one of you, Kiefer and Quade?" She guessed, remembering how he had removed one of the beads and tossed it into Quade's grave.

Xander looked at her, then nodded once. After a moment, he added, "It was my father's. His mother made it for him. He had only one brother, who died years ago. When I was born my father gave the bracelet to me, but it had only one bead—his bead. So my mother had more made after each of my brothers was born." He ran his fingers over the two remaining beads like it was a rosary, saying a silent prayer over each one.

"I'm sorry about Quade—"

"Don't," he cut her off. "Don't apologise. Quade was a soldier. This is war. This is what we do." His words echoed Rainer's back in the Gnome Kingdom, but they sounded hollow to her ears. She disagreed, but didn't think Xander needed to hear that right now.

"Tell me about him."

Xander looked at her quickly, brows knitting together. She thought he might refuse, but he sighed and said, "He was a terrible actor."

She laughed. "What?"

"When we were younger, we shared a room. Not officially, but every night they'd come to my room and we'd stay up talking, playing games and telling stories until we fell asleep." A smile ghosted at the corners of his mouth as he remembered. "I'd sneak down to the kitchen—I wasn't a particularly good sneak back then, they'd know I was coming and have a basket of summer fruits, cakes and biscuits waiting for me. Which I would pretend to have stolen. It was our little secret."

Aria smiled, thinking back to the midnight snacks she and Jasper used to have while they watched horror movies in her room. Scotch eggs, cheese and onion crisps and fig rolls, washed down with lemonade. Nothing as fancy as the Gnome princes' picnics, she imagined.

"Kiefer was the best at making up stories, he'd act out all the battles and make Quade play the enemy, fencing with old, wooden practice swords." His expression turned from wistful to strained. His voice dropped so low she barely caught his next words. "How am I going to tell him?"

She wished there was something she could say or do to ease his pain.

The following day, they crested a grassy knoll and Aria spotted smoke on the horizon. "Is that the Salamander Kingdom?"

Xander, walking beside her, squinted into the distance. "Yes. The smoke is probably from the metalworks. Smith's shoes are Salamander made, it's the finest quality in the Five Kingdoms." He said it without emotion, but she could tell he missed the stallion.

They walked on, closing the distance between them and the plumes of smoke that blurred the line between land and sky. Evening stained the blue sky with rosy pinks and golden oranges, and the heat of the day eased off, leaving behind a refreshing coolness.

They made camp that night in the corner of a small meadow, under a single, lonely oak tree. They unpacked and arranged their bedrolls around the base of the tree, for protection from rain showers. They didn't bother with a fire, wanting to avoid attracting the attention of any animals that may be in the area, they were not blessed with much cover out here in the hills.

They set about sharing the remaining bread and fish from the inn. Coulter had topped up his flask with some Ondine-made liquor, and he passed it round the group while they ate.

Xander took the first watch and sat whittling a small fallen branch with his pocket knife, reminding Aria of Kiefer. She wondered if Xander was thinking about him too. She lay in her blankets looking up at the stars through gaps in the canopy of leaves.

Rainer and Coulter were lying on their sides facing one another, speaking in low voices. The hum of their conversation soon lulled her to sleep.

Aria awoke sometime later. The sound…she wasn't sure if she had dreamed it. She opened her eyes and saw that the sky was now coal black and dotted with stars, like pearls scattered across a bolt of black silk. It fascinated her that the same constellations she could see back home in Hartwood were visible here, in this other place. Whatever magic allowed the first Fair Queen to create this realm within the human world, vast and undetectable, must have been incredibly powerful and complex. She was both here and not here, close to home and impossibly far away.

Looking around the camp she realised Xander was still supposed to be on watch, but had fallen asleep at his post. She couldn't bring herself to wake him, he was finally resting soundly, and after everything he'd been through he deserved a good night's sleep.

She sat cross-legged on her pile of blankets and watched over the group of boys she realised she had come to think of as friends. It was strange to her, barely a week earlier she had been terrified for her life, convinced she was about to be murdered by these boys. Now, she was sitting with weapons in her reach, looking at them as they slumbered peacefully around her. If she had wanted to she could have slit every one of their throats while they slept.

Or run.

But she found she didn't want to leave.

It wasn't because she was curious about her real father, although she was. Now she knew the lengths he had gone to in order to protect her she wasn't sure she wanted to get to know him. She couldn't imagine feeling anything but hatred and disgust for the man who had killed her parents' child. The thought of having anything in common with him, recognising any similarities between them, made her nauseous.

No, something had formed between Aria and the Gnomes as they travelled across the Five Kingdoms, a bond that tied them together, connecting them with strands of grief and anger, but also friendship and trust.

The noise came again, from behind her she now realised. She froze, listening so hard she thought her eardrums would rupture. When the sound didn't come again she turned her head as slowly and smoothly as her fear would allow, refusing to let the terror take over her entire body.

A strange light caught her eye and she thought back to the dracae that had almost drowned her. Fear tried to force its way up her throat but she swallowed it back down. This light was different somehow.

Slowly, so slowly she was barely moving at all, she got to her feet and started to approach the source of the light. Her bare feet were soundless on the soft grass, her blood roaring inside her head.

The source of the bright white light was motionless. As she neared she could see that it wasn't a flame or a torch. It looked like a large animal. Like a horse. Or a deer.

The White Hart of Hartwood.

27

ARIA GASPED. She'd been right, the hart truly existed, she hadn't dreamed it when she was a little girl.

The creature allowed her close enough to touch, only stamping a foot and shaking its enormous silver-white antlers when she reached out to stroke its fur. She snatched her hand back, shocked at her stupidity. She didn't know whether the stag was one of the Solitary, but it didn't seem like a normal deer, with its ghost-white fur and soft glow. Steam poured from its nostrils, warming the cool night air and ruffling her hair.

Aria studied the stag, eyes wide, pulse still racing. It stood taller than any horse and was crowned with at least eight feet of glistening antlers. It was both strangely majestic and incredibly intimidating.

The stag huffed and steam shot out of its nose again, making Aria jump, a yelp escaping her throat. She took a step back as it tossed its head again, antlers cutting through the air. She got the feeling the beast was trying to communicate with her.

It started to lower itself to the ground.

"Aria? Aria!" Xander's panicked voice reached her from the camp. She heard him rip his sword from its sheath, and Rainer and Coulter throw off their blankets and grab their weapons.

"I'm OK. I'm right here," she called in a stage whisper, turning her back on the stag. Xander was running towards her now, wielding his sword in both hands, the others not far behind. She heard a huff and looked over her shoulder to see the stag, now back on its feet. With a grunt it galloped off, disappearing over the fields and out of sight.

Xander reached her first and stared after the stag. "Was that-?"

"The White Hart," she breathed, a combination of awe and adrenalin coursing through her.

Xander must have seen the fire in her eyes because the next moment his silver irises turned molten and his hands were on her cheeks, sinking into her hair, and drawing her in to him. Their lips met in a kiss that erased every moment that had gone before—every fight, every misunderstanding, every hurt. There was only this moment, now, and nothing could come between them.

Xander brushed a thumb along her jaw, sending a shiver down her spine. Her skin felt hot under his cool touch. Her breath caught in her chest as she slid her arms around his neck and his hands moved to her waist, pressing her flush against him.

A cough made them both jump and they pulled apart, embarrassment rushing into the gap where Xander's warmth had just been. Aria turned away and pressed a hand to her mouth, not wanting to meet their eyes.

"Was that the White Hart?" Rainer asked, his tone suggesting he knew full well that it had been.

"Yes," Xander said, clearing his throat.

Aria turned to face them, hoping the moonlight hid the heat in her cheeks. "I saw it once when I was younger, in the woods behind my house. Nobody believed me, but I knew what I saw. And I was right." She grinned, but they didn't return it. "It must have sensed me—my abilities—and come looking for me. Right?"

Xander shook his head, a strange look in his silver eyes. "Aria, the White Hart isn't one of the Solitary." He looked in the direction the stag had run, scanning the horizon.

"What do you mean?" Her blood cooled quickly, raising goosebumps across her bare arms. "What about the glow, you can't tell me that's normal?"

Rainer rubbed his jaw, where a shadow had formed since leaving Aberness. "No, it's not an animal. Rumour has it the first Fair Queen was able to transform into an animal form. A white stag."

Aria felt a chill grip her, ice sliding down her spine. "Queen Oriana? But surely she died centuries ago?"

"Yes, of course. But her descendants live on."

Coulter spoke in a low voice. "Oriana's descendants are spread across all five kingdoms. Any one of them could have inherited her ability for transforming into the stag."

Rainer shook his head. "Oriana only had one daughter. Only Forbia's descendants could have inherited the ability. And Forbia took the Celeste throne on her mother's death."

Aria's breath misted in front of her face. "So, that wasn't just a deer? That was a *person*?" She felt betrayed—exposed and vulnerable.

Xander looked her in the eye, that old intensity back in his gaze. This time, when it made her shudder, it wasn't from fear. "I'm not sure, but I plan to find out."

The next morning, they packed up quickly and set off for the Salamander Kingdom. There were only a few hours' walk between Aria and the truth. Her real father, her true heritage, her destiny.

She hadn't expected to feel this nervous.

She had expected the nudges and winks she and Xander received from the others. She smiled benignly while the boys laughed and teased them, but inside she was torn. She wasn't sure she wanted to stay in the Fair Realm.

She needed to return to her real life, she missed her parents and Jasper. She wanted to take the dogs for a long walk and have a movie night with her best friend. Normal stuff.

She didn't want to be the Salamander Queen, much less the Gnome Queen.

In five years, or ten, he would be ruling the Gnome Kingdom and she would be living her normal life in Hartwood. Or somewhere else entirely.

They trudged onwards at what seemed like a slower pace than usual to Aria. They were all exhausted by the previous days' hike. Or maybe the others were as reluctant to reach the Salamander stronghold and say goodbye as she was. Once they delivered her to her father and their mission was complete, would they go straight back to the Gnome castle? How would she get in touch with them?

"You can send a message with a rider," Xander said, when she voiced her worry.

"What if they don't believe I am who you say I am? How did you even find me?"

Xander gave her a small, reassuring smile. "Ossian told us where to look, and what to look for. We watched you, to be sure, but you are his daughter, Aria. Just look at your eyes, you're one of us." She laughed then, remembering the bronze shimmer she'd noticed back in Aberness.

"They will know who you are on sight, Aria," Xander added. "The family resemblance is uncanny."

Aria raised an eyebrow. "You mean the hair?" She pictured Bazyl with his auburn locks, several shades darker than her own.

Xander laughed. "Well, yes, but you also have your father's strength and determination. And stubbornness. And your mother's beauty." His words hung in the air between them. Aria wanted to grab his hand and pull him towards her, kiss him right there in front of the others. She resisted.

"Have you ever seen my mother? A photo, or a painting?"

He shook his head. "I've only heard it from others."

Aria walked on in silence for a minute, watching with distant interest as the terrain changed from lush, grassy fields and heathland to rocky outcrops. "Who was she? I know she was a Celeste, but nothing else. How did my father meet her?"

"She was a Celeste," he confirmed. "A very powerful healer."

"A healer?"

Xander nodded. "Yes, one of the last truly talented Celeste healers. Most only have a slight affinity for it, but from what I've heard Neviah was the strongest Celeste in generations. It's no wonder you're so powerful."

Aria missed a step, stumbling on a loose rock. Xander's arm shot out like lightning, steadying her. She hadn't thought to ask Rainer what her mother's powers had been, she'd assumed they were the same as her own, a connection with the Solitary.

They trudged on, the ground underfoot now mountainous, sloping upwards steeply. The smoke plumes were close now, just beyond the next peak. When they reached the edge of the cliff, Aria looked down and saw a town laid out beneath them, far below. *Penny Crag.* Warehouses and factories with enormous chimneys that spewed black clouds. She could hear the distant sounds of machinery, metal clanging and engines whirring.

A path had been carved into the rock, zig zagging downwards sharply all the way down the cliff face to the town. Aria started towards the path but Xander called her back. "We're not taking that route," he said. "Too obvious. We would be open to attack from Demitree and his men." His tone was unconvincing. Aria's eyes narrowed.

"Bazyl? He hasn't caught up to us so far, what makes you think he will now?"

"I just don't want to take the risk."

"What are you not telling me? I already know Bazyl and his men want me dead, but we defended ourselves before. What makes you think we couldn't do it again?"

Xander ran a hand through his hair, exasperation weighing heavy in his tone. "Because, Aria, we didn't defend ourselves, we escaped. There's a difference. And there are a lot of Salamanders down there. If even one per cent of them are on your brother's side, they'd outnumber us ten to one. It's too dangerous."

She narrowed her eyes at him, but despite her misgivings, she conceded. The tension in his frame made her nervous though, she didn't like the set of his jaw. But she couldn't argue with his maths.

They hiked over rocky terrain, seemingly away from the town at the bottom of the cliff. Aria assumed they were taking the scenic route and would circle back round to the castle at some point.

She slowed her pace eventually, reluctant to show any signs of fatigue, she still had her pride. She fell back, leaving Xander at the fore. Rainer and Coulter fell into step on either side of her. She narrowed her eyes at them. "I'm not going to run if that's what you think."

Rainer looked at her quickly, too quickly. He gave a short laugh. "We just want to be prepared, that's all. An attack is unlikely," he added, hurriedly, "but we've been caught off-guard before."

Aria raised an eyebrow. That was an understatement. In a quiet voice, low enough that the prince in front couldn't hear, he added, "If anyone—or anything—does attack us, Aria, you run. OK? Back the way we came. We will fight them off and come back for you. Just keep moving, we will find you."

Aria was a little scared by his tone. She supposed it made sense, they had been attacked several times during their journey. This close to their destination, it was understandable that they would be hyper-cautious. "OK," she said, and kept walking, flanked by the Gnome King's Guards.

A sound to their left had the boys drawing their weapons quicker than Aria's eyes could see. A sword, an arrow and a hatchet were all aimed at the source of the sound.

A grey-blue mountain hare hopped out from behind a shrub.

Aria let out a breath and a giggle escaped her lips, turning into a full belly laugh that finally relieved the tension that had been building for hours now. Gradually the boys joined in, although their laughs sounded nervous and forced. Weapons were re-sheathed and they continued on their way.

They picked their way through montane moorland, scrubs of purple heather dotted along their path, the smoky plumes of the Salamander factories far away to the east. The air was thin up here, and

Aria's boots were rubbing in at least three places. On the bright side, she thought she could see the looming shapes of tall buildings in the distance on the other side of the mountain. A city? A castle? Perhaps this was the Salamander stronghold.

Before she could ask, a battle cry rent the air and a dozen men surrounded them on all sides, appearing as if from thin air.

They had been camouflaged to the rocks. They wore grey, their faces painted to match, and silver flashed as they drew their weapons.

28

Xander and the others drew their weapons, instinctively forming a horseshoe with Aria in the centre. They were outnumbered three to one.

Four of the grey men charged forwards, their movements graceful and fluid, like dancers. With the painted skin and pale clothes, they looked like ghosts. The rest of the attackers kept their distance, weapons pointed at the Gnomes. Aria tried to find Bazyl among the men, but she didn't recognise any of them.

Xander lunged with his short sword, forcing one of the men to leap backwards. Coulter had foregone his bow and slashed at the air with his long, curved blade, keeping a grey man at bay. He cried out as his opponent's sword nicked his arm, slashing his tunic and leaving a red line across his skin.

Aria felt terror grip her for a second, she saw Quade's body being thrown against the tree by the troll's gigantic club, his gelding lying on the forest floor, soaked in blood. But as quickly as the image came it was gone, and she saw Coulter fighting back with renewed energy.

Rainer fought off two of the men with his hatchet, slicing at one and spinning round to deflect the others' blow with the handle of his weapon. One well-placed swing left a bright red line down the front of a grey shirt. The man stumbled backwards, looking down at his chest in surprise. Blood soaked through the material, red staining the grey until he fell to the ground, clutching his abdomen. Rainer swung his hatchet at the second man, who took a more defensive stance after seeing his comrade almost sliced in two. Rainer lunged and the man leapt backwards. Rainer took his chance and yelled over his shoulder to Aria, "Go!"

Aria froze, like a deer in headlights. She didn't want to leave them behind, she wanted to fight. But she didn't have a weapon.

The only thing she could bring to the fight was her ability, and she didn't think there were any Solitary for miles around. She had been mentally screaming to them for help ever since they had been ambushed, and nothing had come to their aid so far.

She was on her own.

When he saw that she still hadn't moved, Rainer shouted again. "Aria, go, now!"

His desperate voice broke through her fear and she turned on her heel, sprinting as fast as could in the direction they had come. Instantly, two of the men standing back from the fight set off after her.

"No!" Aria heard Xander's scream and it tore at her heartstrings. The ground shook under her feet, a rumbling that filled her ears and vibrated her bones. She staggered as the earth shuddered, breaking apart. She fell onto her knees and turned to see an enormous crack splitting the ground from Xander's feet all the way to her own. She looked down into the crevasse that had opened in the rock, and then up at Xander's face. He was breathless, chest heaving, fists clenched at his sides.

He had created an earthquake. His Gnome powers had done this. Aria's face was slack, her mind reeling as she took in the scene. The men pursuing Aria had been knocked off their feet by the tremors. In fact, only the Gnomes were still standing. They spread out, weapons raised, keeping the grey men at bay. Xander took a step towards Aria, a single step, and the man nearest her launched himself forward, tackling Aria, pinning her arms behind her back. She felt something cold bite into her neck.

Xander froze. He didn't utter a sound. He didn't appear to be breathing. Aria struggled against her assailant until she felt a warm trickle of blood slide down her neck and pool in her clavicle.

"Move, and she dies."

"You wouldn't." Xander tried his best to sound confident, but it was unconvincing, even to Aria.

"By order of the Celeste King, I would." He sounded smug. Aria hated him for that. "Drop your weapons."

When the Gnomes didn't move he screamed it. "Drop your weapons!"

Reluctantly, they let their weapons drop to the floor. The other grey men got to their feet and grabbed the Gnomes, forcing them forwards. The others collected their dropped weapons.

"Start walking. We're taking you to New Hartwood."

Aria couldn't feel her feet and her hair clung to her damp forehead. She thought she would collapse from exhaustion, until the city she had seen from a distance rose into view.

They had descended the cliff face via a treacherously steep path, making Aria long for the manmade switchback that had led down to Penny Crag. Now, they came around the mountainside to see dozens of shining skyscrapers rising out of a sea of metal and glass.

This must be New Hartwood. She wasn't sure what she had expected of the Celeste Kingdom—if she had expected anything at all—but this wasn't it.

The man holding Aria's wrists in a pincer grip nudged her forward, she had paused to look up at the sky, where the tallest buildings disappeared into the clouds. They were dragged through remarkably clean, paved streets until they reached a large courtyard. An ornate fountain stood in the centre, sculpted from tiles that refracted the light.

The Celeste citadel loomed over them, standing out amongst the clean lines of the uniform edifices that made up the city. It looked more like a Picasso painting of a building than a real one, a collection of sharp edges and glass facets, all combining to create a curved, almost-spherical structure. It reminded Aria of the book about Gaudí Jasper had been sent by his grandmother one birthday, the twisting, organic design and mosaic tiled surfaces.

Except, the Celeste citadel looked brutal and unnatural.

Men and women dressed in varying shades of white and grey sat on marble benches around the edges of the courtyard, enjoying the late afternoon sunshine. Aria watched as a man in blue overalls carrying a toolbox approached the fountain. A hushed silence fell upon the square as all eyes turned to him. Before Aria could see what he was doing, she was pushed through the glass doors of the citadel into a vast atrium, bathed in sunlight thanks to the glass walls and ceiling.

Rainbows glimmered overhead, but when Aria turned to look at them they vanished, reappearing just on the edge of her vision. It was like a greenhouse inside the citadel, the heat was sweltering and Aria felt sweat trickle down her lower back. Exotic plants would have thrived in here, but there wasn't a single potted plant or even a vase of flowers in sight.

The grey men pushed them into a large lift with no buttons. Only the four Celeste restraining them were able to squeeze into the box with them, the rest took up positions by the glass doors to the building.

One of the men took out a key card and swiped it in a slot labelled with the symbol for the Greek letter *alpha*. Another slot below it was labelled with the symbol for *omega*.

The lift was smooth and soundless as it delivered them to their destination. Aria couldn't tell which direction they were travelling in, or how many floors they passed, but when the doors opened she saw a large room with no windows.

Underground, then.

If the Solitary hadn't heard her mental screaming all the way to the citadel, they certainly weren't going to hear her down here.

"Ah! Welcome, welcome. Come in. Thank you, Walden."

Aria couldn't see the owner of the disembodied voice, but the man holding her pushed her into the middle of the room and took a step back, hand resting on the handle of his knife. She gave him a glare over her shoulder and rubbed her wrists.

The Gnomes were dragged out of the lift, but they didn't rush to her side when the Celeste King's soldiers released them. Instead, they fell in behind her, forming a sort of barrier between her and the grey men.

The large, subterranean room appeared to be lit by some sort of incandescent lights. Not candles, or oil lanterns. *The Celeste had electricity?* The bulbs cast a purple-white glow over the cold marble floor, giving it the look of a hospital. Or a morgue.

"Princess Ariadne! What a pleasure to finally meet you," the voice said. She scanned the room, but she still couldn't lay eyes on the speaker.

"It's just Aria, actually." She was impressed to find her voice didn't shake. Inside, her heart was racing like a rabbit's, and her limbs felt leaden.

A man appeared as if from thin air, but Aria caught a glimpse of a reflection as he strode into the centre of the room.

Mirrors. He'd hidden himself in plain sight, like an illusion at the fayre.

He stepped into view. He was tall and thin, with lank blonde hair that curled around his ears and brushed his collar. He wore all white, trousers and a long-sleeved tunic, topped with a sort of chainmail cape, like a shimmering bolero. On his head was a lethal looking silver crown. Something about it reminded Aria of the spinning wheel from the tale of Rumpelstiltskin.

"*Actually*," he said, mimicking her, "my sister named you Ariadne. She told me. Before you were born, of course. Before you killed her." His words cut like a knife. His sister.

Aria felt all the air rush out of her lungs in one big *whoosh*. None of the Gnomes moved a muscle behind her. "You're—"

"Your uncle? Yes." He said, voice high and reedy. "You can call me Auberon."

29

E SMILED THEN, and Aria had never seen anything so terrifying. His lips were thin and cruel, but his eyes were the worst part. Ice-blue, cold and piercing, like looking into the heart of a flame.

Deadly.

Aria could see nothing of herself in him. Had her mother looked the same way? Ethereally beautiful and monstrous?

"Your mother was my sister. Neviah." He studied Aria openly. "I can see you inherited her beauty." His smile was wolfish.

Aria shuddered. Her revulsion rekindled the fire in her belly, and she let the hatred fuel her. "So, did you bring me here for some kind of twisted family reunion?"

The Celeste King laughed, a rattling, scraping sound that set Aria's teeth on edge. "By the Elements! No, child. Nothing quite as sentimental as that."

"Then what am I doing here?" She hoped he couldn't hear the quaver in her voice, that her deliberately bored body language masked the fear that rooted her to the spot. She doubted it, but she wasn't about to give him the satisfaction of seeing her afraid. She wanted to hear him explain himself. She wanted to keep him talking, give Xander and the others time to assess the situation and come up with an escape plan.

"As soon as my sister told me of the prophecy, and her suspicion that it spoke of her own unborn child, I knew you would be special. I had to see what you were truly capable of." He closed the distance between them in a second and Aria saw movement out of the corner of her eye. Xander's hand moved to his hip where the handle of his sword would be, if the grey men hadn't confiscated their weapons.

The Celeste King didn't even glance in his direction. He stood in front of Aria, so close she could smell the strange, chemical scent on his breath, and slowly traced the back of a finger down her cheek. She suppressed a violent shudder, gritting her teeth so hard she thought they would break. She didn't close her eyes, didn't dare with him standing so close.

"You see, *Aria*." He pronounced each syllable like it was a separate word. "My sister was a very powerful woman. A healer. A prophetess. You were bound to inherit something of her abilities—those of our family line." He looked her up and down, making her skin crawl under his scrutiny. His tone was derisive. "With any luck, the only thing you inherited from your Salamander father was that hair."

Knowing what she did about her father, Aria didn't disagree.

The Celeste King turned and walked away, draping himself over an enormous white throne, one leg over the padded velvet armrest.

"That is why I had the Gnome Prince here bring you to me." He waved a hand in Xander's general direction, but his eyes didn't leave Aria's face, waiting for her reaction. He wasn't disappointed.

Aria's lungs ceased to function. She opened and closed her mouth several times, but it was like the air had been sucked from the room. To compensate, her heart went into overdrive, pumping blood around her body so quickly she thought she would faint. She turned to Xander, hoping he would deny it. The guilt on his face told her everything she needed to know.

"Aria, I didn't—" He stammered before trailing off pathetically.

She glanced at the faces of the other boys and knew immediately. They had all been involved. They had delivered her to the enemy. Even Rainer, who was avoiding her gaze, staring at the lift as though he could magic himself out of this awkward situation if he could only reach the lift doors without being killed first.

Finding her voice, Aria whispered, "Why?"

The king grinned. He was enjoying this. "*Why?*" He repeated her question, cupping a hand round his ear as though he hadn't quite heard her. "To kill you, of course!"

"*No!*" Xander's cry should have been gut-wrenching, but Aria felt numb. He launched himself forwards, but three grey men grabbed him before he could gain more than a yard. "You lied to me!" He yelled, thrashing against his restraints. "You said you wouldn't hurt her, you said you only wanted to stop the prophecy. You promised me!"

The King studied Xander in silence. He shifted on his throne, cleared his throat. "Yes, about that. I lied." He threw back his head and laughed, thoroughly amused at his deception. When he finished laughing, he leaned towards Aria and held his hands out wide, palms up. "I toyed with the idea, briefly. You see, I thought I could train you in your abilities myself, teach you our ways—the Celeste way. I considered making you my queen, ruling the Five Kingdoms side by side. Just think how powerful our children would be." He sighed. "It could have been bliss." He sounded wistful.

Aria gagged.

"But, now…Well, it's far too late for all that. From what I hear, your abilities have blossomed beautifully, and the Solitary are naturally drawn to you. It's taken me years to coerce them around to my side, and you managed it in a matter of weeks." He sounded genuinely impressed. But then he shook his head. "You're much too dangerous to be allowed to live. I can't have you raising an army of Solitary against me." He gave an absurd chuckle.

"Therefore, Aria, my darling niece, you must die." He said it like it was the only option, the only one that made sense. Almost like he was sorry for that.

Something in his voice pushed Aria past bone-chilling terror to blood-boiling anger. She held up her hands. "Wait a minute. Let me get this straight, because it's been a long day. A long month, actually." She was damned if she was going to go down without a fight. "First, I'm knocked out and kidnapped by this bunch of arses—" she gestured behind her to the Gnomes. "Then they tell me my parents aren't my parents. No. No, apparently I'm the daughter of some lizard king." She thought she heard a smothered laugh from Rainer at that. "I'm a princess! With *magical* powers!" She forced a laugh, which sounded maniacal to her own ears. "Then, we're attacked by all manner of monster, and I have to watch people I care about die in front of my eyes. And then—then!" She was on a roll now, gesticulating wildly to emphasise her point. "Then, I find out I was dumped on my parents' doorstep one day, and their real baby was murdered. *Murdered.* By my real father!" Her voice had risen until she was almost shrieking. "And after all that, you're telling me I was never going to meet him? I was just brought here to you, to be killed? Is that seriously what you're telling me?"

She could feel the tension building in the group of men behind her. She dropped her voice so they had to strain to hear her. "Well, I'm not having it."

Auberon squinted at her. "You. Are. Not. Having. It?" He enunciated every word like she was speaking a foreign language, his voice colder than ice, and twice as brittle.

For several beats, nobody in the throne room moved a muscle. The silence stretched on for so long Aria began to wonder if she had made a grave mistake.

But then the King threw his head back and laughed so loudly Aria thought it might be fake. He laughed for longer than seemed normal. She stared at him, questioning his sanity.

"You are a feisty one, Ariadne, that's for sure." He took a silk handkerchief from his chest pocket and dabbed the corners of his eyes. "I can see how you managed to ensnare the prince over there. What a shame he's already betrothed. Camellia, isn't it?" He winked at Xander.

Her stomach plummeted. Xander was *engaged*? Had their kiss been just another in a long line of deceptions? She burned with rage, and more than a little shame.

"It's not like that, Aria. I swear—" Xander blurted, until a gasp told her a Celeste soldier had punched him in the stomach. She didn't turn around, not wanting to let him see the hurt and humiliation on her face.

Auberon carried on. "If I were a few years younger I might have fallen for you myself." She felt revulsion creeping under her skin and wanted to scratch it out. He had to be insane. She was his *niece*.

He picked up a small silver bell from a table beside the throne and shook it, an incongruously pretty tinkling sound filled the room. A panel slid open in the wall next to the lift doors and a man in a dove grey uniform and a white apron that reached his knees entered the room. He strode towards the King, spine ram-rod straight, holding a polished silver tray topped with a beautiful china tea set. He placed the tray on a side table next to the throne, bowed deeply to the king, and left the way he had come.

Auberon proceeded to pour himself a cup of tea, adding a splash of milk and two sugar cubes. "Where are my manners. Tea?" He held the pot out to Aria who shook her head, utterly bewildered. He took a sip, murmuring in pleasure, and set the cup back down in its saucer.

"You remind me a lot of my sister, you know, Ariadne. She was feisty too. And beautiful. And smart, strong, stubborn…" He trailed off, looking at a point just above Aria's head where memories lived. She wanted to take her chance to look around the room, find an escape route now she knew the Gnomes weren't going to help her get out of this situation. But she found herself listening to her uncle's ramblings, enthralled by the idea of her mother, wondering whether they truly were alike. She realised the King's voice had turned bitter.

"I warned her about the dangers of interbreeding. I told her not to mess around with that Salamander wastrel, but no, no, she wouldn't listen to me. She wouldn't take her big brother's advice. Instead, she left me here to rot and ran away with that Ossian. I should have stopped her, gone after her. But I was too angry. Too proud…And then you came along." He spat the last part, fixing Aria with a glare that made her muscles tense, like they wanted to shrink away from this monster. She couldn't tear her eyes away.

You didn't look away when a shark was circling.

He took a sip of tea, closing his eyes as he did so. Calmly setting it back down, he added, "Basically, you've stolen everything I've ever loved—my sister, my Solitary creatures. You're a threat to my position, and I'm afraid I have to kill you."

Aria felt like she'd been punched in the gut. She grasped at the first thing that came to mind. "What would my mother think if you killed me?"

"Good question. I'll be sure to ask her when I use your blood to reanimate her."

30

THE ONLY SOUND IN THE ROOM was the gentle thrum of the incandescent lights. Auberon's smugness was palpable as he waited for Aria's reaction, still draped languorously over the white marble and velvet throne.

"*What?*" Aria felt sick to her stomach.

Rainer's voice came from behind her. "That isn't possible. Is it?"

"It speaks!" Auberon chuckled to himself. "Thank you for asking, sir. In fact, it is possible. I have had my best men working on it for, well, almost eighteen years."

"Alchemy is against the law," Xander ground out. "It is unnatural. If you have been dabbling in—"

"Oh, I wouldn't call it dabbling," said Auberon, offended. "My alchemists have finally perfected the elixir of immortality, after years of failed trials. And just in time, too. A few more weeks in the Human Realm and you would have lost your Fair abilities permanently. I'm not usually a patient man, but this was definitely worth waiting for. With Neviah alive I can continue the Celeste royal bloodline without contaminating it, or watering it down." He extricated himself from the throne, unfolding his long limbs as he got to his feet and approached Aria. She fought every single instinct telling her to take a step back.

"You see it's really quite simple," he said, still several feet away. "All I have to do is drain every little drop of your blood, perform the ritual, and transfuse it into—"

The sounds of a struggle broke out and Aria was grabbed roughly from behind. Something cold kissed her throat. From the height of the body pressed to her back, she could tell it was Rainer. She stiffened, trying to avoid accidentally cutting her throat on the blade he had obviously wrested from one of the grey men.

"Take one more step and I will spill *every little drop* of her precious blood all over your shiny white tiles." Rainer's voice was barely more than a growl, and Aria's stomach plummeted. She had trusted him.

Auberon paused, eyes narrowed slightly. Aria couldn't turn her head to look, but she thought the scuffle when Rainer grabbed her meant the other Gnomes were now being held by the Celeste guards. They were at an impasse.

"What more do you want? I've already agreed to allow trade between our kingdoms in exchange for the girl. Is that no longer enough? Because this is beginning to seem a little like extortion, if I may say so."

Trade? That was what this was all about?

They had brought her to the Celeste King like a lamb to slaughter, and all so Gnome could trade with Celeste again. Were they really that desperate for healers? Aria remembered Xander telling her about the sickness that plagued her father and had killed thousands of Fair. It sounded awful, but was it really worth knowing they had given her over to be exsanguinated for some sick ritual that was supposed to bring her dead mother back to life?

"Perhaps, gold?" Auberon mused, eyes dancing.

"We both know your fool's gold isn't worth a bean," Rainer ground out next to Aria's ear. His breath moved her hair and tickled her skin. She tried to pull away, and felt the blade bite into her neck again.

Auberon laughed. "Worth a try." There was a tussle behind them as the Gnomes struggled against their captors and Rainer stepped to the side, dragging Aria along with him. He stood with his back to the lift doors, Aria could now see both Auberon and the other two boys, who were fighting against the four Celeste who restrained them. Xander looked at Aria with turbulent eyes.

Auberon held his hands up, trying to placate Rainer like he was a cornered animal, which she supposed he was. Auberon forced a laugh, but panic shone in his eyes as they darted around the room. "There is really no need for all this. If you spill her blood, you get nothing and I'll still be able to make the elixir. I don't actually need every drop, it was something of an exaggeration." Aria hoped he was bluffing.

Apparently, he was, because in the next second he lunged forwards, arms outstretched, his face contorted with rage and desperation. Rainer was too quick for him, he tossed the knife in the general direction of the King, who threw himself onto the tiles, narrowly avoiding the missile. Rainer picked Aria up and threw her unceremoniously over his shoulder and ran to the lift, hammering the button with the heel of his hand. He didn't turn his back on the room, watching the guards who held his friends, and the king, who had recovered himself quickly and was now dusting off his white trousers, that smug look back on his face.

"I think you'll find you need a key card." His mouth quirked in the ghost of a smile, but it didn't reach his eyes now. A hollow ding resounded through the throne room. Nobody moved.

The lift doors opened in what felt like slow motion.

And then Bazyl and Kiefer burst into the room, followed by three other men in leather and chainmail with weapons Aria couldn't identify in the blur of movement. Rainer practically threw Aria into the lift before turning to join the others in the ensuing melee. She stumbled to the door and tried to peer into the room, but a throwing knife whistled past her and she flattened her back against the metal wall of the lift.

"Aria?"

She hadn't heard that voice in a long time. In the commotion, she hadn't noticed the other person standing in the far corner of the lift. Now, she took him in, studying every inch of him.

When she was finally able to speak, her voice came out as a sob. "Jazz?"

31

"**W**HAT ARE YOU DOING HERE?"

Aria took a step towards her best friend, but she'd barely moved when Rainer and Coulter appeared at the lift door, holding Xander up between them. A dark red stain marred his tunic.

Kiefer and Bazyl were still fighting outside the lift doors, Kiefer firing arrow after arrow at the remaining Celeste soldiers. "Swipe the key!" He yelled over his shoulder. Aria turned to the control panel, and her heart sank.

"Here." Jasper held out a card like the one the Celeste guard had used earlier. There was no time to ask where he had gotten it from. She took it and swiped it in the slot next to the letter *G*. The doors started to move at once and the two boys jumped in before they closed, Kiefer firing one last arrow through the rapidly narrowing gap. The doors sealed, leaving them in complete silence, the only sound their ragged breaths as the lift began to rise.

Rainer and Coulter put Xander down, and he slumped against the opposite wall. When he touched a hand to his side it came away wet and red.

Nobody spoke. Maybe they were all holding their breath until they got out of there, like she was. She couldn't order her thoughts, everything she had heard in the throne room, everything she'd seen since entering the Fair Realm, it all played on a loop in her mind, sped up to double time. She should be angry. Furious. And she was, but right now she just felt numb.

Kiefer glared at Xander across the small space, anger and disappointment warring on his face. And something else. Sadness.

"Kief—" Xander began in a breathless voice, but Kiefer cut him off.

"The King's Guard brought word from the castle when they arrived in Hitherham." He practically spat the words at his brother. "Father succumbed to the fever. He passed away almost two weeks ago."

Xander's expression didn't change as he absorbed the news. Aria realised everyone in the lift was staring at him now, she scanned their faces, a crease forming between her eyebrows. Xander closed his eyes, steeling himself for something. Aria wasn't sure what, until Kiefer spoke again, his tone bitter.

"The King is dead. Long live the King," He placed his right hand on his heart and one by one the other Gnomes crammed into the lift did the same.

"Long live King Balthasar," Rainer breathed.

Bazyl Demitree watched the exchange with quiet interest, eyes moving from one face to the next. Aria had no idea why he was here, unless the Gnomes had decided to hand her over to him for a better offer. She wouldn't put it past them at this point.

The lift doors opened onto the marble-floored atrium, early evening light giving the citadel a peach-pink glow. The floor was littered with the bodies of Celeste guards, and four men dressed in the same way as Bazyl—chainmail vests, leather trousers and heavy-looking boots— stood by the glass doors. Bazyl jogged across the space to speak with his men, and Kiefer ushered the rest of them out of the lift.

Aria's mind turned to the Salamanders they had left fighting in the underground throne room, how would they escape?

Kiefer held a hand out for the key card. "We need to send the lift back down." He swiped it in the slot and dropped it on the floor of the lift. "Let's hope they get in before the doors close." He reached a hand out towards her and when she flinched away hurt flashed in his eyes, quickly replaced by a sad smile. "It's good to see you, Aria."

Jasper put a hand on her arm. "Come on, we have to get out of here."

She looked at his face, drinking him in. "I'm so glad you're here, Jazz." She threw her arms around his neck and squeezed, but it was brief. They needed to leave, now. "How did you get here?"

"With Baz. He told me what had happened, how you'd been taken. I couldn't let them go without me, Ri. I had to come and find you." His eyes burned into hers, that sea glass green a reassuring constant. She wondered if he'd noticed her newly-glimmering, bronze irises. "I almost got to you on that first day, after the barghests attacked. But by the time I caught up to Baz you'd already gone."

She worked to keep her face blank, but inside she screamed. If she'd waited just one minute more she might have seen him, might have been able to avoid all this.

But why had Bazyl brought Jasper from the Human Realm—to use him as leverage? As a hostage?

They picked their way across the lobby and Aria avoided looking too closely at the bodies of the guards, she didn't want to know whether they were unconscious or…something worse.

Bazyl saw her coming and took a step towards her.

"Aria." He grinned, but it slipped when she didn't smile back. "I'm sorry about all this, it's not exactly how I imagined us meeting."

"We met at the fayre," she said, her voice cold and hard. He faltered.

"Yes, we did—"

"So, you came to Hartwood to bring me home?" Her tone held a note of mockery.

"Actually, I came to Hartwood to protect you," he said, coolly. "Not bring you here. That said, since you're already here I had better take you to the stronghold. Auberon will almost certainly have raised the alarm." He gestured to his men who began to move towards the exit, weapons at the ready.

"He's not dead?"

Bazyl shook his head, his dark eyebrows knitting together so they appeared to be one. "No. Injured, but alive. The coward disappeared when we took our eyes off him. Probably had a secret door somewhere in that room."

"Mirrors," Aria said, more to herself than Bazyl.

"Mirrors?" He squinted at her and she looked up.

"He appeared as if from nowhere when we first arrived, but I saw his reflection. He uses mirrors to create an illusion, a hiding place."

Bazyl pushed a hand through his thick auburn hair. "Well, that information would have come in useful down there. There's nothing we can do about it now, though. We need to get you to safety as quickly as possible."

They followed the Salamanders to the entrance where the Gnomes stood, Xander propped between Rainer and Coulter, his face pale and breathing ragged. Kiefer seemed to be ignoring his older brother—and now king—by engrossing himself in conversation with one of Bazyl's men.

How had they come to be together? When had the escape plan been formulated? She couldn't figure it out. Didn't the Gnomes hate Bazyl? Or had that been yet another lie?

She caught Rainer's eye, his expression of shame and regret tugged at her. She opened her mouth to speak, not entirely sure what would come out, but a hollow ding filled the atrium, making her pause. The lift doors opened and the remaining Salamanders spilled out.

"Let's move," Bazyl said, taking charge. "Our bikes are hidden nearby."

Bikes?

Jasper grinned at her, and she got the impression he knew something she didn't.

"Don't worry," Bazyl added, seeing her expression. "You'll be with me."

"I can ride a bike," Aria muttered, and he smirked before turning back to his men.

"Aria's with me. Jasper, you go with Brent. Brent, take it easy, he's not a hardened Salamander like us." Bazyl winked at Jasper, who blushed faintly and rolled his eyes. Aria's mouth fell open. Was her alleged-brother *flirting* with her best friend? And at a time like this?

The sound of steel on leather filled the air as belts were tightened and weapons unsheathed. And then they were moving, pushing through the glass doors into the courtyard, which was now empty, no doubt thanks to the Salamanders arrival and the ensuing battle.

The Salamanders took the lead, jogging two-by-two, with Bazyl and Aria behind them, followed by the Gnomes. The square was silent, eerily so. Aria could hear the distant sound of leather slapping on stone echoing off the tall buildings that surrounded them. It seemed to be getting louder.

Just as Bazyl and Aria reached the entrance to the side street, the sound reached a crescendo and dozens of Celeste soldiers dressed in grey poured into the square from the opposite corner.

A cacophony of shouts and gunshots erupted, making Aria jump. Her scream was cut short by Bazyl who grabbed her arm and yanked her around the corner, pinning her against the glass.

32

"**G**UNS?" ARIA HISSED. "They have guns?"

"Apparently so," Bazyl murmured, pressing her flat against the glass wall, his hands either side of her shoulders as he peered around the corner, trying to see what was happening without being spotted. Or shot. "That's new. They're aether powered by the looks of it."

"The Gnomes are in the square!"

"They can take care of themselves, you're my priority."

The noise from the Celeste guards' weapons had lessened somewhat, although Aria couldn't guess why. The Gnomes were hugely outnumbered, there was no way they were going to make it out of there.

"What's happening?" Her voice was small and choked.

"Half of the Celeste guards went inside the citadel, probably the King's close guard. The rest are firing on the Gnomes who are using the fountain for cover. Kiefer has taken out a few of the Celeste with his bow." He looked at Aria, removing his hands from the wall behind her. "Come on, we need to get to safety. They'll be fine."

Aria hesitated, casting a glance in the direction of the courtyard, but all she could see was a sliver of the marble paving, the shadow of the fountain looming large. She nodded to Bazyl and they ran, heading for the other Salamanders who had waited at intervals along the alley, eyes on their leader and prince.

They had barely reached the next crossroad of streets when Aria heard a scream that turned her blood to ice. It was Coulter's voice.

Rainer.

She slipped through Bazyl's grip and tore down the alley, back the way she had come, not stopping until she reached the corner and burst into the courtyard. Bullets were still flying, but she heard the gunshots as though they were miles away, like a recording with the volume turned right down. Aria couldn't tell if she was moving or not, but in a second she was standing over Rainer's immobile form.

He was collapsed on the edge of the fountain, blood dripped into the water, clouds of red growing and spreading. Coulter crouched next to him and tore off his leather body armour and tunic, using it to staunch the flow of blood from Rainer's shoulder. He was mumbling something over and over to Rainer, but Aria couldn't make out the words. His tunic was soaked through and his hands came away dark red and shaking. He wiped his face on his forearm, smearing blood across his forehead.

Aria dropped to her knees on Rainer's other side and took his large hand in both of hers.

She couldn't breathe, couldn't think. The only thing running through her mind was *not Rainer*. He couldn't die, she wouldn't accept it—wouldn't allow it. He had to be OK. Any anger she was still holding onto over his part in the deception of the last few weeks was forgotten as she clutched his bloody hand between hers. She willed him to live.

With a sudden gasp, Rainer's eyes flew open. He tried to sit up, but Coulter pinned him down by his good shoulder, a sob of relief tearing from his chest. "Don't you dare, Conroy Rainer. Don't even think about it." Rainer laid back against the tiles and closed his eyes, chest heaving. Aria brought his hand to her face and kissed the back of it, squeezing his fingers as she did.

His eyes found hers then, as he tried to catch his breath. "Aria. I'm sorry. I never—never meant for this." She shook her head as he struggled for air, but he went on. "I wrote to Kiefer and Bazyl. But it was too late. I couldn't—"

She furrowed her brow as he gasped, but the image of Rainer handing off a note to a maid in Aberness rushed to the surface of her mind. He'd sent for back up. They hadn't arrived in time to stop Auberon getting his hands on her, but they'd intercepted before he could do any damage. And she had Rainer to thank for that.

Kiefer was still firing on the Celeste soldiers, only a handful were still standing, but it was enough. With Rainer and Xander both injured, and only Kiefer with a long-range weapon, they were woefully outmatched.

Aria had to think fast. She picked up Rainer's knife from where he'd dropped it on the marble floor. She stepped out from behind the fountain, putting herself in between the Gnomes and the Celeste. They immediately ceased firing.

Aria held the knife to her own throat. She fought to keep her voice steady. "Your King needs me alive. If you spill a single drop of my blood, he will have you executed." She was making an assumption, but when they didn't argue, she knew she was right. "Let us go, or I will slit my throat right here, and you'll have to explain to your King how you let me die."

There was complete silence across the courtyard. Aria hardly dared breathe while she waited for their response. She started to get the very real feeling she had brought a knife to a gun fight.

After a moment, a low hiss passed between the soldiers and they all lowered their weapons one by one. She had judged them correctly, none of them were willing to die for this mission.

A discordant drumbeat of boots on stone sounded behind her and she saw the Celeste raise their weapons again, this time pointed over her shoulder at the Salamanders.

"No!" She leapt to the side, knife back at her neck. A single bead of blood slowly rolled down to pool in her collarbone from where she accidentally nicked her skin. The Celeste froze before lowering their weapons once again when the Salamanders ignored them and jogged towards the Gnomes.

Bazyl appeared at Aria's side. "Aria, come. Quickly now." He placed a reassuring hand on her waist and guided her away from the soldiers. She refused to turn away from the Celeste, knife still poised at her throat.

They quickly cleared the square, Kiefer and one of the Salamanders carrying a deathly pale Xander between them. Rainer clutched Coulter's tunic to his wound, Coulter's arm wrapped tightly around his waist as they made their way out of the courtyard. They needed to get to a healer as quickly as possible. Aria hoped the journey to Penny Crag was a short one, she couldn't see either boy surviving long without medical attention.

Jasper appeared on Aria's other side once they turned the corner into the alley. He took her hand in his and gently wrested the knife from her shaking grip. It clattered to the floor and he pulled her to him, her face crumpling and tears threatening to spill over.

She couldn't allow herself to fall apart now, she had to keep it together, at least until they made it to safety. She pulled away from Jasper's embrace, pressing the heels of her hands into her eyes, forcing back the tears.

"We need to keep moving." Bazyl gestured for Aria and Jasper to walk on ahead of him. Jasper slipped his hand into hers and they followed the others down the alley in silence.

They gathered in a smaller courtyard, hemmed in on all sides by towering buildings. There were no windows on the ground floor, nobody wanted a view of the bins while they worked.

The Salamanders began throwing open the lids of the large black bins and digging through the rubbish bags, pulling out shining hunks of metal. The bikes.

Motorbikes. Of course they weren't going to pedal all the way to Penny Crag, her sitting on the handle bars while Bazyl steered.

The men dusted off their sleek silver and black vehicles, straddled them and started the engines. Jasper threw a leg over Brent's bike, gripping onto his jacket. He flashed Aria a grin and she grimaced, eyeing Bazyl's bike with trepidation. She'd never been on a motorbike before. Her mum was going to kill her when she found out.

She cast a glance at the Gnomes, injured and exhausted, tensions running deep between them. She didn't know how they were going to get back to the Gnome Kingdom, and she didn't care. They had betrayed her. A cold fury filled her belly and she turned away from them.

"We don't have time for a lesson on the basics, Aria," Bazyl called over the revving of several engines. "Hop on, let's go." She hesitated for a second longer before taking a deep breath and sliding into the seat behind him. She wrapped her arms tightly around his middle, clinging on for dear life. The scent of smoke and leather hit her nostrils as he gunned the engine and the bike lurched forward, carrying them towards the Salamander stronghold.

With one last look back, Aria's eyes caught Xander's briefly, before the bike turned a corner and he was gone.

The wind whipped her face as they sped away, stinging her skin and tangling her hair. She knew she'd look terrible when they finally arrived, but she didn't care. She let the hot tears rush over her cheeks, closing her eyes tightly and letting the wind dry her face.

33

THE SALAMANDER STRONGHOLD was on the other side of Penny Crag. It was constructed of red brick, half-hidden by ivy and surrounded by a wide, deep moat. The bridge had been lowered in anticipation of their arrival, they rode across it, Aria worrying the entire time the bike would crash through the aged wood and dump them into the murky water below.

When they pulled up at the enormous double doors two girls with hair mere shades away from Bazyl's were waiting to greet them. The younger girl looked about twelve and had waist length curly hair as bright as the sun. She ran towards them. "Ariadne!"

Aria looked at Bazyl, who smiled warmly at the girl. "Aren't you going to welcome me home, Sable? Or have you forgotten what I look like?"

Sable giggled and leapt at Bazyl, hugging him and beaming brightly. "Of course not! I missed you, Bazyl. Lark is dreadful at hide and seek."

She added the last part in a conspiratorial whisper.

"She is, isn't she," Bazyl agreed. "She always gives up too soon."

Aria laughed and they both turned to her.

"Aria, meet Sable. Our little sister."

"Less of the little, old man!" Sable said, standing up straighter and trying to look grown up.

"And this," Bazyl said, waving the other girl forward. "This is Lark."

Lark's smile was hesitant, but she held out a hand for Aria to shake. Aria took it. "It's lovely to meet you both."

She could hear the strain in her own voice, but she couldn't help it. She'd suddenly gone from being an only child to having three siblings. On top of everything else, it was a little overwhelming.

Bazyl watched her with curiosity, but when she turned to him, chewing her lip, he took the hint. "Shall we go inside?" He ushered them towards the huge doors. "Is father home? I think it best if we get cleaned up and have something to eat before seeing him. Don't you agree, Aria?"

She nodded gratefully, she hadn't eaten or bathed in a while and the motorbike ride had played havoc with her hair. She couldn't meet her father looking, and smelling, like a scarecrow.

"I'll show you to your room," Sable volunteered. "It's next to mine."

"I will order a bath be brought up," Lark said. "And then, shall we all go down to the kitchens to eat? We can get to know each other over some of Cook's homemade toffee." She was trying to make Aria feel welcome, like part of the family—which, she supposed she was—and all Aria could do was nod stiffly.

Once the heavy door closed behind her and silence settled over the plush, green bedroom, Aria let the tears fall.

Aria stood in front of the enormous, free-standing mirror. She pushed her damp hair behind her ears and ran her fingers over the sharp points that had formed at their tips.

The transformation was complete, she finally looked like one of the Fair.

She wore a borrowed dress, a forest-green, brocade gown with full sleeves and an empire waist. It was a little loose after weeks of barely eating, and it made her look like one of them, the Salamander royal family. A Demitree. She wasn't sure how that made her feel.

She jumped when someone knocked on the door. It opened a crack and Jasper's head appeared. "Hey, are you almost—whoa." He stepped into the room and shut the door, striding towards her with his hands up, reaching for her ears. He stopped a foot away and his hands hung in the air between them. "So, it's true then. You really are one of them. I mean, you're still you," he added quickly, grinning, "but you look different. And, you know, you have magical powers."

Aria laughed. It felt good. "Yeah, I guess I do. But what about you? You're here, with Bazyl, my…"

"Brother? Yeah, it's mad." He flopped backwards onto her bed.

"How the hell did that happen?"

"You remember Mark, the guy I was supposed to be meeting that night?" Aria nodded. The blue-eyed doughnut vendor. "Well, he stood me up. I know, how dare he, right? So I was on my way back to yours to see if you wanted to watch a film. When I got there, the doors were wide open and all the lights were on, and then I saw this guy in your room. It was Baz—I recognised him from the fayre, the cute redhead you were talking to outside the fortune teller's tent."

Aria rolled her eyes. "Please stop crushing on *Baz* and continue."

Jasper snorted. "Anyway, he asked me if I'd seen you or knew where you were. Obviously I didn't, and when he said you'd been taken by some other guys and he was going after you I insisted on going with him. He tried to talk me out if it, but I said I'd just follow him anyway. I didn't realise quite how far we'd be going, but I wasn't about to go back until we found you. Especially once I realised what was really going on."

Aria was touched by Jasper's loyalty. The vision the hag had shown her drifted to the surface of her mind. "So mum and dad are OK? I mean, they were fine when you left?"

"Yeah, I think so. I didn't actually tell them what had happened, I thought we'd be back in a few hours." He rubbed the back of his neck, a sheepish look on his face.

Aria breathed a sigh of relief. "And Bazyl just let you tag along? They didn't bring you by force or anything?"

"No, but I reckon they knew they'd need me to convince you. Plus, who can blame them for wanting a bit of eye candy around."

Aria tossed a pillow at Jasper and he caught it deftly. She noticed the watch she'd given him that night was still on his wrist. "Wait—is your watch broken?"

Jasper frowned, studying the watch's face. "I don't think it's broken. I think it's just stopped." He shrugged. "Maybe the battery died. Anyway, what about you, what happened after I left your house that night?"

Aria caught Jasper up on everything she'd been through since the fayre as they made their way down to the kitchens. They walked through the wide hallways, bare feet sinking into thick rugs lain over the stone and wood. The walls were draped with huge colourful tapestries that kept out the cold and made the castle feel almost cosy. The wall hangings depicted battle scenes, but unlike the tapestries Aria and Jasper had seen on school trips to museums, these battles weren't fought with swords or bows and arrows.

The tapestries showed the Fair using their abilities. Streaks of red fire, blue water, and white air were splashed across the fabric. Gnomes created earthquakes, the landscape splitting in two, men sprawling into the crevasses. The aether magic performed by the Celeste was depicted as a swirling, purple phenomenon that reminded Aria of the aurora borealis.

Aria froze on the bottom step of the staircase, almost tripping Jasper up. Straight in front of her on the wall was an enormous tapestry of a moonlit forest. And there, in the midst of the dark trees, like a luminescent spectre, was the White Hart.

It was a perfect depiction of the creature Aria had seen the night before under the full moon. It appeared to be a life-size rendering, antlers the size of a small tree protruding from its vast head.

"The White Hart of Hartwood," Jasper said, mildly intrigued. He knew of Aria's history with the animal. But he was a scientist, he didn't believe in mythical creatures, or magic.

That is, he hadn't believed. Before.

Perhaps that had changed since she'd last seen him.

"I saw it again, last night," she said, and Jasper raised an eyebrow. She went on. "We were camping in a field near the Salamander border and I woke up in the night, and there it was."

She remembered Xander's expression when he'd found her, the relief that had turned to white-hot passion in response to the awe and wonder he saw in her face. She pressed her fingertips to her lips, remembering their kiss.

But that had been before. She wiped the tingling sensation away.

"It's not an animal, or a Solitary creature. Apparently, it's a person."

Jasper opened his mouth to respond, but the soft shuffling of slippers on stone announced the arrival of Sable, her fiery locks glowing like embers in a shaft of sunlight from the high windows.

"That's the White Hart," she said, proud to show off her knowledge. "The First Fair Queen could transform into a stag. She died a long time ago, but sometimes people still see the stag. I saw it here—"

"There you are!" It was Lark, appearing from the same archway as Sable. An expression of exaggerated surprise barely hiding the tension in her body.

"I was just telling them about the White Hart."

"That's just a story." Her words were too quick, her smile clearly forced. "Come on, the kitchens are this way. Cook has made shortbread." She gestured for them to walk ahead of her, Sable leading the way. They followed the scent of hot chocolate and buttery biscuits down a stone corridor, the heat of the ovens wrapping around them like a blanket as they neared.

The kitchens were smaller than Aria had expected for the size of the castle. A rectangular table took up one corner, two long benches and two ornate chairs providing seating. They positioned themselves around the table while a ruddy-faced woman with a stained apron and greying hair poking out from under a white cap bustled around them. She plonked five large mugs of hot chocolate onto the table, humming softly as she did, followed by platters of sugar-dusted shortbread, sticky-looking toffee squares and a freshly-baked chocolate cake on a metal stand

"Where do I submit my application?" Jasper was looking at the spread like he hadn't had a proper meal in days.

"Application for what?" Lark asked.

"Becoming a Salamander," he said through a mouthful of biscuit crumbs. "If this is how you guys eat all the time I'll move in tomorrow. I'll muck out horses and wash dishes—whatever it takes."

Lark and Sable giggled as they watched him pile a plate high with cake and shortbread, taking big swigs of hot chocolate between bites.

Aria barely heard them. She couldn't face eating, cradling her mug for warmth more than anything else. Her mind kept flicking between the vision the hag had shown her of Bazyl torturing her parents, Quade's violent death, the heart-breaking betrayal she'd suffered in the throne room. All of her worst experiences from the last few weeks ran on a loop and a sick feeling of foreboding crept over her now clammy skin.

King Ossian had killed an innocent child and planted her in its place, and now she was going to have to face him, almost eighteen years after he chose to discard her.

Maybe he blamed her for her mother's death, the same way Auberon did?

Bazyl appeared at the door to the kitchen, grinning when he saw the array of treats laid out on the table. "Cookie, you are too good to me." He kissed the beaming chef on her cheek and slipped into the chair at the head of the table. He popped a piece of toffee into his mouth, which got stuck in his teeth, but that didn't stop him talking through it. "So, do you have any questions before we take you to meet our father?"

Aria blinked for several seconds, trying to separate the two images of Bazyl—the cold, murderous one the hag had conjured, and the teenage boy sitting across from her with his two devoted younger sisters and disarming manner.

He continued to chew the toffee, licking his teeth and sipping from his mug in an effort to dislodge it.

"Uh, no. I can't think of anything right now."

"Well, there's no rush. We can all get to know each other a bit. We've got time. Now you're here, we've got forever." He grinned, the toffee finally unstuck.

"Actually, I'm not staying. Not for long, anyway." She saw his smile falter and added, "I don't belong here. I know there's a prophecy and everything, but I belong back in Hartwood. I've got a family there, a mum and dad who miss me and want me back. I can't stay here."

34

A PAGE IN A RED TUNIC STEPPED INTO THE KITCHEN and bowed before them. "Prince Bazyl, your father is ready for you and the Princesses Ariadne, Lark and Sable." He bowed again and swept out of the room.

"Thanks, Keegan!" Bazyl called after him, shoving another toffee in his mouth and pushing his chair back. "We should go. Father isn't known for his patience." Sable nodded conspiratorially to Aria. "Jasper, it might be better if you wait here. Cookie will look after you." He winked, and Aria wasn't sure if it was aimed at Cook or Jasper.

She followed Bazyl as he weaved through the maze that was the Salamander stronghold, ascending staircases and moving along corridors lined with yet more tapestries showing scenes from various historical events. Aria paused briefly in front of one that seemed to depict the creation of the Fair Realm, until Sable bumped into her back and she was forced to keep moving. She would study that one more closely later.

After what felt like a mile hike up hill and down dale, over plush carpets and stone staircases, they reached a set of large double doors engraved with what Aria assumed to be the Salamander crest—the hilt of a sword rising from flames. Underneath the image were the words *Forged in Fire*.

Bazyl paused at the door and turned to Aria. "Ready?" She took a deep breath and nodded. Bazyl knocked.

The doors opened onto a large room with high, arched ceilings, vast oil paintings of flame-haired kings and queens lined the walls. At the back of the room on a raised dais were two oversized, ornate thrones studded with rubies and citrines that caught the light and cast a warm glow over the room.

"Ariadne! By the Elements, is it really you?"

An enormous, bearded man stood from one of the thrones and came towards her, arms open wide. The woman sitting beside him on the other throne—Bazyl, Lark and Sable's mother by her dark auburn hair—remained seated, a smile fixed on her delicate features.

"It's just Aria," she said coolly, impressed at the steadiness of her own voice. The King heard the ice in her tone and dropped his arms, coming to a stop a few feet in front of her.

"Of course. Well, my name is Ossian." He paused briefly. Was he waiting for her to curtsy? "This is my wife, Tala." The Queen dipped her chin ever so slightly in greeting, hands on the arms of her throne, legs crossed demurely. Aria nodded back.

Ossian turned to Bazyl. "Bazyl, my boy. Welcome home. Well done, son." He beamed, every inch the proud father. Aria sneaked a glance at Bazyl who was grinning ear to ear. They embraced in that masculine way of chest bumping and back slapping.

"Sorry," Aria interrupted, studying the King's ruddy face and substantial size. "You look fine, have you recovered from your illness?"

Ossian's thick eyebrows drew together almost comically. "Illness?" He scanned the faces of his children. "What's this about an illness?"

A fist clenched in Aria's chest, squeezing so hard she could barely breathe, let alone think straight. "So you're not dying?"

"Elements, no! Whatever made you think that?"

Anger rose up so forcefully she forgot to be respectful. "Then what the hell am I doing here?"

"Aria—" Bazyl said, but she cut him short.

"You were never ill, were you? They lied to me about that too. I don't believe this!" She gave a bitter little laugh, shaking her head. "I was dragged here against my will for nothing. All so Xander could hand me over to Auberon to have my blood drained for some bizarre ritual." Bazyl watched her with a worried look on his face, the reunion clearly not going as well as he'd hoped. "This was a complete waste of time. Do you know how many people I care about that I've had to watch die? How many times I've been attacked by the Solitary and the Celeste King's Guard just so he could use me to resurrect his dead sister?"

Ossian's face blanched. The room fell silent in the wake of Aria's outburst.

In a deathly quiet voice, Ossian said, "What did you just say?" He stepped forwards and gripped her upper arms in his meaty fists, cutting off the circulation. "What is Auberon planning to do to Neviah?"

A chill gripped Aria as tightly as Ossian did, her mind blank as she looked into the dark eyes of the King. Her father. The man she had come all this way to meet.

This was the man she had expected, not the jolly, bearded giant of moments ago. He shook her and she saw Bazyl twitch out of the corner of her eye, as though he had been about to intervene and stopped himself.

Ossian's grip tightened. "What did you say!"

"He said he had men, alchemists, experimenting with reanimation. He said he'd found a way, but he needed my blood for it to work. All of my blood. He wants to kill me and bring her back. But, it's not possible, right? He's insane."

She knew from the King's expression that it was true. Auberon might be insane, but the ritual was very possible.

"He has crossed the line this time." Ossian released her, and she knew there'd be bruises from his finger marks tomorrow. "I returned Neviah's body to him out of courtesy, out of respect. Not for this, this…twisted and *unnatural* charade. He has to be stopped. Aria, did he say anything else about the ritual? Anything at all?"

He stepped towards her again and she took a step back without thinking. "No, only that his alchemists had been working on it for years, and he needed to transfer all my blood into her body. He didn't tell me anything else."

Bazyl put a hand on her shoulder and she flinched away. "Father, I think we should let Aria get some rest, she has had a long and difficult journey. We can continue this conversation in the morning."

Ossian considered Bazyl's words. "That is a very good suggestion, Bazyl. Gather the men, we will have a strategy meeting to discuss this new information. Lark and Sable, please show Aria to her room and make sure she has everything she needs."

They all started to move, except Aria. "I want to be in the meeting."

Ossian had already turned away from her, but he turned back, his dark eyes hard. "Absolutely not. This is not your concern, Aria."

"Not my concern? I'm the one he wants dead!"

"That is exactly my point!" Ossian took a steadying breath, pushing a hand through his thick red hair. "Aria, I hid you in the Human Realm eighteen years ago for a reason. I wanted to protect you from him—from anything that might cause you harm. Auberon, the prophecy, the war. I will not put you in danger now because you want to feel involved."

All the air whooshed out of her like he'd punched her in the gut. She glanced at the Queen who had stayed silent throughout the entire exchange. Tala just watched them, keen interest simmering beneath her serene expression.

"What about my parents' child?" Aria's nerves were alive with electricity as she waited for Ossian's answer. Several moments passed before he spoke, voice almost too low to hear.

"What about her?"

"You didn't care about protecting her." Ossian looked stung, Aria thought she saw tears shining in his dark eyes. "You left me in her place, you gave me the security she should have had. And then you killed her."

Aria blinked back tears of her own, her throat thick. Ossian's expression had gone from pained to bewildered.

"What?"

"The Gnomes told me what I am—a changeling. They told me you'd killed my parents' real child." The tears that had begun to collect at the corners of her eyes now ran freely. The atmosphere in the throne room was so heavy Aria could hardly breathe. Lark and Sable stared at their father, aghast.

Ossian's expression hardened. He strode past them towards the double doors and growled, "Follow me."

It was an order.

Aria looked to Bazyl who nodded, a sombre look on his face, and lead the way down the corridor behind their father.

They walked quickly through the halls, down the stairs and out into the grounds. Dusk painted the sky with splashes of pastel, like a watercolour canvas. The stronghold's gardens were well tended, with box hedges around the perimeter and swaths of colourful flowers lining the paths. The temperature had dropped slightly, and goose bumps rose along Aria's arms as they followed Ossian through the maze of bee orchids and foxgloves. She was about to ask Bazyl where Ossian was leading them when he stopped next to a bench in a sun-drenched corner of the garden. A large buddleia climbed a wooden pergola and draped over the bench like fragrant bunting. A kaleidoscope of butterflies perched on the purple flowers, wings fluttering in the gentle evening breeze.

Ossian took a seat on the edge of the bench, hands clasped between his spread knees, head hanging. He sat in silence for a moment before looking up at Aria, squinting slightly in the last of the sunlight. "This is where we buried her."

Aria looked around. There was no headstone, no bronze plaque on the bench. It was a pretty spot, but nothing signified there was a grave here. "I don't understand why you brought me here. So, you buried her. It doesn't change the fact—"

"I didn't kill her, Aria." He sighed. "I loved her, as if she were my own."

"You—what? But she is dead."

Ossian gave her a sad smile. "Yes, she passed away just over a year after I brought her here. She was very sick, it was one of the reasons I chose her."

Aria tried to absorb this.

"Her name was Harmony. It was one of the names her—your—

parents had decided on. I was carrying a handwritten note with the name your mother had chosen for you. Ariadne." Her mother. He meant Neviah. "When I heard them speaking about musical names I tore the end off the note and left it on the table in the hospital room. I'm glad my suggestion stuck, Aria."

She chewed her lip. She'd never been gifted musically, it had become a favourite joke just how badly her name suited her. Would Harmony have been a talented musician, if she'd survived?

Ossian went on. "I gave your parents a healthy child, a chance to see their daughter live, and I gave you the future you deserved. Your life would have been in danger every day if you had remained in the Fair Realm. I could not bear to see you live under lock and key, not when there was another way. Harmony was a sweet, joyful child. She made the pain of losing you almost bearable. Losing Neviah."

Aria thought she saw Ossian's jaw quiver, before he rubbed a hand over his face. "I summoned every healer in the kingdom to help her, but none could cure Harmony's ailments. Without the aether magic of the Celeste healers, nothing worked. She succumbed to her affliction, and we buried her here. The gardens had been her favourite place." His eyes glistened.

"There's no marker," Aria said. "Nothing to say she's buried here."

Ossian gestured to the flower bed where the buddleia was planted. Aria crouched beside it, searching, and spotted a smooth stone nestled in the roots. She picked it up and brushed the dirt off. It was engraved with the word *Harmony.*

Aria remembered the stone they had placed on Quade's grave. She swallowed hard.

"I did not kill Harmony, Aria. I would never harm a child. The Gnomes lied to you, or perhaps they were misinformed, but either way

I am no murderer. I cherish the months I got to spend with her, she was my connection to you for that first year of your life. I still come here every so often and spend an hour with her, enjoying the gardens that she so loved. She is not forgotten." He ran a hand over his face, wiping his damp eyes, and stood.

Aria was lost for words. She didn't know how to feel, let alone what to say. She had believed her father a killer, that he had abandoned her and callously disposed of the other child, and now she knew the truth she struggled to erase the image of him as a cruel, cold-hearted king.

So far, it seemed everything she'd been told about the Salamanders had been a lie.

"I'm sorry." She replaced the stone marker and stood, emotions warring in her heart and on her face.

Ossian bowed his head. "It is forgotten. Now, come. You need rest. Tomorrow we will discuss your return to Hartwood."

Aria lay back on the pile of silk pillows atop her four-poster bed, staring out the window at the star-studded sky. She had thought about going in search of the tapestry depicting Queen Oriana and the creation of the Fair Realm, but she wasn't convinced she could find it again, and didn't want to wander the halls alone.

She'd browsed the bookcase and selected a leather-bound book of children's stories, they were surprisingly similar to the ones she had grown up with, save for the fact the Fair children knew them to be true. It hadn't helped to quieten her mind or answer any of the questions she still had after meeting her father.

She'd wanted to ask about her mother, the prophecy, the White

Hart, but instead of answers she had been left with more questions.

A soft knock came at the door, followed by a creak as the handle turned and it began to open. Aria expected to see Lark's pale face peering through the gap, come to check Aria had everything she needed, but it wasn't the princess.

Jasper stood in the doorway. "Are you awake?"

"Yeah. Come in, Jazz." She sat up, shuffling backwards to lean against the cushioned headboard. Jasper closed the door behind him and sat cross-legged at the foot of the bed.

"Are you OK?"

Aria laughed darkly. "Am I OK? That is a good question."

She'd changed out of the green gown and into a pair of striped cotton pyjamas Lark had given her, Jasper had borrowed a t shirt and some plaid pyjama bottoms from Bazyl. It was just like their old sleepovers. Except they were in a castle in another realm where magic existed, and Aria was a princess...

"I'd be rocking in a corner if I'd gone through everything you have in the last few weeks. In fact, how are you so calm about all this?"

"I'm still trying to get my head round half of it. I'm sure I'll have a melt down when it all sinks in. Probably when I'm back at home in Hartwood and can't explain to Mum and Dad what's wrong."

"So you're still planning on going back to Hartwood? What about your family here?"

Aria sighed. She'd been wrestling with the same question herself before he came in. In Hartwood she was an only child, she loved her parents and the dogs more than she could describe, but here she had a brother and two sisters who she wanted to get to know. She wished she could somehow split her time between the two, but it wasn't that simple when they lived in two different realms.

"I don't know, maybe I can visit. The crossing between the realms is only open on the solstice and the equinox, so I'd have to spend months here at a time. Or meet near the crossing for one day."

"That's true. Shit, what the hell are we going to tell our parents when we get home?"

Aria shuffled over and lay flat on her back next to Jasper, legs dangling over the edge of the bed. "Well we've got time to come up with a good explanation."

Jasper turned his head to look at her. "We might as well make the most of it then. Midnight snack?" Aria grinned and leapt off the bed.

35

Aknock came at the door and Aria squinted in the morning light. She elbowed Jasper, who groaned and pulled the covers over his head. They'd stayed up until the early hours of the morning eating treacle tart and drinking a spiced milk drink Cook had concocted for them.

"Aria? Are you decent? I'm coming in." The door started to open and Bazyl's auburn head popped into the room. "Come on, lazy bones. Father has sent for you." He noticed the person shaped lump under the covers next to her and quirked an eyebrow. "You don't dilly dally! Been seducing the staff?" He teased. "Keegan, is that you under there?"

"It's just Jasper." Aria pulled the covers off him, causing Jasper to cry out and roll over, burying his head under the pillows.

"Jasper?" Bazyl repeated, sounding confused. And disappointed. "I thought…"

"We were up late and crashed, that's all Bazyl." Bazyl's face brightened considerably and Aria threw a pillow at him. He caught it and placed it on the chair by the door.

"Well, leave him to sleep. You hurry up and get dressed. Father wishes to speak with you."

Realising what this meant, Aria threw the covers off and dashed to the cheval mirror where she had draped the green dress. "Just give me a sec."

Bazyl hesitated, eyes on the curve of Jasper's back where his t-shirt had rucked up, exposing a few inches of tanned skin.

"Bazyl!"

"Sorry." Aria thought she saw a blush creeping up his neck before he disappeared behind the door.

They zigged and zagged through the stronghold's corridors until they reached the room where the strategy meeting was to be held. The door stood open, and inside was a vast table covered in maps with small pebbles scattered across the landscape of the Fair Realm. At least, that's what Aria assumed. A wide blue line weaving its way through the middle must be the River Aspid that carved through Aberness. And there were the Caelum mountains between Salamander and Celeste.

"Why did he change his mind?" Aria asked, running a hand over one of the maps, tracing the faint line that marked the border between the two realms.

"Hm?" Bazyl mumbled, leafing through a pile of papers absently.

"Ossian. What made him decide to let me in on the meeting?"

"I—"

The door swung open then and Ossian entered. He filled the space, making the room seem suddenly smaller. "Ah, Aria, there you are. Thank you for joining us."

She straightened her spine and nodded. "Thank you for letting me attend the meeting, I know you said—"

Ossian interrupted her with a shake of his head. "Aria, the meeting has already taken place. This morning, before you awoke." Her face fell. He pushed on as though he hadn't noticed. "I asked you here to discuss logistics for your return to Hartwood." He took a seat at the head of the table and gestured for them to do the same. Aria sat down across from Ossian, blood thrumming in her ears as she waited to hear what he would say.

"As you know, the Autumnal Equinox is still a few weeks away. The crossing will be closed until then." Ossian scrubbed a large, scarred hand over his beard. "However, the journey will take a fortnight at least, even on our fastest horses. So I propose that you remain here at the stronghold for one week, regain your strength and use the time to help us understand Auberon and his plans. You're our only source of information on this ritual his alchemists have discovered. We need to find out as much as we can about what he plans to do before you leave."

Aria laid her palms on the table top, covering the Salamander and Celeste Kingdoms with her splayed fingers. "Alright, I'll help as much as I can, but I really don't know anything."

"You've seen the inside of the Celeste citadel and spoken directly with Auberon himself, that's more than almost any other living soul. You might not think you know anything useful, but I can guarantee that you do."

She nodded, conceding. "And then you'll take me home?"

Bazyl, sitting next to her, spoke then. "I'll escort you myself. And you can rest assured that we will stop King Auberon. Without the information you've gathered from inside the Celeste citadel, we wouldn't be in such a strong position. You have given us the opportunity to end Auberon's tyranny. Your contribution to the cause is invaluable, Aria."

Ossian nodded. "We'll send for you when we're ready for a formal debrief."

Aria pushed her chair back with a screech and stood. "Well, if that's everything, I think I'll go and spend some time with my sisters. If I'm leaving in a week I'd like to make some memories before I go." She strode around the table and through the door before either of them could respond.

Once outside the room, she slowly made her way back to her bedroom, studying the tapestries she passed on the way. She wanted to learn as much as she could of the history of this realm while she had the chance, she wasn't sure if she'd ever be coming back once they returned to Hartwood.

She found the one that depicted the creation of the realm and tried to commit it to memory, admiring the whorls of purple that represented Queen Oriana's aether magic. She would learn as much as she could, study the maps and any history books she could find. She might not be able to stay and take the throne or fulfil the prophecy, but she'd be as useful as she could before she left this place forever.

36

ARIA KICKED OFF HER BLANKETS AND PULLED ON HER BOOTS. Dawn was still an hour away and she stumbled in the darkness, almost tripping over Jasper's bedroll. He was already up, sitting a short distance away with Bazyl, their hushed voices carrying on the light breeze.

She folded her blankets and bundled them into a saddlebag for Bazyl's men to carry back to the Salamander stronghold. They would shortly be arriving at the crossing and saying their goodbyes before Aria and Jasper returned to Hartwood.

The past three months had been an experience she would never forget. Aria didn't recognise the girl she had been before, she felt like an entirely different person. Even Jasper had changed, not only was he more open minded, he had discovered a sort of inner peace, a calmness that Aria envied. Watching him with Bazyl, the easiness between them as they talked and laughed, their knees touching, heads bent together,

Aria felt a pang of jealousy. But it wasn't for Jasper, her feelings for him were nothing more than friendship now, and she was happy he had found someone who made him smile. She was jealous of their bond, the burgeoning relationship between them. The secret looks and shy touches. She longed to have that intimacy with someone. She felt lonely, like she didn't quite fit. Not quite human, not quite Fair.

She thought of Xander then, and what had almost been between them.

She understood Xander's reasons for doing what he did—even if she didn't agree with it. He had seen nothing but suffering among his people since the day he was born. His father had been dying from a fever he had seen kill again and again. All he had wanted was peace and security for his kingdom, at any cost.

She could almost believe he hadn't seen Auberon's betrayal coming, that he had wanted to believe Auberon would keep his word so badly he had convinced himself it was true. No matter how much evidence there was to the contrary.

It was unlikely they would see one another again, he had returned to the Gnome Kingdom for his coronation and impending nuptials, and she was leaving the Fair Realm. She didn't know if or when she'd return, but not before Auberon had been defeated and the Five Kingdoms were at peace. That much Ossian had made clear.

She ran her fingers over the pointed tips of her ears absentmindedly. They had grown on her in the past few days, poking out of her hair and making her resemble an elf. She might even miss them when they were gone.

In addition to the pointed ears and glittering irises, she now possessed the ethereal look of the Fair. Her features appeared sharper, more defined, giving her an alien look she definitely wouldn't miss.

Bazyl had assured her she would look the same as she always had as soon as she crossed through the Veil, that there was no trick to appearing human. It was just a physical response to the aether magic running through the air like an electrical current in the Fair Realm.

"Ready to go home?" Bazyl asked as she approached where they sat around the long-dead fire. She wasn't sure how to answer. She was desperate to see her parents and the dogs again, but the thought of never returning to this place, never seeing her siblings or the Gnomes again, was like a stone in the pit of her stomach.

She hoped the war would be over quickly so she could visit someday soon.

She forced a smile. "Ready when you are."

Bazyl stood and Jasper followed suit. They were still a short walk to the crossing, having spent the night camped out nearby watching for any Celeste guards or Solitary creatures that were loyal to Auberon. They left the horses in a small grassy clearing with two of Bazyl's men and set off on foot.

They arrived at the crossing, the archway formed of two bent and entwined trees where Aria and the Gnomes had first entered the Fair Realm, quicker than Aria had expected. Something fluttered wildly in her stomach as they neared it, she was nervous, but there was something else as well. She could feel the magic, the aether, in this place. She remembered noticing it when she had first come here, but it felt exponentially stronger now. Like a current of electricity that rippled through her with every heartbeat. Every breath.

Bazyl and Jasper were speaking in hushed tones behind her. "I will see you on the Winter Solstice," Bazyl whispered, hands gripping Jasper's forearms.

"It's only a few months. It'll fly by." He slid his arms around Bazyl and they embraced. Aria wasn't sure whether Bazyl's promise to visit would stand the test of time, but she hoped so, for Jasper's sake. She smiled when they both turned to her.

"Thank you, Bazyl. For everything." She hugged him tightly and he squeezed back. "If it weren't for you and Kiefer…well, you know. Good luck with everything, I hope it goes smoothly with Auberon."

He gave her a wink. "We'll be fine, don't you worry."

She grinned. Bazyl would make a great king someday, and she hoped to see it for herself. But first, she had another year of school before she could even think about the future.

"Then I suppose this is goodbye, for now." Aria thought she saw silver lining Bazyl's eyes, but it was probably just the glimmer of his blue irises in the low dawn light. "Best of luck, Aria," he said with a lopsided smile. They hugged once more and then it was time to go.

Aria and Jasper stepped up to the arch. This time, Aria saw something between the trees, the forest rippled slightly like a sail in the wind. With one last glance over her shoulder at Bazyl, she grabbed Jasper's hand, squeezed, and stepped forwards, pulling him with her.

They were finally going home.

Aria's heart thudded like a sledgehammer as she walked up the driveway towards the bungalow. Jasper slipped his hand in hers as she slowed, sensing her panic.

"I'll be right here the whole time," he whispered, squeezing her fingers. She gave him a weak smile that was more like a grimace.

"Here goes." She reached out and tried the handle, the door was unlocked. They stepped into the hallway and Aria noticed the lamps were lit. Of course her parents hadn't been sleeping since she'd gone missing, they must be beside themselves. Her whole body shook as she took another step further into the house, glancing around for her parents.

Light was coming from under the door of her dad's study. She tightened her hold on Jasper's hand and walked towards the door, but before she reached it her mum appeared from the kitchen doorway holding two steaming mugs. Aria froze, her mind going completely blank.

"Mum—"

"Aria! There you are, we were starting to worry." Her mum smiled at them both and sipped from her mug. "Why didn't you tell your dad you were going over to Jasper's for a couple of hours?" She turned to Jasper. "Happy birthday by the way, love."

Aria and Jasper glanced at each other, their expressions carefully blank despite the questions flying through Aria's mind. She opened her mouth, but Jasper got there first.

"Sorry, Mrs C. It's my fault, I had a date tonight but he stood me up, so I called Riri and she came straight over."

Aria's mum gave Jasper a sympathetic smile. "Don't worry, love, you were probably too good for him anyway." She took another sip from her mug and stepped around them, heading for the study. "You're welcome to stay over, Jasper, but please let your mum know first." She gave Aria a pointed look and let herself into the study, closing the door behind her and leaving Aria and Jasper standing in the living room in deafening silence.

Aria's legs finally gave out and she collapsed onto the sofa. They were home, and it was Jasper's birthday again.

No time had passed while they'd been in the Fair Realm. How was that possible? Did her abilities allow her to manipulate the crossing? Or was this always the case with travelling between realms?

She had so many questions and no way to answer them. She looked up at Jasper, who's expression of confused amazement mirrored her own.

"I guess we were never gone." He shrugged, sitting down beside her on the leather sofa.

Aria grabbed his left arm suddenly, pulling his hand towards her. He was still wearing the watch she'd bought him, it was ticking again, the hands making their slow circles around the face. The watch read five to midnight on the twenty first of June. It was as though they'd never left.

Aria blinked, a slow smile spreading across her features as a laugh bubbled up in her chest. When it broke free she fell back against the sofa and laughed until her stomach hurt, Jasper joining in a moment later.

They were home, they were safe, and they weren't in trouble.

Ossian, Bazyl and the Salamander King's Guard were going to rid the Fair Realm of the Celeste King.

A calmness settled over Aria and she closed her eyes. Everything was going to be alright, on both sides of the Veil.

When she opened her eyes she was still on the living room sofa, Jasper was gone and a blanket had been draped over her. Stretching, she stood and folded the blanket, placing it on the chair, and turned off the table lamp, leaving the house in darkness.

She made her way to her bedroom, running her fingertips along the furniture and walls, reminding herself of the texture and feel of home. The light was still on in her room, spilling out from under the door into the hallway. Aria opened the door and took in the scene before her. It was like she'd never been gone, music played quietly from her laptop speakers, her phone sat on the bedside table, charging. The blue wrapping paper from Jasper's present was strewn across her bed. Aria smiled, shut the door and set about preparing for bed, turning off her laptop and changing into her pyjamas.

She turned off the light and got into bed. Had she locked the French window? She couldn't remember. She slid out of bed and went to the door, parting the curtains to check the handle. Her hand paused above it, her eyes drawn to the woods behind the bungalow. Something was out there, in the trees on the other side of the low garden fence. Something that shone with brilliant white light.

The White Hart huffed a cloud of steam into the night air before turning and disappearing back into the woods. Aria shivered, staring at the spot where the stag had been for a long time afterwards.

Note from the Author

Dear reader, I want to thank you for buying or borrowing this book and taking a chance on a new indie author. I hope you enjoyed Aria's story, but this is only the beginning. If you'd like to find out what happens next, book two in The Fair Chronicles, *The Solitary King* will be released in 2021.

Reader reviews are really important for authors as they help new readers to discover our books, so if you'd like to leave a review for *The Fair Queen* you can go to Amazon or Goodreads.

If you have any feedback, or noticed any errors in this edition, please send an email to me@lyndseyhallwrites.com.

ACKNOWLEDGEMENTS

Writing this book over the last five years has gotten me through some of the most challenging times of my life, and also some of the best. So many people have supported me as I've written (and rewritten) *The Fair Queen*:

My parents, Angela and Philip, who always encouraged my creativity and gave me the strong work ethic that meant I never gave up on this book, and decided to just publish it myself instead of waiting around for someone else to love it as much as I do. And Tony, who always believes in me and is first in the queue for a signed copy. And my brothers, who probably won't read this, but I love you anyway.

The amazing friends who read very early drafts of this book and loved it, despite its many flaws: Daniella, my soul sister and best friend, love you and your face. Thank you for being my person. Lorna, thank you for feeding my reading habit for decades, sorry I never return your books. Beckie, thank you for loving this story almost as much as I do, and sharing it with other people you knew would love it too. Beci, your friendship and influence are definitely part of the reason I believed in myself enough to write and publish this book, thank you for always being there for me. Roshini, thank you for being the model of kindness and generosity in my life, you may have slipped into some of the softer characters in the story—and I promise you, there will be a second book! And Abbie, your love and enthusiasm for me and my story means so much to me, thank you for being my sister and supporter, especially when my reservoir overflows.

The online writing community that has been instrumental in teaching me how to craft a story, self-edit, and self-publish, and kept me sane along the way:

Kristen Keiffer of Well-Storied, Faye Kirwin of Writerology and Christine Frazier of Better Novel Project—thank you for the Twitter chats and abundant resources for new writers, you made me realise my dream was achievable.

The brilliantly clever and creative team behind the finished product you're holding in your hands, they're like my very own Glam Squad:

My editor, Lara Ferrari, thank you for taking a very rough draft of *The Fair Queen* and helping me to shape it into the book it was destined to be. I'm so proud of this final version, and I hope I did your edits justice. My cover designer, Natalie Narbonne, who designed this gorgeous premade cover, as soon as I saw it I knew it was the cover of *The Fair Queen*. Thank you, it's a dream come true every time I look at it. My interior formatter and designer, Julia Scott, thank you for polishing these pages and making them as pretty as the outside of the book.

Thank you to my friend and awesome graphic designer, Esmée, for creating the gorgeous book trailer for *The Fair Queen*. It was a major bucket list moment and I adore it.

And finally, Matt and Joey, my everything. Thank you for doing life with me, this is for you.

ABOUT THE AUTHOR

LYNDSEY HALL lives in a small village somewhere in the middle of England. She grew up surrounded by books, and thanks J.K. Rowling for her love of fantasy (and her gran for introducing her to the boy wizard when she was eleven). She loves to travel and try her hand at  new things, but is most at home when curled up in a chair with a cup of tea and a good book, usually accompanied by at least one dog. She's fortunate enough to share her home with two cherished humans and two beloved dogs.

THE FAIR QUEEN is her first novel.
A sequel, THE SOLITARY KING, will be released in 2021.

Website: lyndseyhallwrites.com
Twitter: @lyndseyhall_
Instagram: @lyndseyhall